The
DRAGON'S
PEARL

Unknown Lands

Surmountable
Mountains

The
DRAGON'S
PEARL

SIMON & SCHUSTER
BOOKS FOR YOUNG READERS

New York   London   Toronto   Sydney

By

Devin Jordan

Based on a story by

Virgil Howard

and

Bill Ryan

SIMON & SCHUSTER BOOKS FOR YOUNG READERS
An imprint of Simon & Schuster Children's Publishing Division
1230 Avenue of the Americas, New York, New York 10020

SIMON & SCHUSTER BOOKS FOR YOUNG READERS is a trademark of
Simon & Schuster, Inc.
For information about special discounts for bulk purchases, please contact Simon & Schuster Special Sales at 1-866-506-1949 or business@simonandschuster.com.
The Simon & Schuster Speakers Bureau can bring authors to your live event. For more information or to book an event, contact the Simon & Schuster Speakers Bureau at 1-866-248-3049 or visit our website at www.simonspeakers.com.
Book design by Laurent Linn
The text for this book is set in Brioso Pro.
Manufactured in the United States of America
2 4 6 8 10 9 7 5 3 1

Library of Congress Cataloging-in-Publication Data
Jordan, Devin.
The dragon's pearl / by Devin Jordan.—1st ed.
p. cm.
Summary: Sixteen-year-old Marco Polo, with his best friend Amelio, sets out
from Venice, Italy, in 1300 to rescue his father from weird creatures
of the Unknown Lands of the East, who are commanded by one
whose sinister plans threaten the entire Earth.
ISBN 978-1-4169-6410-0
ISBN 978-1-4169-9576-0 (eBook)
1. Polo, Marco, 1254–1323?—Childhood and youth—Juvenile fiction.
[1. Polo, Marco, 1254–1323?—Childhood and youth—Fiction. 2. Adventure and
Adventurers—Fiction. 3. Supernatural—Fiction. 4. Animals, Mythical—Fiction.
5. Kidnapping—Fiction.] I. Title.
PZ7.D76223Dr 2009
[Fic]—dc22
2009006541

FIRST
EDITION

To my mom, who taught me that anything is possible
if you put your mind to it

The
DRAGON'S
PEARL

"The inhabitants of Kesmur are adept, beyond all others, in the art of magic; insomuch that they can compel their stone idols, although by nature dumb and deaf, to speak. They can likewise perform many other miracles. . . ."

"In India they have the power of diabolical arts, with men who can produce darkness and obscure the light of day. . . ."

"In Bascia, the people are extremely skilled in the art of . . . the invocation of demons. . . ."

"[And] I have only told the half of what I've seen."

—THE TRAVELS OF MARCO POLO, 1300 AD

"I had snuck into my uncle's room days before, and after
covering every inch, I found the secret compartment
concealed in the base of his bed. Inside, my uncle had hidden
his pack containing everything he had mentioned that terrible
day. A map of the Unknown Lands. A blank diary set
to record my father's rescue. And, unexpectedly, I also
found a strange, softly glowing blue pearl. . . ."

—FROM THE JOURNALS OF MARCO POLO

Insurmountable
Mountains

Part One

VENICE

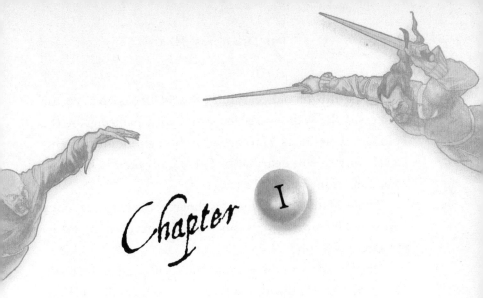

Chapter I

Marco Polo glared at the menacing knight standing at the other end of his family's trophy room. The sixteen-year-old boy saw his curly brown hair, piercing blue eyes, and thin, wiry frame reflected in the knight's enormous blade and polished armor. This was a matter of life or death; it would take only one slice for that knight to cut him in half.

"This is the house of Niccolo, Maffeo, and Lorenzo Polo," Marco said in the most confident voice he could muster. "You are an intruder, and I order you to leave."

The knight tightened his armored fingers around his sword.

Marco blinked.

Nothing changed. The knight was still there, silent and menacing as ever.

"Fine," Marco said. "You can't say I didn't warn you."

Marco glanced around the trophy room, trying to figure out a plan. The room was lined with enormous wooden

bookcases full of old, carefully bound books. Above the bookcases the walls were decorated with paintings of the Polo family, artifacts Marco's father brought home from his travels, and shields bearing the Polo family crest. There had to be something he could use. . . .

Before Marco could finish his thought, the knight let out a yell, raised his sword over his head, and came charging madly in Marco's direction.

Quickly, Marco jumped onto the shelf of a nearby bookcase, yanked a shield with the Polo crest off the wall, and positioned himself behind it as he leaped back down.

Within seconds, the knight's powerful blade smashed against the shield. Marco's body shook from the impact.

"Coward!" Marco said. "If you came here to kill me"—Marco lifted his shield to fend off another attack—"at least fight fair and give me a weapon!" The knight's sword hit Marco's shield again. "Or are you afraid, because I'm the finest young swordsman in Venice?"

Marco glanced quickly past the knight between blows and spotted one of his grandfather's wooden canes lying on the floor.

Before the knight could stop him, Marco dove, rolled between the knight's armored legs, and broke into a run toward the cane.

Snapping it up, Marco turned and pointed it threateningly in the knight's direction. "Ha! Who's the scared one now?"

With three quick swipes of his sword, the knight cut the cane into pieces.

Changing tactics, Marco flexed his legs, shot forward, and

pushed into the knight, using his shield like a battering ram. The knight stumbled, caught by surprise. Marco pushed harder into the knight, slamming him into a bookcase, and the sword slipped from the knight's hand at the moment of impact.

Marco snatched up the sword with a triumphant shout and immediately brought the blade to the knight's chest. "I told you not to mess with Marco Polo!"

The knight raised his head and said something that was muffled by his metal headpiece. It sounded like "mmmm mm mmm mmmmm!"

"What?" Marco asked, confused.

"Mmmm mm mmm mmmmmm!" the knight said with urgency. He motioned toward the tall bookcase behind him, stacked full with hundreds of books, wobbling dangerously from the recent impact.

Marco looked up at the bookcase and his eyes grew wide. "Oh, no . . ."

The bookcase wobbled once more, then pitched forward, everything inside crashing down on Marco and the knight, instantly burying them both under a sea of books.

Chapter 2

Marco's grandfather, Lorenzo Polo, slowly opened the door to the trophy room.

His wrinkled face grew stern as he saw the toppled bookcase, the enormous pile of books, and Marco in the middle of them, alongside a figure wearing the metal headpiece of a knight. Two armored hands lifted off the headpiece, revealing the pale face and blond hair of a fifteen-year-old boy.

"Marco Polo and Amelio Strauss," Marco's grandfather said in his stern, commanding voice.

The two boys turned as one, shocked to see Lorenzo standing by the open door. Lorenzo's long, tousled gray hair hung around his shoulders, and his thick eyebrows were arched into an angry V.

Marco's and Amelio's faces immediately flushed with embarrassment.

"What in the world is going on in here?" Lorenzo asked. "Amelio, are you wearing armor? Did you take that from the armory?"

"No, sir! Or yes, sir, I am wearing armor, but it's—"

Marco interrupted him. "It's my fault," he said, getting up from the pile of books. "All of it. I snuck into the armory last night, and I took the suit of armor. I made Amelio put it on."

Lorenzo's face radiated disappointment. "Why?"

"I wanted him to act like a knight. Invading the house. To be sure I could protect us."

Lorenzo looked at Marco incredulously. "Protect us, Marco? From what?"

"In case anything happened!" Marco said, his voice rising. "My father's been gone so long, and . . . I needed to know that I could. I even told Amelio to go rough on me, take me by surprise. . . ."

Lorenzo held up his hand and Marco grew silent. Lorenzo looked at his grandson's earnest face, so much like his own when he was a boy, and took a deep breath.

Lorenzo turned to Amelio. "Amelio Strauss, stand up and listen very closely to what I'm about to say."

Amelio stood, armor clanking, still holding the metal headpiece in his hands. He lowered his head in respect.

"I knew your grandfather very well, and I've known your father since the day he was born. Generations of your family have lived and worked at the Polo household, and for that we are extremely grateful," Lorenzo said. "Because our families have a special relationship, you and I are going to make a deal. Very soon, you will leave this room, head down to the armory, and take off that armor. You will polish it and return it to its rack. Then you will leave the armory, forget it exists, and I will never see you in there again. Is that clear?"

"Yes, sir."

"Good," Lorenzo said, nodding his head. "In return, I will do what old men do and forget I saw you here today. That will save me from growing upset—at my age, one should grow upset as infrequently as possible. Are we agreed?"

"Yes, sir. We are, sir," Amelio said, unable to fight back a slight smile.

"Then go and do what I told you before I start remembering."

At that, Amelio ran out of the room as fast as he could, armor clanking loudly with each step.

With Amelio gone, Marco looked at his grandfather warily. "I don't suppose you're willing to forget about me, too?"

"Unfortunately, when it comes to my grandson, my memory's quite a bit sharper." Lorenzo looked down and saw several books on the floor by his feet. He picked one up and thumbed through it. "Marco, did you know some of these books are over a hundred years old? Look at the artifacts on the walls. Do you realize what your father went through to find them in the first place?"

Marco studied the artifacts on the walls for the thousandth time. The mounted ceramic plate covered in strange, cryptic symbols, with two dueling dragons in its center. The fist-shaped black rock hanging next to it, always ice-cold to the touch, even when Marco stole it one night and held it for hours over a fire. Marco spent far too much time imagining the adventures his father found himself on to obtain these and the rest of the artifacts . . . and far too little time going on any adventures himself.

Lorenzo put his hand on Marco's shoulder, his grip loving but firm. "I know it's been hard on you since your father went away again. But you know better than to play in this room. Tell me, Marco, have you even finished your warehouse inventories yet?"

Marco looked down at his feet. "Not quite."

"The inventories that were supposed to be done yesterday?"

Marco didn't say a word.

Lorenzo sighed. "You're not a boy anymore, Marco. You're training to become the chief accountant for the Polo trading venture, and it's a huge responsibility. Your father and uncle risk their lives to open new trading routes, and they've expanded our business farther than anyone imagined. But you and I have to hold up our end of the bargain back home to keep things running."

"Yes, Grandfather."

"There are some things I have to attend to, so we'll finish this conversation later. For now, pick up every one of these books, then go straight to the clerk's chambers—and stay there—until your inventories are finished. Is that understood?"

"It's understood."

Lorenzo sighed again, patted Marco on the back, then walked out of the room. Seconds later Marco heard Lorenzo's voice calling from the hallway. "And Marco, don't think I didn't see my ruined cane! We'll talk about that later!"

Marco walked over to the pieces of the cane, picked up the largest one and held it until Lorenzo was out of earshot. As soon as he was, Marco grunted with frustration. Then he dropped it on the floor, kicked it across the room, and watched it crash into the opposite wall with a loud *thwack!*

Chapter 3

A short distance away from the Polo household, in a cavernous, dimly lit chamber, hundreds of dutiful clerks sat at identical wooden desks, writing in dusty ledgers with neat, precise strokes of their pens.

This chamber was the heart of the Polo trading venture, and—though it was owned by Marco's family—everyone was instructed to treat Marco just like any other trainee. Most paid him no attention at all.

Sitting at his own wooden desk, surrounded by ledgers and inventories, Marco did his best to ignore the work in front of him. No one in the chamber was saying a word, and in the silence, he listened to papers being shuffled, throats being cleared, a fly buzzing over his head.

Marco glanced up at the fly. *I wish I could be you,* he thought. *You've never been forced to stare at an inventory in your life—which means you've been spared the most boring task in the world. And you can fly out of here whenever you want. If my family gets their way, I'll be stuck in here forever.*

As if it were trying to taunt Marco, the fly landed on his desk, took several steps, and grew bored. Then it flapped its tiny wings twice as fast as before, zipped off, and flew out of the chamber.

Marco watched it go. As he did, he saw a clerk making his way back to his desk with a satisfied look on his face, several official-looking documents tucked under his arm.

Or maybe you're the one I wish I could be, Marco thought. *You wouldn't know an adventure if it smacked you in the face. And if one did smack you in the face, you'd probably collapse in fright. Your wooden desk is all you want from the world. Well, that's not enough for me.*

It's not enough for me.

At that moment, Marco saw a skinny boy with light blond hair going from desk to desk, delivering mail. Amelio!

Marco waited as Amelio made his rounds, handing out mail at each desk.

"Hey, Marco," Amelio whispered.

"Hey!" Marco said. "You're not usually here this late—did they put you on second shift mail duty?"

"My father put me on first *and* second shift. Someone heard your grandfather yelling, and . . . well, it got back to my father. Now he's making me do double shifts all week."

Marco grimaced. "This is my fault. If I hadn't slammed you into that bookshelf my grandfather never would have heard us, and—"

"No," Amelio said, "it's my fault too. If I hadn't sliced up your grandfather's cane—"

"You didn't have a choice! Otherwise I would have taken it and used it to . . ."

Both boys broke into terrific grins.

A clerk at a nearby desk looked pointedly in their direction and put a finger to his lips. "Shh!"

The boys kept smiling but lowered their voices.

"Are you hurt at all?" Amelio asked.

"Nah. Maybe a bruise or two, but they're the most exciting bruises I've had in months. You?"

"About the same. And, for what it's worth, if I really was an invading knight and saw you fighting in there—I'd think twice about messing with you again."

"Thanks," Marco said proudly.

"Anyway, now I'm just bringing around the mail shipment from Constantinople."

Marco hesitated. "Is there anything from my father?"

"Not today," Amelio said. He cleared his throat. "But, you know, letters can take a long time to arrive, especially when your father's so far away."

Marco sighed. "It's fine. When my father's off on his adventures, he doesn't have much time to write."

Amelio looked awkwardly at his feet.

"Hey, you want to see what I found earlier?" Marco said, suddenly brightening. He glanced at the clerks all around them to make sure no one was watching, then reached under a pile of invoices on his desk and pulled out a manuscript. Marco flipped it open to the first page. "I found it in the trophy room when I was putting away those books. I already read fifty pages. It's a history of the Mongol Wars!"

Amelio's face immediately grew pale.

Marco continued, oblivious. "I can't believe this stuff actually happened! Entire Mongol armies—by all indications, coming straight from the Unknown Lands—crossing over the Insurmountable Mountains. They went on to kill hundreds of thousands of our finest knights, almost conquered all of Europe . . . until they were called home to elect a new leader, entirely disappeared, and were never heard from again."

"And that's all for the best, don't you think?" Amelio interrupted, his voice growing high and nervous.

"It's for the best that they left, sure. But where does that leave us now? No European has ever traveled past the Insurmountable Mountains. And we still don't know where the Mongols went, which means we'll be unprepared if they ever come back again. I mean, look at this!" Marco flipped to another page in the book, featuring the image of an old, wizened dragon looking down over a hand-drawn map. The map showed Europe and the regions immediately on the Mediterranean, including Constantinople and Bukhara to the east. But a mountainous barrier neighboring Bukhara was marked with the words THE INSURMOUNTABLE MOUNTAINS. And everything beyond it was colored a deep, charcoal black and marked THE UNKNOWN LANDS.

Amelio looked at the map and his eyes clouded over darkly. As a counter to Marco's excitement, he exuded apprehension and fear.

"What's wrong?"

"Nothing," Amelio said.

"That expression on your face isn't nothing."

"Look, Marco, it's one thing to play around in your house, all right?" Amelio began, his voice suddenly passionate. "But the Mongols are the most ferocious killers in the world. You said it yourself, they came out of nowhere and slaughtered hundreds of thousands of our finest knights. I'm glad that they left, and I don't even like thinking about the possibility they could come back again." Amelio shivered. "Never mind thinking about what it's like in the Unknown Lands. Now I'm going to go finish handing out the mail. Maybe you should finish your inventories, all right? And put that book back where it belongs."

Without saying another word, Amelio reached into his bag of letters and walked over to the next clerk's desk.

Marco frowned, disappointed.

After a while, he turned back to the spread on his desk. To his left were his ledgers, still unfinished. To his right was the book with the hand-drawn map. Marco zeroed in on the map, focusing on the area marked THE INSURMOUNTABLE MOUNTAINS.

He gazed at it for several minutes, deep in thought. Amelio was his best friend, but he lacked a sense of adventure. With a desperate curiosity Marco wondered where the Mongols had gone, how one could cross those mountains, and what they might find in the Unknown Lands beyond. . . .

Chapter 4

The following morning Marco rubbed the sleep from his eyes and made his way downstairs. His bedroom was on the third floor of his large and impressive house, next to his father's, uncle's, and grandfather's. The second floor held the trophy room, and the first had a hallway, the armory, a parlor, a dining room, and a kitchen.

As Marco padded his way down each flight of steps, then walked past the row of framed paintings hanging along the first floor hallway, he imagined his grandfather already in the dining room, finishing his breakfast and preparing to lecture Marco for sleeping in. Luckily, Marco had an excuse on hand—the night before, he'd spent hours working in the clerk's chambers. Sure, he spent most of that time finishing the book on the Mongols, but he spent some of it on his inventories, too, and before he went to bed he completed all of his leftover forms. If his grandfather scolded him, he was ready to use that fact like a shield, and he hoped it would deflect any further attacks.

Soon, Marco arrived at the dining room and peered inside. To his surprise no one was there, and the long oak table in the center of the room gleamed like it hadn't been touched. He wrinkled his forehead in surprise.

Marco turned back to the hallway just in time to see Giuseppe Strauss, Amelio's father, coming in the front door with a large stack of papers in his arms. Giuseppe and Amelio lived in the servants' quarters only a quick jog away from the main house.

"Hey, Giuseppe!"

"Good morning, Marco." Giuseppe offered Marco a tight smile. Giuseppe had the same pale skin and blond hair as Amelio, but he was much taller and his features were more stretched out.

"What's Amelio doing today?"

"He's in the clerk's chambers—first and second shift. He'll be busy the entire day."

Marco immediately turned red, remembering Amelio was forced to take on more shifts because of what happened in the trophy room. "I'm really sorry about that—what happened yesterday, with the armor. . . ."

Giuseppe shrugged as he always did when Marco apologized. "It's nothing." This only made Marco more embarrassed. It was usually his fault whenever Amelio got in trouble and everyone knew it. But Giuseppe would never say a harsh word to any of the Polos, so he let everything slide. It was impossible to know for sure, but Marco hoped, deep down, Giuseppe didn't think too poorly of him. . . .

"Either way, I swear it won't happen again."

"No matter. To be honest, I'm surprised you're even here—I thought you'd be down by the docks with your grandfather for sure."

"You know where my grandfather is? I was just looking for him in the—"

"Didn't you hear?" Giuseppe interrupted.

"Hear?"

"Your uncle's ship pulled into the harbor this morning! They sent a messenger, and your grandfather went down to the docks to meet him straightaway."

Marcos eyes grew wide. "Is my father with him? Are they back?"

But before Giuseppe could get out an answer, Marco had already broken into a run and charged straight out the front door.

Chapter 5

Marco bolted down Venice's streets, seagulls screaming overhead.

To a visitor Venice might seem like an endless maze of backstreets and alleyways, but Marco had been exploring since he was old enough to walk. When he was a boy, his father spent hours taking him down every path, telling him incredible stories about the imaginary creatures that lived and swam under the canals. It truly was an amazing city—which was why Marco hated being forced to spend even an hour of his day cooped up in that horrible accountant's cave.

But today, right now, all of that was left behind. His uncle's ship had come in! And his father along with it!

Charging forward and taking a shortcut, Marco turned a corner after a church and ran alongside a minor canal. A man in a gondola used his oar to briefly match Marco's pace—until Marco pulled ahead, turned another corner, and was gone. The route took Marco zipping down a long strip of shantytowns, where the city's poor lived in cramped apartments.

Finally, winded and chest heaving, Marco arrived at the harbor, the strong smell of saltwater pumping through his nose. The sheltered harbor of Venice was a gateway to the open sea, with galleys and cargo ships bobbing proudly up and down, enormous sails stretched out above them while dockmen loaded cargo down below.

Marco stopped in front of the nearest ship and yelled to a sailor prying open a massive crate with the help of a crowbar.

"Hey! Did you just arrive from Constantinople?"

"Our ship leaves for Constantinople in one week's time—if you're looking for new arrivals, they're farther down."

Marco continued running along the strip, yelling to any sailor he saw, but he was told to keep going by each one in turn.

Finally, Marco made his way to a ship with a sailor on deck who looked somewhat familiar. "Hello, sir! Did you just return from Constantinople? Were you sailing with the merchants Niccolo and Maffeo Polo?"

The sailor turned slowly to acknowledge Marco. "I did return from Constantinople," he said, his voice flat. "Why do you care who I returned with?"

"My name's Marco Polo—Niccolo and Maffeo are my father and uncle. Were they sailing with you? Are they still on board?"

The sailor gazed blankly at Marco. "Your uncle Maffeo sailed home with us, but he was alone. Niccolo Polo was never on this ship."

Hearing this, the excitement rushed out of Marco's body like a balloon that had been slit open. His knees felt suddenly weak. "My uncle came back alone? Why? Where . . . where is he now?"

"Your uncle met your grandfather here an hour ago. But they left straightaway for the Palazzo Ducale, to speak in front of the council."

"The council? Why would they—"

"I'm not the one to say. If you want to know more, you'll have to go to the council yourself."

His excitement now entirely replaced by a dark and creeping dread, Marco turned on his heels and ran as fast as he could in the direction of the Palazzo Ducale.

Chapter 6

The Palazzo Ducale was another ten-minute run from the shipyard, and by the time Marco arrived he was entirely out of breath. This building was the center of the Venetian government, containing the Palace of the Doge, the law courts, bureaucratic offices, and the city jail.

Marco usually loved the square in front of the palazzo—the beauty of the architecture, the hustle of people charging inside and out, the street musicians who performed while passing around their hats for change. But today he felt only confusion, and his head was buzzing with questions. Why had his uncle returned alone? Where was his father? And why would his uncle and grandfather be addressing the council? He couldn't just wait—he needed to find out what was happening.

Pushing forward by instinct, Marco headed for the palazzo's closest entrance. It was early yet and there would be only one guard on watch at each entryway. There were conference rooms throughout the palazzo, but if Marco's uncle and grandfather were there they could only be in the third floor council chamber—that's where the most powerful trading families in Venice were met and entertained.

Without stopping to think, Marco stepped inside the palazzo's closest entrance. He glanced over the room's high ceilings and polished marble floors, taking in the enormous paintings covering every wall. A heavyset guard with a thick black mustache was in the center of the room, laughing and flirting with an attractive, dark-haired young woman, and behind the guard—in the room's far right corner—a grand and twisting staircase led to the palazzo's second and third floors.

Marco headed toward the guard. "Good morning," Marco said.

The guard continued flirting, his concentration focused on the young woman.

"Good morning," Marco repeated, louder this time.

The guard breathed in deeply, nodded apologetically to his companion, then cleared his throat before glaring at the boy in front of him with clear displeasure. "Good morning."

"If I needed to meet with the council, what would I have to do?"

"The council is in an important session. They won't be seeing anyone else for the rest of the day, boy—strict instructions. You'd best be on your way."

"But I need to get up there and join my family. They may need me up there. Are you sure they won't admit anyone else?" Marco persisted.

"The only people seeing the council today are in the room with them right now, and they'll be in there for a good long time. Absolutely no exceptions, no matter who you are. Got that?" the guard barked. Seeing Marco's disappointed expression, the guard continued. "These are my instructions from on high. Now, if you'll excuse me, I have business I need to attend to. You'd best be on your way." With that, he turned away from Marco, put his hand back on the young woman's shoulder, and gave it an affectionate squeeze.

On any other day Marco might have taken this for an answer, or tried his best to argue his way in, or come up with some clever strategy to sneak inside without being noticed. But after hearing what the guard said, his adrenaline was flowing, his heart was pounding furiously in his chest, and he could think of nothing other than his need to know what was being discussed and what had happened to his father.

As soon as the guard's attention was again swallowed up by his companion, Marco bit his lip, counted to three, then ran as fast as he could, making a furious beeline for the winding marble stairs.

"What? I don't believe it!" the guard shouted incredulously as Marco whipped by. He turned to his companion. "Don't move." Then he charged after Marco, his footsteps echoing throughout the chamber, heavier, slower, and several seconds behind. By the time the guard reached the base of the steps, Marco was already halfway to the second floor.

Marco pushed forward at top speed, his head throbbing, barely able to comprehend what he'd just done. He had no choice now but to think fast—if the guard was able to catch him, it would be a complete disaster. Marco had been up these stairs before, when he first came of age and was formally introduced to the doge. There would be a landing on the second floor and another on the third. After the third floor landing there would be a sturdy door, a small marble hallway, then the impressively ornate entrance to the council chamber. If Marco could make it to the small hallway in time, he might be able to turn back, bar the door and stop the guard in his tracks. . . .

Without another thought Marco set his plan into motion. He arrived on the second floor landing, the guard just behind him, then started straight up toward the third without looking back. The guard was a bit quicker than he looked, but Marco was bursting with energy and barreled onto the third-floor landing with several seconds to spare.

With just enough time to understand what was about to happen—but not enough to stop it—the guard touched down on the third-floor landing, reached out his hand toward Marco, then felt the impact as the sturdy door slammed shut in front of him. By the time the guard tried the handle, Marco had already swung closed the latch.

Gulping for breath, Marco leaned against the marble hall-way wall and tried to calm down. That wasn't the smartest thing he'd ever done, but it worked. The guard's fists rained furiously against the door but they both knew it was no use—Marco had done it, and, at least for the moment, he was safe.

Once he'd calmed down enough to regain some of his composure, Marco continued pushing himself, traded his previous recklessness for something resembling stealth, then moved toward the heavy double doors at the other end of the hallway. Just beyond, a meeting was already in session and Marco crept toward it. As carefully as he could, he looked through the crack between the doors to the council chamber and listened closely.

Chapter 7

The council chamber was among the most beautiful rooms in the Palazzo Ducale. The ceiling was impossibly high, painted gold and covered in intricate carvings. On every wall there were paintings of former doges in elegant attire, long gray beards hanging from their chins. An enormous marble table dominated the room, with ornate, high-backed chairs all around.

Through the crack in the door Marco saw the entire council had convened. Fifteen stern-faced nobles—representatives from each of Venice's oldest and most powerful families—were spaced evenly around the marble table. One noble wore a dark green vest over a stiff, collared white shirt. Another wore a satin jacket with brass buttons bearing his family's insignia. A third was still wearing his dark blue captain's uniform, as though he'd just returned from a long journey at sea. The withered, ancient doge himself sat at the head of the table, a long purple cape draped around his shoulders and pooling at his feet.

And standing in front of them, addressing everyone gathered, was Marco's grandfather, Lorenzo, and his uncle, Maffeo Polo. Maffeo had strong, proud features, a broad and muscular frame, and a head full of dark, unruly curls. As Maffeo spoke, Marco saw his face twist into a grimace, and the rest of the council looked on with expressions of shock and dismay. Growing nervous, Marco moved closer to the door and listened as hard as he could.

"Gentlemen," Maffeo said, "you know our caravan to be made up of the strongest men. We only grew more formidable over the course of our cursed journey, facing many trials and growing stronger from each. If our attackers had been ordinary thieves, they never would have been able to surprise us.

"Instead, they proved themselves to be . . . anything but ordinary. We had been riding toward camp through the desert night, with nothing around us for miles, when we saw a pack of travelers holding their ground up ahead. They appeared to be men—average men—lost and confused in the dark. But after all that followed, I have no doubt they were something else entirely."

Feeling increasingly uneasy, Marco tried to make out his grandfather's face through the crack between the doors. Lorenzo was standing by Maffeo, his eyes full of sadness, his long hair hanging limply around his neck. Marco felt a twisting in his gut—something was terribly wrong.

"As soon as we noticed them standing there," Maffeo said, his hands starting to tremble, "several of us called out in welcome. They did not reply, or even acknowledge they heard us. We continued toward them, still unafraid—as I said, they looked more than anything like lost and disoriented strangers.

"It was only once we were within striking distance that I noticed their eyes narrowing and their bodies growing tense. I am disgraced to say it, but at the time I did not feel concern. Then, without provocation, one of them leaped straight for the throat of the man next to me, with a speed and savagery unlike anything I have ever seen. Barely a moment later all of them were upon us, a flurry of deadly rage, each one faster and stronger than the next. These were not men, or men as we have known them. They snarled as they attacked, ripping into us with nails and teeth that were suddenly sharp as blades. Their eyes were deep and horrid, and they reveled as we bled.

"I wish I could report there was a lengthy battle. But in truth, even our bravest men were unprepared for the speed and savagery of their attack, and it was over quickly. In less time than I've taken to speak these words, not one of us remained standing."

"For my part I found myself cast to the ground, badly injured. It was a struggle to stay conscious. And it was only ther   very one of our men had fallen—that our attack-
e   narrowed eyes, the largest of them looked to
                    ʾind him, and take him on your back to
                    ian. They say this one has what we've

                              ey did as they were told. As I
                              ound a single one of us, his face
        ɟɪoʊ   ʌs my brother, Niccolo Polo, alive
        ʿhev   ∠ for him with purpose. . . . They
                              him up. Those of us still able tried to
sto   injuries there was little we could do. I
screamed ̭   ould, and I . . ."

Maffeo paused, lowering his head in defeat. "From that point until morning I remember little. Brief flashes of consciousness, mixed with fear and pain in the dark. My brother was gone."

Crouching outside the council chamber, Marco found his entire body had gone numb. His breath came in short, sharp bursts as he heard his father's fate, and the air felt unusually cold in his chest. He couldn't move, he could only keep listening. . . .

"In the daylight, we cleaned and bandaged our wounds and took stock of what had happened. Though we were desperate to go after my brother, we had heard terrible stories of Arghun and his growing army. If these beasts worked for Arghun and took Niccolo to him, we knew our numbers would not be sufficient. So we returned to Venice—to you, my dear council, to beg for assistance."

"I submit to you now with humility. You were right to forbid travel past the Insurmountable Mountains to the Unknown Lands, to keep us away from that which we did not understand. We ignored your warnings, and in doing so, we sealed our own fate. My brother and I, with that map in our possession, were blinded by possibilities for adventure, the opportunity to open new and profitable routes of trade. We moved quickly into the Unknown Lands and kept our plans secret. But our actions now threaten to carry the highest price."

Marco let the words flow past him. A map, a secret plan, his father and uncle in the Unknown Lands. It was all too much.

"If our misdeeds affected us alone, we would not be here before you today. But past the Insurmountable Mountains a new evil is spreading, something unlike anything even the

Unknown Lands have known before. We heard of it in rumors and hushed whispers, in terrified cries in the night. And then we came across it ourselves, my brother taken hostage by the sorcerer Arghun and his band of dark soldiers. Arghun and his forces are unlike any we have ever faced; their numbers are monstrous and growing, even the Mongols cower at their sight. If we allow this evil to continue unchecked, it will not stay contained. It will grow past the Lands, across the Mountains, and one day force its way into Venice itself—and, by the time it does, we may find ourselves unable to stop it. It is for this reason, for the sake of Venetian and Mongol alike, that I request a small army.

"Our largest merchant ship is leaving for Constantinople in one week's time, and I ask to be on it—accompanied by our bravest men, outfitted with our finest weapons and armor. Before this evil can strengthen and continue to spread, we will travel back to the Unknown Lands and strike. Together we will put an end to this sorcerer and his beasts, rescue my brother at Mount Dragoian, and show the world the might of the people of Venice. And through your wisdom, and our force, we will secure the safety of my brother and our citizens far into the future."

With that, Maffeo stepped back and waited for the council's reply. Lorenzo, just next to him, hung his head in despair, looking like he'd aged twenty years in a day.

The rest of the council began talking quietly among themselves. Marco could only make out some of what they were saying:

"—none have ever dared travel—"

"—they were warned—"

"—outrageous—"

"—who knows what horrors—"

"—the land of the Mongols—"

"—magic and beasts—"

"—when certain lines are crossed—"

"—they'd slaughter us all—"

Before they could continue, the council was interrupted by a series of loud and angry bangs—followed by a deafening crash—as the small hallway door across from Marco was slammed into again and again, then knocked completely from its frame by four furious palazzo guards.

Snapped out of his numbness by the sight of four guards heading straight toward him, Marco leaped up. He immediately started backing away in the only direction he could—through the double doors, and right into the council chamber.

Several council members stood up in shock, surprised to see a sixteen-year-old boy stumbling into the chamber, and even more surprised to see four guards drawing their blades in pursuit. Maffeo and Lorenzo's eyes grew wide. "Marco?"

Marco looked around the room, almost everyone now on their feet, and froze. He was surrounded. There was nowhere to turn.

Marco's brief hesitation proved enough for the guards to finally catch up with him, one grabbing him from the left, one from the right, and two from behind.

"We've got him!"

"Honorable Doge, this boy broke through our defenses—"

"We have no idea how it happened."

"Get away from me! Get away!" Marco shouted, struggling as hard as he could.

"Enough!" The doge, who had remained seated, now rose from his chair. He pointed his long, grizzled finger at the group of guards standing next to Marco.

"I know this boy. He should not be here—but, like his father, he has always been reckless, and his presence does not surprise me. He has come in search of his loved ones, and he has reason to be upset. Release him."

"But sir . . . the boy broke into the council chamber."

"He's been eavesdropping on your conversation."

"He's some kind of—"

"Release him!"

The guards let go of Marco, who was red-faced and breathing heavily.

Stepping away from the grand table, the doge moved slowly toward the Polos. He looked at Lorenzo, about to collapse, at Marco, growing more upset by the second, and at Maffeo, exhausted but determined. "We have all been given much to think of this day. And you Polos have issues of your own to discuss," the doge said. "Please go home and try to heal, safe in the knowledge that we, the council, have heard your pleas, and will employ all of our wisdom to accomplish what is right. In two days' time we will meet again, and the council will answer your request."

Chapter 8

The following night, Amelio, Marco, and his uncle Maffeo walked back along an empty stretch of docks toward the Polo residence, listening to the waves lapping gently against the creaking wooden ships.

"I still can't believe you broke into the council chamber," Amelio said, looking at Marco with something like awe. "And the way you shut out that guard—I could never—"

"I don't know," Marco said, with uncharacteristic bashfulness. "I wasn't thinking clearly. I just wanted to find out what happened to my father."

"And your father is going to be fine," Maffeo said, putting his arm around Marco's shoulders. "Arghun's forces kept him alive for a reason, and we know just where they're headed. In one week's time I'll be on my way toward them with an army by my side, and before you know it, I'll be bringing your father home again."

"I still can't believe you were in the Unknown Lands," Marco said.

"Nor can I," Amelio whispered.

"I'm sorry we didn't tell you. Both of you."

"How did you even do it? Get past the Insurmountable Mountains, survive the Mongols . . . ," Marco started.

Maffeo breathed in deeply. "Some time ago, your father and I found an unmarked map in our travels. We didn't recognize the places it depicted and turned it over to several men skilled in cartography for assistance—and, after much research, they believed it to be a map of the Unknown Lands."

"Spending time with the map, the cartographers identified three sets of coordinates that seemed to be marked off. Though they were skeptical at first, they soon agreed the coordinates illustrated a path through the Insurmountable Mountains themselves. Amazed, and unable to resist an attempt to prove this theory, we decided to investigate. If the path existed we would take it through to the Unknown Lands, where we might open new and profitable routes of trade. So as not to anger the council we swore to undertake our work in secret.

"Your father and I put ourselves to the task, gathered our bravest companions under cover of a trip to Constantinople, and set about our journey. The hidden path through the Mountains was, indeed, just as the map had shown. And though the trek was among the most difficult we've ever made, we found ourselves in the Unknown Lands—a place of impossible wonder, far different from anything we could have imagined."

Maffeo's eyes went wide with amazement as he spoke. "In the East, the rules of the world are altered. Some men have power over the elements. Others have control over beasts. I've come across animals that walk upright and live among humans, and beings beneath the sands that are unlike any creatures you've ever seen."

"It sounds incredible," Marco said, awestruck.

"More incredible than anywhere in all the world. Marco, in one strange city I rode on an animal with a nose bigger than my body, and a body as big as our house. In another, even the mundane was enhanced—I ate meals that tasted like nothing ever dreamed of in Venice, and saw beautiful buildings that put our palazzo to shame.

"But for all of this wonder there is darkness as well. Almost as soon as we arrived, we heard whispers of an evil spreading, a new danger unlike any that had come before. It was given a name—Arghun—and those who dared speak of him said he was an Eastern wizard corrupted by his own power, who had spawned hosts of monstrous creatures prepared to do his will. No one knew his plans or whereabouts, but all were fearful of his next moves.

"As we continued on our journey, we never imagined Arghun's next moves would involve our caravan. But they did nonetheless, and all of us were caught by surprise.

"I still don't know why they came for us. But I do know, if Arghun's forces wished us dead, they should have finished the job. Instead we lived, and now even the mightiest of his creatures will see they can still be slain by the steel of Western swords. Even now, as we speak, our bravest man, Aziz, is at the Polo estate in Constantinople readying supplies for the journey ahead. Aziz was with us in the Unknown Lands, and is as loyal and strong as any man alive. He would gladly lay down his life to destroy this sorcerer and bring your father home.

"Since meeting with the doge, I've rallied each member of the council to our cause. Many expressed fear and anger, insisting we never should have gone to the Lands in the first place. But after much discussion, and pulling in every favor I'm owed, most have committed to provide us with the Venetian soldiers we seek.

"Next week I will board a ship with our men, meet with Aziz in Constantinople, and retrace our steps to where we'd been. I promise you, Marco, it will not be long before I bring your father home."

Marco didn't hesitate. "And I'll come with you. I'm prepared to fight to save my father, and you'll need all the manpower you can get."

Maffeo gazed down at his nephew. "You're a brave one, Marco, you know that? But I'm afraid you're staying right where you are."

"Why? You just said that you—"

"Do you honestly think your father would have you put in this kind of danger? Why, I suspect, he would strike me down the moment I rescued him if I brought you along!"

"But you could use my skills with a blade, you know you can! I can fight! I can help you—"

"Marco!" Maffeo said. "Your heart is in the right place, but I've given you my answer. You're staying here with your grandfather Lorenzo."

Marco refused to give up. "How much longer will it be until you leave on your journey? One week?" he asked.

Maffeo nodded gravely.

"Then I have one week to convince you to bring me along.

To show you what I'm made of so you'll reconsider."

"You're just as stubborn as your father, you know that? I shouldn't be surprised." Maffeo sighed. "The answer will still be no—but if you'd like to spend the week attempting to change my mind, you're welcome to try."

For the first time all day, Amelio saw Marco smile.

The night sky was a deep, dark blue, and they began to pass houses as they walked closer to their own. The orange light of kindling fireplaces and waxy candlesticks glowed softly in the front windows they passed.

"While I was away, did your grandfather Lorenzo treat you well?" Maffeo asked, moving on to lighter topics.

"He had me spend too much time in the accountant's chamber instead of practicing my swordplay . . . but he did treat me well. He wants what he thinks is best for me," Marco said.

"And how about you, Amelio? Has your father, Giuseppe, been giving you too much work too?"

"He gives me a lot, but I try to keep him happy. I can handle it."

Maffeo ruffled Amelio's hair. "I know you can. If only my nephew didn't keep getting you into trouble, right?"

Both boys smiled again, and Marco spoke playfully in his own defense. "Hey, I don't get us into too much—"

But before Marco could continue, they arrived at their house and everyone stopped short. The front door had been left wide open.

"That's very odd," Maffeo said, looking at it strangely. He took a step inside the house and listened carefully. The only sound he heard was Lorenzo snoring—Lorenzo's snores seemed to grow louder, and his hearing slightly worse, with every passing year.

Then Maffeo heard something else from another room, much like glass shattering. It was followed by a loud thump, like something heavy had been knocked aside.

"What was that?" Amelio said, growing nervous.

"I don't know," Marco said, straining to hear more.

Maffeo pulled a dull short sword from the sheath on his belt. "I'm going inside to have a look. Both of you, promise you'll wait here until I come back out to get you."

Marco's eyes grew wide. "But this is just what I meant—what if you need backup—"

"*Promise me*," Maffeo said in a voice Marco had never heard from his uncle before. It was authority mixed with fear, and it left little room for dissent. "This is out of your league. I don't know what's up there, and until I do I want you someplace safe."

"We promise," Amelio said, looking at Marco and hoping his words were enough to bind them both.

Maffeo squeezed Marco's and Amelio's shoulders thankfully, then pushed forward into the house and left the boys outside.

After several minutes passed with no word, both boys began to grow nervous. "What do you think is going on in there?" Amelio said.

"I don't know, but I'm going to find out." Marco turned and scanned his house's large front lawn, his eyes finally touching upon a giant oak twenty feet away.

Then, without another word, Marco broke into a run toward the tree.

Amelio watched as Marco jumped up at the tree's base, wrapped his arms around the lowest hanging branch, and pulled himself on top of it. Marco climbed onto a higher branch, then again once more, until he reached a height in the tree that was level with the second story of his house. From that vantage point, if he squinted, he could just see through the window of the trophy room by the light of a single candle.

Marco focused his eyes, and what he saw in the trophy room made his blood run cold. In the window he made out his uncle's shadowy silhouette, dull blade drawn before him. Then someone—no, some*thing*, more beast than man—pounced in his uncle's direction, knocking him onto the ground and out of sight.

Chapter 9

Amelio, listening closely at the front door of the house, turned back around just in time to see Marco falling from the second-story tree branch.

"Are you all right?" he shouted as his friend hit the ground.

But Marco was back on his feet, dusting himself off and charging toward Amelio within moments.

"Your knees, they're bleeding! Why didn't you climb down?" Amelio said.

"There was no time, my uncle's in trouble!" Marco yelled. "I saw him through the window, we have to get upstairs!"

"But we promised him—"

Marco rushed past his friend, straight into the house, and along the first-floor entryway. Then he turned and bounded up the stairs as fast as he could. Hitting the second-floor landing, Marco could see the door to the trophy room at the other end of the hall. It was open by a narrow crack, and through it he saw frenzied movement.

Marco exploded down the hallway. When he was almost at the door, he raised his shoulder to crash through it—and, just as his shoulder made contact, a stronger force pushed back hard from the other direction, knocking the door shut and barring his way. Marco pushed at the door again, then again, but something prevented the door from moving. "No!" he shouted, slamming into it with all his might.

It was only when Amelio bolted up the stairs to join his friend, and the two boys pushed together, that the door finally began to give. When they combined their strength a sliver of space opened between the door and the trophy room, and while Amelio pushed one final time, Marco was able to slide his body through it. Then the space slammed shut behind Marco, barring Amelio from the room.

Once inside, Marco saw that the candle had gone out and the room was dark.

It took a second for Marco to regain his bearings, and in that time a large figure flashed past him, then crashed headlong out the trophy-room window.

Marco rushed after it, and from the shattered window, he saw something unlike anything he'd seen before scrambling to its feet on the ground below. It wore no clothing and was easily seven feet tall. It was hairless, with scaly gray skin that was peeling in chunks and wide, horrible eyes that were entirely milky-white. In its mouth Marco saw hundreds of sharpened teeth. Its frame, though thin, looked sinewy and strong; its movements were fluid like an animal's. And, where its hands should have been, it had a pair of enormous and jagged claws.

Once the creature was standing, it looked up toward Marco and, making eye contact, let out a single, terrible shriek. Then it ran, impossibly fast, away from the Polo household. In no time at all it had entirely disappeared.

Before Marco could process what he'd just seen, he heard a low groaning sound behind him. He whipped around, ready for anything, and saw the heavy force that had first prevented him from pushing into the room.

It was his uncle Maffeo. The full weight of his body was slumped against the door. Maffeo was holding his hands weakly over his stomach, his sword on the ground beside him. Marco saw deep slashes and a large red blotch on Maffeo's shirt, the redness quickly spreading.

"Oh, god . . . no, please . . . ," Marco said, running over and falling onto his knees next to his uncle.

"Marco . . ." Maffeo looked at his nephew, weakly lifting a hand toward him. There was blood everywhere.

"We're going to get you some help. Hold on, stay as still as you can," Marco said, tears running down his face.

Maffeo moved his lips, but his wounds were deep and it was already a struggle for him to speak.

"What? What is it?"

"Aziz . . . ," Maffeo said. "Tell Aziz . . . he knows what to . . ."

"Aziz?" Marco said, frantic. "The warrior in Constantinople? What should I tell him?"

"Listen closely, Marco . . . my bed. My bed. Go to my bed. Find the map. . . . Take the . . ."

Then Maffeo's body started to shake. He breathed in sharply one final time and everything abruptly went silent.

Chapter 10

One week later, Marco stood in the Polo dining room opposite his grandfather Lorenzo and refused to give up.

Lorenzo looked at Marco with eyes that were red from days of crying, his finely wrinkled face appearing years older. He leaned heavily on his cane as if he could barely walk without it. "Marco, you must understand," Lorenzo said. "One of my sons has died."

Marco held his ground. "He died trying to do what was right. And your other son—my father—still has a chance!"

"Not from the council, he doesn't."

"Not if we don't fight! If we don't convince them to send their men—"

"Marco, you don't get it!" Lorenzo said, raising his voice. His hands began to tremble. "Calling in everything he was owed, your uncle Maffeo might have been able to gather some support to go back to the Unknown Lands to save your father. Not much—I know the council—but some. But now, without him, there will be no army. With the way he died, they're all too scared—"

"The way he died proves there's a threat to us all! A threat we can't just walk away from!"

"But they *will* walk away, Marco! They're horrified. Some of them don't believe our story; they insist it was an ordinary thief, or some terrible accident. And the rest would rather die themselves than send more men to meet the same fate. You must understand, the council has no appetite for blood, and they're terrified by what resides in the East. They'd rather walk away now, and forget what your father and uncle discovered, than risk more lives and climb in deeper. As far as the council is concerned, Marco . . . it's over. They will never again speak of the Unknown Lands."

Marco looked at his grandfather with fire in his eyes. "And you? The ship my uncle would have taken leaves for Constantinople tonight, and another won't leave here for three weeks' time. Would you walk away now too, when my father could still be alive? Would you let Venice remain at risk and my uncle go unavenged?"

Lorenzo put an old, grizzled hand on Marco's shoulder. "Right now, what I would do is cherish what I have and mourn what I've lost. I would rather learn from our mistakes and keep you here, where I can watch over you, and we can both be safe." The two looked at each other, and Marco saw his grandfather begging him with his worn and tired eyes . . . but he refused to relent.

Just then, Marco and Lorenzo were interrupted by the unexpected clanking of dishes, followed by footsteps approaching the dining room door. They both looked up to find Amelio cautiously entering the room, a silver tray of tea and biscuits in his hands.

"Hi . . . I heard your voices and thought you might be able to use these. If you're hungry, that is. Or thirsty. Just in case." Amelio looked down at his feet, trying his best to be a comfort without knowing exactly what to say.

"Thank you, Amelio. I'm fine for the moment—but the sentiment is appreciated." Lorenzo gave Amelio a gentle smile. "Why don't you stay here with Marco while I attend to things upstairs? I have a feeling, right now, my grandson could use a friend."

Amelio nodded and set down the tray of tea and biscuits on the polished dining room table while Lorenzo made his way from the room.

Once Lorenzo was gone, Amelio turned to Marco. "How are you feeling?"

"Like there's something I have to do."

Amelio instantly grew serious. "What are you talking about?"

"If our roles were reversed . . . if it were me trapped over there, instead of him . . ."

"Marco, stop it!" Amelio said, appalled. "How can you still be thinking about this? You're not talking about fighting in your house wearing armor, or breaking into a room of men who have known your family since you were a boy. You saw what those fiends can do!"

"I can't just leave him, Amelio. You don't understand."

"I do! I know how much your father means to you. I've known him since I was born—he's been like my own family! When I was younger, he used to—"

But Marco had stopped listening. He spoke over Amelio as if he weren't even there. "The trading ship my uncle would have taken leaves tonight. And my uncle said Aziz would be waiting in Constantinople to travel to the Unknown Lands to save my father. Even without a Venetian army, Aziz may have another plan. It's worth the risk."

Amelio grew frantic, doing everything he could to talk Marco down. But it was too late. Marco was already absorbed in his memories, thinking about his uncle's bedroom—how he had snuck into his uncle's room days before, and after covering every inch, he'd found a secret compartment concealed in the base of his bed. Inside, his uncle had hidden his pack containing everything he had mentioned that terrible day. A map of the Unknown Lands. A blank diary, set to record the rescue of Marco's father. And, unexpectedly, Marco also found a strange, softly glowing blue pearl.

Marco told no one, took the pack to his room, and hid it away. With his dying breath, Marco's uncle had told him where to find it, and Marco knew what that meant.

That pack held everything Marco would need to begin his journey. If no one else would save his father, Marco now had everything he needed to do it himself. . . .

Chapter II

Later that night, Marco felt the darkness in his room like it was alive, thick and swirling just over his bed. He lay quietly in the dark, counting each breath, until every bit of noise in the rest of the house died down. Even then Marco remained perfectly still, waiting for the late-night scratch of his grandfather's cane, or, farther downstairs, the sound of Giuseppe creeping back inside to finish some nearly forgotten chore. Eventually, after a very long stretch of darkness and silence, Marco convinced himself it was safe.

Steeling his resolve, and refusing to think any more than he had to, Marco crept out of his bed. With his fingertips leading the way, he felt around his room and put on his clothes without making a sound. His uncle's pack had plenty of room left inside, and before lying down, Marco had stuffed it full with clothes, money he had saved, and a quill pen to record his journey in his uncle's diary. Marco put on the pack and tested its weight. It didn't feel like it would slow him down.

Marco knew he would have to move quickly—if he didn't, he wouldn't go at all. The council, the Unknown Lands, what happened to his uncle in the trophy room: If he let himself stop to think, it was terrifying. But if he was impulsive, like always— what his grandfather always told him was his greatest flaw—he would push forward and do what was right. He'd have some kind of chance to save his father.

So Marco cleared his head and started moving. He made his bed and, on his pillow, left the note he'd written for his grandfather hours before. He kept it short.

> Grandfather, I will not let you lose another
> son. I'm boarding the ship for Constantinople.
> I know the journey will be hard, but I will
> soon return with my father. I love you always.
>
> Marco
>
> P.S. There's money in my desk for your
> ruined cane. I'm so sorry, for everything.

Marco ran his fingers over the paper one last time.

Then he crept out of his room, moved past his grandfather's bedroom—listening to the faint sound of his grandfather snoring—and padded down the stairs. He slunk past the second floor and the first before making his way down the main hallway. Finally, Marco slipped out the front door of his house and closed it tightly behind him.

At night Venice was particularly beautiful, the moon and stars twinkling in the water of the canals.

Marco saw his reflection shimmering in the water just beneath him as he walked quickly down Venice's streets. The air was cold against his face. After several blocks, the scenery of his youth began to turn sinister—the enormous houses of the aristocracy suddenly dripping with shadows in every crevice, the temporarily abandoned merchant carts, covered in blankets, looking for all the world like lumbering fiends. Even the storefront windows, which gleamed so brightly during the day, now seemed to hold only menace within.

Choking back his fear, Marco took his familiar shortcut to the harbor. As he passed through the streets of the shantytown he picked up speed. This area—always full of screaming, yelling, and racket—was, for the first time, entirely silent. Marco knew he would soon arrive at the harbor, and once he was there and boarded that ship, there would be no way for him to turn back.

Chapter 12

The enormous ship was already boarding when Marco arrived. A string of merchants was lined up beside it, pulling wooden carts piled high with every manner of goods. When he was younger, Marco would wait by the ship for hours to see his father off, wanting more than anything to be on the boat as well. Now he would finally get his wish, but he wouldn't be on the ship with his father. Instead, he would be entirely alone.

But Marco still had one more obstacle to overcome. Everyone boarding already had a ticket—except Marco—and tickets were no longer being sold. Luckily, he'd been around these ships long enough to have a plan. Several men in uniform were on the ship's deck, checking rosters, collecting tickets, and inspecting each merchant's goods as they came on board. Every now and then a merchant would take his son along with him, and Marco used to watch enviously as those boys helped their fathers present their carts for inspection. The men in uniform usually smiled and almost never checked the boys' tickets as well. All it would take, Marco suspected, was an older merchant who might be in need of a helping hand. . . .

Waiting until the moment was right, Marco spotted a thin, reedy man pulling a cart that was clearly too heavy for him. Marco rushed over, wasting no time.

"Sir, my father's up ahead and he hates seeing anyone struggle. He has my two older brothers helping him and doesn't need me—he asked that I help you instead."

"Are you sure?" the reedy man said, his voice a curious mix of surprise and relief.

"It's no problem at all. I'm strong for my age. Put the cart on my shoulders, I'll take it on board."

It worked almost too well. Marco found himself on the ship's deck in record time, his uncle's pack tight around his shoulders and a five-lire piece from the skinny merchant in the palm of his hand.

Walking over to the side of the ship, Marco breathed in deeply and leaned over the edge. Venice was to his left, the most majestic city in all of Europe. And the sea was to his right, waters he'd longed all his life to travel. Being on a boat like this was all he had ever wanted. But now that he was finally here, he felt so—

Before he could finish that thought, Marco heard someone shouting, then two firm hands slapped down on his shoulders from just behind him.

Chapter 13

"What do you think you're doing?"

Marco whipped around, preparing for the worst—and was shocked to find himself face-to-face with Amelio.

"What am I doing? What are *you* doing?" Marco asked.

Amelio's blond hair was matted with sweat, and his eyes were filled with rage. "I'm trying to stop you from making the biggest mistake of your life! Look around you!" Amelio gestured at the merchants moving past them on the ship's deck, each one exhausted, easily twice their age, pulling heavy carts to the storage area below. "You don't belong here!"

"Amelio—"

"Don't 'Amelio' me! Look, I had a feeling you were going to try something like this—you're my best friend, but you never knew the difference between brave and stupid. I was lying in bed when I heard the door to your house open. . . . I followed you here."

"You followed me?" Marco asked, incredulous.

"I tried to reach you before you boarded, but you had too much of a head start."

"How did . . . how did you even get on the ship?" Marco said.

"You're not the only one who knows how to get on without a ticket. We watched your father leave from here plenty of times. That man over there—" Amelio pointed to a heavyset man several yards away, leaning against his cart and trying to catch his breath. "I ran over and offered to help him with his goods."

"Amelio, I know what you're trying to do, but I don't have a choice. I'm going to rescue my father."

Anger flashed across Amelio's face. "You do have a choice. What you don't have is a *plan*. You don't know the first thing about Constantinople, do you—or this soldier, Aziz. What does he even look like, Marco? How do you know he'd take you to the Unknown Lands, or that he'd have any idea how to rescue your father once you get there?"

Marco's anger grew to match Amelio's own. "So what would you rather I do—stay in Venice and let my father die?"

As the boat rocked gently, and merchants rushed past, Amelio glared at Marco. "You know, my father always said you were trouble, and I defended you. I said, when it mattered most, you wouldn't be so reckless—you'd have all the sense in the world." Amelio looked at Marco with new eyes. "But I was wrong. You haven't given any real thought to this . . . or to the people you're leaving behind. You're so desperate for adventure, you'd rather get yourself killed trying to—"

This was the limit of what Marco could take. "Hey! I didn't ask you to follow me here, all right? I've made up my mind! If you're going to stand around and insult me, why don't you just go home?"

"I came here to get you to listen to reason—but if you don't want to hear it, maybe I will!"

"Maybe you should!" Marco worked himself into a frenzy. "You know what, that's an order! I'm sick and tired of you holding me back, of . . . of you forgetting who works for who around here!"

The instant those words escaped Marco's mouth, he desperately wished he could take them back.

"Who works for who?" Amelio said, clearly hurt.

"Amelio . . . I didn't mean—"

"No, you did mean it," Amelio said, swallowing hard. "And you're right, my family does work for yours. Next time, I won't forget that." Amelio patted Marco on the shoulder, refusing to meet his eyes. "Good-bye, Marco. You want to make this fool's journey? You go ahead and do it without me."

Without another word Amelio turned and walked away, heading for the ramp where he'd boarded the ship. Marco watched him go with a heavy heart, wishing for all the world there was something, anything, he could do or say.

Chapter 14

Amelio was halfway across the deck when shouts rang out all around him. "Anchors up, we're ready to sail!"

"Take your positions!"

"We're about to embark!"

Merchants who hadn't yet brought their carts below deck quickly began lugging them forward, and the entire floor of the ship started trembling under the massive shifting of weight.

Caught in a sudden stampede of merchants, Amelio's breath quickened. He pushed ahead as fast as he could, trying to get to the ramp he'd climbed to board the ship. But every time he took a step, his path was blocked by a merchant or his cart.

"Excuse me—I have to get through, excuse me—"

"Wait in line, boy!"

"Get out of the way!"

"You're going to get run over!"

Amelio darted and weaved, slipping between and around carts, desperate to get ahead. As he drew closer to where he needed to be, he saw a gruff sailor with several days' beard anxiously completing his paperwork by the ramp. But before Amelio could approach him, he felt a sickening jolt of motion under his feet, and another round of shouts filled the air.

"Anchors up!"

"Here we go!"

"No!" Amelio charged the rest of the way to the sailor, reaching him just as he finished writing.

"What was that jolt?" Amelio asked, sounding desperate. "Did the boat start off?"

"We're on our way," the sailor said. "Ramp is up, we're at sea from now until Constantinople."

"We were supposed to have more time!" Amelio grew frantic. Over the side of the boat, he could still see the Venetian shore. "I have to get off this ship!"

The sailor looked at Amelio like there was something wrong with him. "You just got on. You didn't buy a ticket for nothing."

"I didn't buy a ticket, I . . ." Amelio felt sick to his stomach. "Please, I need your help. . . ."

"Wait a minute—I remember you," the sailor said, fully taking in Amelio's blond hair, pale face, and skinny frame. "You came on board with your father, didn't you? Heavyset man, wheezing, big, full cart. The cart was three times bigger than you are."

Amelio spoke quickly. "I came on with him, but he wasn't— he's not my father. I don't even know him. Listen, I can't stay on this boat!"

As soon as the words left his mouth the ship lurched forward, and, as it began to drift from the shore, another round of cries rung out.

"To Constantinople!"

"No! I have to get off!"

The sailor began to grow angry. "Listen, kid, I have things to take care of. I don't know why you want to get off, and I don't care—no one leaves the ship once it's in motion. Now come with me, you can't go wandering about on your own. I'm taking you back to your father."

With that, moving faster than Amelio imagined he could, the sailor shot out his hand and grabbed Amelio roughly by the wrist. Amelio struggled but the sailor ignored it, yanking him forcefully, and unstoppably, back toward the center of the ship.

Chapter 15

Amelio struggled desperately, trying to get away from the sailor. "You can't do this! I can't stay on this ship! He's not my father, he's—"

The sailor yanked Amelio's arm roughly. "If you don't stop squirming—"

Just then, the sailor saw another boy with clear blue eyes and curly brown hair rushing toward them. Without missing a beat, Marco's face twisted up with fury and he started screaming at Amelio.

"Where did you dart off to? Where have you been? You can't run away like that, what's wrong with you!"

Before Amelio could respond, Marco's tone softened and he turned apologetically to the sailor. "I'm so sorry, sir. He's my little brother. Our father got seasick down below, and this one got scared and ran off. My father sent me to get him—I promise, he'll be punished severely. I can take him from here."

Suspicious, the sailor turned from Marco to Amelio.

"This true?"

Amelio said nothing, scared and still furious at Marco. But, with the ship pulling farther away from the shore, he realized he had no choice. Amelio forced an apologetic tone. "I'm sorry, sir. My brother's telling the truth. Our father's a traveling merchant, but he gets ill when he's on the seas. I just . . . got scared and tried to get off. I'm lucky my brother found me in time."

"I'll make sure he stays out of trouble from here," Marco said, relieved to find Amelio playing along.

Still suspicious, but eager to get on with his work, the sailor took his hand off Amelio. "All right, that sounds fair. But this is your one chance—it'll be a different story if I have to speak with either of you again. We have a ship to run, we're not here to babysit. You boys make sure you stay out of trouble."

"We will, sir, I swear it," Marco said.

Without further delay, Marco pulled Amelio over to the other side of the ship. The wind blew in their faces as they left the sailor behind.

"I'm so sorry, Amelio," Marco whispered. "What I said earlier, and I . . . I watched you walk away. I saw the anchors go up, then that sailor grabbed you. This seemed like the only way to save you."

But now it was Amelio's turn not to listen, and as they arrived at the boat's edge, Amelio's expression melted into one of horror. "Marco, how is this happening? How am I still on this ship?"

"You never should have followed me—"

"You never should have come here in the first place! What am I going to do?"

"I . . . I don't know," Marco said. Amelio was on the verge of tears.

"What's my father going to think? He's never going to forgive me. And he never liked you to begin with."

Marco looked hurt. "You always said your father did like me. . . ."

"Well, now that there's no chance he'll ever change his mind, you might as well know the truth. And this is only going to make it so much worse. . . . What have you gotten us into?"

Amelio slumped down against the side of the boat. After a time, Marco slumped beside him.

For a long while neither boy spoke, taking in the motion of the waves, the hard wood beneath them, and the cold, salty air. Across the deck, merchants gazed out at sea or prepared to head down to the cabins below.

Staring blankly ahead, Marco put his hand on his friend's knee. "I'm so sorry, Amelio. I never thought you'd get pulled into this. And I'm terrified." Marco paused for a moment. "But if I had to have someone along with me . . . if it had to be anyone in the world . . . I'm really glad it's you."

Marco and Amelio continued staring ahead, breathing in the salty air, and they both lapsed back into silence.

Chapter 16

The following morning Marco woke at dawn and quickly got dressed. The area below deck was packed full with cabins, and the night before, he and Amelio had claimed one as their own. Each cabin was basic—bare except for a scratched wooden table and two hard mattresses wrapped in stained sheets—but they were both so exhausted they fell asleep as soon as they lay down.

Now Amelio was still snoring gently, his arms and legs tangled in his sheets. Marco wrote him a short note, saying he was going for a walk, then grabbed his uncle's pack and quietly made his way from the cabin.

Up on deck the sun was shining brightly and the wind was crisp against Marco's face. Merchants were milling about and, overhead, sailors were working on the boat's mast and gazing out at the ocean from the crow's nest. The ship had covered some distance during the night and there was now nothing but water in every direction, interrupted by the occasional gull sweeping down from the sky.

Marco always wondered what his father felt when he left Venice, and now he knew. There was the exhilaration of being on the open seas, the sadness of leaving behind everything he loved, mixed with the strange excitement of the impending unknown. Marco breathed in deeply and felt only a trace of the previous day's fear and apprehension. This was the riskiest thing he'd ever done . . . but it felt right.

Walking over to the side of the ship, Marco sat down where he and Amelio had slumped the night before. Seeing no one nearby, he took off his pack and rifled through it, his fingers eventually landing on his uncle's rolled-up map.

Marco took out the map and spread it in front of him—when it was unrolled, it was nearly two feet in length. If it weren't for this map, Marco knew, his father and uncle would still be in Venice, sitting around the dining room table with his grandfather Lorenzo. If his family never found it, they would still be whole.

But, by the same token, the map now allowed Marco to set out and rescue his father.

Marco ran his fingers over its drawings. The map had been made entirely by hand, and many sections were drawn in painstaking detail. Marco placed his fingertip on the northern part of Italy, the black dot that represented the city of Venice. From there he traced the route their ship was about to take, down through the Adriatic Sea and around the islands of Greece before cutting through the Aegean to arrive in the city of Constantinople.

Just outside of Constantinople they would find Aziz. Marco moved his fingertip toward what he assumed would be their next destination after Constantinople, pushing through the Turkish grasslands and passing the Caucasus Mountains to find themselves in the trading city of Bukhara.

On the far border of Bukhara, Marco saw a symbol representing the enormous Iron Gates, the fabled gateway between the West and the East. And, just beyond the Gates, the map revealed the great Insurmountable Mountains, including the hidden, narrow path that wound between them.

Beyond the mountains the map became far less detailed. These were the Unknown Lands, and only select locations were marked—the two most prominent being the Forbidden City in Peking, which was whispered to be the home of the dreaded Kublai Khan, king of all the Mongols; and, several days journey beyond it, Marco saw a symbol for Mt. Dragoian. Almost everything else was lightly drawn, obscure, or illegible, a mystery to the entirety of the Western world.

Marco looked at the symbol representing Mt. Dragoian, felt a slight chill, and—not wanting to think on that place any longer than he had to—turned back toward Constantinople on the map. He put his finger on the exact port where their ship would soon land, then slowly and carefully traced it down the forest paths they would have to take through the cluster of woods on Constantinople's border. After traveling through those woods, Marco and Amelio would find themselves at the Polo estate—and, inside, they would finally meet the man Marco's uncle had told them about, the warrior Aziz.

From there, Marco was sure, Aziz would tell them even more about the fate of his father; Aziz would also help put

Amelio on the next ship to Venice. His friend would be in plenty of trouble, but at least Marco had a plan to get him back home. . . .

As more merchants woke and began walking about on deck, Marco rolled up the map and put it back in the bag with the rest of his things. The strange blue pearl glowed eerily in the darkness of the pack.

Pushing everything aside, Marco fumbled about until he found his uncle's leather-bound notebook and old quill pen.

Flipping through the notebook, Marco saw that every page was blank where Maffeo would have recorded the rescue of Marco's father. That rescue would still come.

With the cold air blowing against his face, and a silent promise to finish what his uncle had started, Marco pressed his quill to the paper and started writing.

"The Adventures . . . of Marco Polo . . ."

"I wrote down all of the nomad's words: 'Arghun was a fire mage, the most dangerous kind of sorcerer you can be. He cozied up to the khan for access, to try and learn the forbidden summoning spells . . . and it worked. Now Arghun's spies are everywhere. Black magic, caravans disappearing, strange creatures in the night. And who knows what terrors the Insurmountable Mountains hold?'"

—FROM THE JOURNALS OF MARCO POLO

Insurmountable Mountains

Part Two

IRON GATES

and

INSURMOUNTABLE

MOUNTAINS

Chapter 17

"We're nearly there," Marco yelled over his shoulder as he hurried down the narrow forest path. "Hurry up!"

Swinging a small sword he found on the boat like a machete, Marco hacked away at the branches crowding them in on all sides. Marco and Amelio had set out from Constantinople's port that morning, when the path leading to the Polo estate was wide and clear. But the closer they got to their destination, the narrower and rockier the path became. Now Marco was practically bushwhacking his way through what he thought would be an open trail.

Several yards behind him, Amelio struggled to keep up.

"Ouch! Marco, these branches are—there are some kind of thorns all over them. Can't we slow down so we don't keep getting—ouch!" Amelio said.

"Hey, you're the one who keeps insisting I get you back home," Marco shot back. "The sooner we get to my family's estate in these woods and find Aziz, the sooner he can buy you a one-way ticket back to Venice."

"Don't you mean find Aziz so he can buy *us* one-way tickets back to Venice?"

Marco increased his speed, pretending he didn't hear the question.

"Are you sure we're even going the right way?" Amelio said, pointing out a rotting gray tree trunk with two long, clawlike branches. "That looks creepily familiar; I think we've been walking in circles. Can we please just check the map?"

"The map?" Marco repeated. "Amelio, the entire time we were on that ship you were either sleeping or getting seasick. I didn't have anything else to do—I basically memorized the entire thing. I've never been in these woods before, but I could probably take us down every path by heart."

"It's not my fault I got seasick," Amelio mumbled defensively.

"It's fine. I stayed with you in the cabin, didn't I? If our positions were reversed, you would have done the same for me."

"If our positions were reversed, I would have let you take a break when we docked in Constantinople so you could have gotten used to walking on dry land again. . . ."

Marco pushed forward, holding tight to the straps of his uncle's pack while he ducked under another branch. "Hey, I wanted to stop in Constantinople just as much as you," Marco said. "But we can't let Aziz think no one's coming and set off on his journey alone. We don't know when he and my uncle were supposed to meet." They arrived at the bottom of a small hill and Marco looked up at the sky. "Plus, the daylight's starting to fade. I'd rather get through these woods before dark. . . . Luckily, we're nearly at the estate."

"You've been saying that for hours," Amelio muttered as Marco sprinted up the hill. "'We're almost there. We're nearly there. We'll be there any minute.' I don't think you even know where 'there' *is*, Marco. Where's 'there'?"

From the top of the hill, Marco looked down at Amelio with a wide, confident grin. "It's there," he said with a sweep of his hand. "*There.*"

As Amelio continued over the crest of the hill, the tall, dark turret of a tower rose into view, followed by the whole of a gray stone building and the black bars of an iron fence. From the hilltop, Amelio could see a coat of arms above the estate's front entrance—the Polo family crest.

"This is it," Marco said to himself, taking it in. "My father described the Constantinople estate to me, but it's another thing to see it in person."

Amelio felt a similar sense of awe as he gazed upon the building, resembling nothing so much as a small castle. But the longer he looked at the Polo estate, the more his feelings gave way to a creeping sense of dread.

"But, Marco . . . doesn't something about it seem a little . . . off?"

Marco's eyes crept from one part of the estate to the next, and he slowly began to see what Amelio meant. Some of the fence's iron bars were bent at jarring angles, as if they'd been forcibly pulled apart. The wide front lawn had been dug up in strange patches. And most of the windows looking into the estate had been smashed, broken glass littering the ground.

"What happened here?" Amelio asked as the extent of the damage sunk in. There was no reply from Marco, just the howling of the evening wind.

After a long pause, Amelio asked the next-most-pressing question. "What do we do?"

"What can we do?" Marco said without taking his eyes off the house. "We need to find Aziz. If he's inside, we keep going."

"And if we find . . . someone else?"

"We'll deal with that when it happens. *If* it happens. Which it won't," Marco said with more confidence than he felt. "We came all this way, Aziz will be inside, and that will be that."

As Amelio watched, Marco clenched his jaw and started down the hill, moving toward the estate with purpose. The sight of the castle had been, for a brief moment, so comforting. Now Amelio thought the cold stone building looked like a ghost house.

Amelio glanced back over his shoulder at the distance they'd already traveled, thinking of the port where they'd disembarked in Constantinople. At this point, he couldn't see even the most obscure outlines of that giant city. All that was behind them was a thick forest landscape, growing increasingly menacing as the sun continued to set. Marco was right—there was no turning back.

"Hey! Hey, Marco! Wait for me!"

Chapter 18

The two boys stood motionless at the stone steps leading to the Polo estate's entrance.

"Feel free to lead the way," Amelio said, eyeing his friend.

Fighting back a wave of fear that rose from the pit of his stomach, Marco approached the front door. There was a steel knocker in its center, and Marco grasped it firmly before rapping three times.

They waited in silence. Nothing happened.

Marco grabbed the knocker and rapped again, harder than before. This time the weight of his hands pushed the heavy door forward, and it slowly swung open with a deep, mournful groan.

"It must have been unlocked," Marco said, trading glances with Amelio.

What they saw inside didn't provide any further comfort.

The house had been completely ransacked. Furniture was tipped over, paintings ripped off the walls. The carpets were torn, and the contents of shelf after shelf had been knocked onto the floor.

"Hello?" Marco said uneasily. "Is anyone home?"

"Hello?" Amelio chimed in, his voice sounding tinny and small in the cavernous space.

To the left of the entrance they saw a large, empty dining room. A place setting remained at the table—a glass of wine still half-full, next to food sitting uneaten on a plate. To their right they saw a richly furnished but disheveled parlor, from the center of which a great stone staircase twisted upward to a second floor. In front of them a long hallway stretched out, eventually pushing back into the recesses of the house.

"I don't like the looks of this, Marco."

"Neither do I. But my uncle told us Aziz would be here."

"If Aziz is still here, why did he trash the place? Or let someone else trash it?

"Let's check this way," Marco said, taking a deep breath, ignoring Amelio's questions and starting down the dark hallway that stretched out in front of them. Amelio watched him go. Then, not knowing what else to do, he forced himself to follow several steps behind.

As Marco pressed ahead into the hallway's shadows, his eyes adjusted slowly to the darkness. Halfway down he saw two wooden doors facing each other, and he opened the door to the left—it was a small pantry. Several rows of shelves jutted out, supporting jars of orange preserves and a delicate ceramic dish filled with expensive, chewy candies.

"At least we'll have something good to eat tonight," Amelio whispered, grabbing a handful of the candies and slipping them inside his front shirt pocket.

Marco turned to try the handle on the door to the right, and upon opening it, he gasped aloud.

"Father!"

Amelio looked past Marco, who stood frozen in the doorway. They were in front of a small sitting room. Propped up on a red velvet armchair, facing directly toward them, was a portrait of Marco's father—but his eyes had been torn out, leaving two large and gaping holes. Across the mouth there was a long, curved slash. The color of the crimson chair bled through the ripped spaces, making it look like Marco's father was staring at them with bloodred eyes and a maniacal, devilish grin. On the floor next to the chair were the casually discarded, scattered contents of a jewelry box.

"Let's keep going," Amelio said, placing his hand on Marco's shoulder and turning him away, propelling him onward toward the end of the dark hallway.

The two boys walked in silence toward a door that came into view at the end of the hall, passing a large bay window on the way. Through the window they noticed a small garden on the side of the house. It had been completely dug up, much like the front lawn—there were vegetables and flowers strewn everywhere, every stone overturned. "Whoever did this was pretty determined," Amelio said with more than a hint of fear.

"What were they looking for?" Marco said, bewildered.

Finally, Marco and Amelio arrived at the final door. They opened it carefully and stepped inside, entering a small, bookshelf-lined room.

"Aziz?" Amelio said.

"Nobody's here." Marco glanced around. "But from the looks of it, this must have been my father's study." Marco headed toward the heavy wooden desk at the back of the room. "Aziz might have used this room too. Maybe there's a clue among all the papers."

Marco rifled through the desk while Amelio took in their surroundings. To his left were two identical, evenly spaced stained glass windows. The glass in each was designed in abstract patterns of blue and orange shapes. Depending on how Amelio looked at them, the shapes resembled a blossoming flower, or a fiery explosion, or a smiling man with a comically oversize hat. Just next to the stained glass windows there was a display case holding a menagerie of animals sculpted in glass: a humpbacked camel, a fox, an eagle with spread wings. Amelio reached in and picked a spiny alligator off a shelf, amazed at how light it felt in his hand.

"There's nothing here but receipts in some language I don't understand," Marco said in a disappointed tone, looking up at Amelio from behind the desk.

But before Amelio could respond, Marco raised his hand abruptly to silence him. Both boys strained to hear a noise in the distance.

It was the sound of footsteps making their way down a staircase.

"Hello!" Marco called out loudly.

Instantly the footsteps stopped. Both boys looked nervously at each other in the silence.

"Aziz?" Marco called out loudly again.

Another moment of silence. Then they heard the footsteps—*click clack click clack*—coming quickly toward them down the hallway.

Chapter 19

"Aziz?"

The figure who appeared in the doorway of the study looked nothing like what either boy expected. He was very tall and extremely thin. He had pale skin, two beady black eyes, a small and upturned nose, and a few wisps of white hair that stretched limply across the top of his head. He wore shabby, disheveled clothing.

"Hello," he said in a strange, high voice.

The man's eyes swept from Marco, behind the heavy desk, to Amelio, standing in the corner of the room by the display case with the glass animals. Stepping fully into the study, the man turned and gently shut the door behind him. It slipped into its frame with a gentle *click*.

"You're Aziz? The warrior?" Marco said.

The man looked at both boys; his nose twitched. "Of course," he said. "I am Aziz." Surprised but determined to stay on course, Marco launched into a speech that he'd prepared in his head.

"At last. This is Amelio," he said, pointing to his friend, "and I'm Marco, the only son of Niccolo Polo. My uncle, Maffeo Polo, who was supposed to have met you here . . . was killed, in Venice, not long ago. He—"

"Polo?" the man cut in. "You are . . . Polo?"

"I'm Marco Polo," he said.

"Polo's son?" Slowly, almost imperceptibly, the man began taking steps toward Marco behind the desk.

As he did, Amelio couldn't help but notice how long the man's legs were, even in proportion to his tall frame.

"The son of Niccolo Polo, and the nephew of Maffeo. I have my uncle's things in my pack," Marco said, gesturing to the bag over his shoulder. "My uncle left me his map, which will help us in our journey as we cross over to the Unknown—"

"The uncle left you . . . *things*?" the man interrupted. "I am, as you say, Aziz. I was looking for something I . . . lost . . . but perhaps I simply did not know where to look."

"Something you've lost?" Marco repeated, staring at the man's face as he stepped up to the edge of the desk—a face that suddenly filled Marco with an undeniable feeling of dread. It wasn't just the sickly absence of color, or the unusually small size of his features. He couldn't place it, but the longer Marco gazed at the man's face . . . the deeper he stared into his beady black eyes . . .

Then, in a flash, he realized what it was.

"Your eyes," Marco said with terror in his voice. "You've been staring at me for minutes. Don't you ever blink?"

The man said nothing. Then, finally, he blinked.

But his eyelids hadn't moved. A *second pair of eyelids*, some kind of milky white membrane, closed just behind the first—coming from the *sides* of his eyes!

"What *are* you?"

The inhuman eyelids slid out again, narrowing the creature's eyes to two thin, vertical slits.

"Why don't you wait here, Polo?" the figure said in its unnaturally high voice. "The others will be here soon, and we shall explain everything. Arghun already has one at Mount Dragoian, but now he needs the other, too—and you may have just what he's been looking for."

From his side of the room Amelio heard Arghun's name and grew pale, beginning to fully understand what they were up against. But this fiend was already too close to Marco; there wasn't any room for his friend to escape. Desperate for something he could do, Amelio turned to the display case just behind him and grabbed the largest, heaviest glass animal he could find, a giant tortoise. Catching Amelio's eye, Marco offered an almost imperceptible nod, validating the plan.

"You're right," Marco said, trying to hold the creature's attention until Amelio could make his move. "I bet I do have what Arghun's looking for. And I'd love to give it to him, just like you said. Why don't we all wait here until the others come? We can all just—"

Before Marco could complete his sentence the glass tortoise flew through the air and crashed into the back of the creature's head with a heavy *thunk*. It let out a shriek before its features twisted into a snarl and it whipped around toward Amelio.

The second the creature took its eyes off him, Marco put his hands under the heavy desk, lifted up with every bit of strength he had and smashed the desk sharply into the creature's back. It pitched forward and fell onto the ground in surprise. Then, quickly finishing the job, Marco heaved the desk forward until it tipped, slamming down onto the creature's long legs and back.

As the full weight of the desk crashed down, the creature let out an inhuman, prolonged, and deafening scream.

Immediately, both boys plugged their fingers in their ears against the sound—it continued growing louder and louder at a pitch unlike any they'd ever heard. For several seconds Marco thought his eardrums would explode under the unbearable noise.

Then, one after another in rapid succession—with the *ratatatatata* sound of a firecracker—the entire collection of glass animal sculptures exploded under the sonic pressure of the creature's wail. Next were the panes of the glass display case itself, until finally—with two deep, booming crashes—both stained glass windows exploded in a cloud of orange and blue shards of glass.

Now the creature stopped yelling and began its struggle to get the desk off its legs, with every other sound in the room drowned out by a painful ringing.

Though he could tell Amelio was yelling loudly to him from the other side of the room, Marco could barely hear his words. Luckily, he could read his lips clearly enough.

"I think I heard something else! There are more of them coming down the hall!"

Both boys looked at the door leading back to the long hallway, then down at the struggling creature, then—at the same time—to the two empty frames where the stained glass windows had been. Through the empty frames they could see the garden outside the house.

Without saying a word to each other, they knew their path. At opposite ends of the room, each boy took a few long strides, cut sideways, then jumped headlong out the windows.

Their fall was cushioned by the soft soil of the churned-up garden. They quickly scrambled to their feet, but before they could choose a direction in which to run something else froze them in their tracks.

Emerging from the trees and bushes just across the garden yard—and moving toward them at full speed—was a tall shadowy figure, carrying a large and jagged saber in its hand.

Chapter 20

It never gets easier, does it?" Amelio said with a nervous gulp.

The two boys briefly stood rooted in place as the dark figure ran toward them. Then Marco withdrew his small sword from its sheath and stepped forward, placing himself between the approaching enemy and his weaponless friend. Crouching into his best battle stance, he raised his blade and waited for their adversary to attempt an attack.

But instead of continuing its rush toward them, the figure slowed as it approached, coming to a full stop just beneath a cherry tree several yards away. There it stood, completely still, scrutinizing the two boys from the shadows.

They could barely make out the figure's face in the inky darkness. Its body looked like a man's—six feet tall and powerfully built—slightly set-off against the moonlit landscape. Catching a shaft of moonlight, the long, curving blade of his saber glinted ominously.

"Both of you," the figure commanded, his voice gravelly and low. "Come with me if you want to survive."

"With you?" Marco replied in a steely tone. "Why should we trust you?"

Before the man could answer, the creature in the house let loose a scream of rage and pain, its horrible screech echoing across the valley.

"That's good enough reason for me," Amelio said. "Let's get out of here."

But Marco refused to let down his guard. "I just learned my lesson—I'm not sure what we've stepped into, but I don't trust *him* any more than I trust *that*. For all we know this could be Arghun himself!"

Amelio turned from the shadowy figure and looked back at the house they'd just escaped. Through the shattered windows he heard the terrible clamor of the creature huffing and puffing, of desk drawers crashing away, and of scratching at the smooth stone floor—these sounds chilled Amelio to the bone. He knew that thing would soon free itself, and once it did, they wouldn't stand much of a chance on their own.

"Marco, we can't afford *not* to trust him," Amelio pleaded. "He would have attacked us already if he meant us harm!"

But Marco said nothing, his gaze fixed on the terrifying figure holding a large blade before them.

"For once in your stubborn life," Amelio said, his fear unexpectedly turning to anger, "can you please listen to me? Just *once*, Marco? Please?"

Marco's stance softened as he gave Amelio a long and searching look. Then, after a brief pause, he slipped his sword back into its hilt.

"Good idea, listening to your friend," the man said in his gruff voice. "Now come this way, quickly." Without wasting another moment, the man turned around and started jogging toward the eastern border of the property. The two boys followed close behind. When they reached a barnlike building at the far edge of the estate, he quickly unbarred the entrance and waved them both in. Then he slammed the door behind them, plunging all three into impenetrable darkness.

Amelio groped around, desperately trying to regain his bearings. In a moment of panic and confusion, he second-guessed himself. What if Marco had been right? What if they'd just walked into a trap?

And then he felt it. A blast of warm, putrid breath hit the side of his face, and an inhumanly strong, furry arm pressed down firmly on his shoulder.

Chapter 21

After several seconds of darkness a candle was lit.

The glow cast by the small flame helped suggest the layout of the room—the junctions of the wooden walls and dirty floorboards, the support beams that crisscrossed the ceiling, the rectangular horse stalls that lined the right side of the barn.

Marco looked around, his eyes adjusting to the gloom. The shadowy man stood in front of a long worktable, gripping a candle. Turning around, Marco saw Amelio by the horse stalls—his eyes shut tight, his body stiff. A dark figure passed over Amelio's shoulder.

Then a sudden breeze blew out the candle, and darkness flooded up again.

A flame was struck; the candle relit. This time the glow was brighter, illuminating even the darker recesses of the stalls.

"Amelio," Marco called out. "What are you doing with that horse?"

Amelio nervously opened his eyes. A large black stallion,

its long muzzle laid on his shoulder, was poking around inside Amelio's front shirt pocket.

"It's just a stupid horse!" Amelio said with noticeable relief. "You just wanted the candies I put in my shirt pocket, huh?" Amelio let out a laugh.

"Shhh—be quiet," the man said, instantly silencing him.

Both boys turned to watch in rapt attention as the man stepped quickly into an empty horse-stall, moved aside several bales of hay, and uncovered a brown pack full of supplies.

"Should we all go back there?" Amelio asked in a whisper. "If we hide, do you think the creatures won't be able to find us?"

"I'm just getting supplies. You can't hide from those things," the man said, grabbing the pack off the ground. "Not once they've gotten your scent. The Abarimon would find you in seconds."

"The Abari-*what*?" Marco said.

"The Abarimon," the man said again, coming out from the stall. "They came three days back under cover of darkness and ripped apart the house. They seem to be looking for something. I escaped to the woods, hiding and waiting. But now you've come along and made them angry. Here," he said, taking two swords in leather sheaths from the brown pack, then throwing them at Marco and Amelio's feet. "Take these. You'll need them."

The boys grabbed the swords nervously and secured the sheaths to their waists. As they did, Marco couldn't help but give voice to the suspicion that had been taking root in his head. "You—you're the warrior Aziz, aren't you?"

The man abruptly stopped what he was doing. "And how

do you know who I am?" he asked, his voice instantly thick with menace.

"Because we came all the way here to find you," Marco said.

"You two came here to find *me*?" the man asked, his eyes darting between the two boys. Then his gaze fixed on Marco, and his jaw fell slightly open.

"The resemblance . . . *you're Niccolo's son!*" he said. "I never— I thought you were two local boys looking for mischief—I tried to shout to you before you entered the house."

"My uncle sent us," Marco said. "He told us he was due to meet you here."

"But where is he? Is Maffeo with you? Does he know they've found us—I've only been hiding in the woods until he could arrive, so we could both avoid a battle and escape—"

Both boys' faces fell at the mention of Maffeo's name, and Aziz stopped speaking mid-sentence, instantly understanding what must have happened. Now he knew why these two were here in Maffeo's place.

" . . . I see. I'm so sorry. . . ."

"I—" Marco began. "I still don't—"

"We'll talk more later," Aziz said, any trace of vulnerability swiftly replaced with a steely-eyed sense of purpose. "I gave my word I'd wait for your uncle, and I was prepared to stand and fight if that's what it would take to hold my ground until he arrived. But if you're . . . if you're here in his place . . . then we can still try to avoid a confrontation. If we move quickly, we may be able to head off before they find us."

Before either boy could attempt to speak, Aziz started giving orders in a firm, clear voice. "There's no time for questions—do exactly as I say. Niccolo's boy," he said, pointing at Marco, "get three horses out of their stalls, saddle them, and bring them to the barn's back door. Can you do that?"

"Yes, sir," Marco said immediately.

"You," Aziz said, pointing first at Amelio, then at a small hole in the wooden planks of the barn's front door, "I need you to keep a lookout while I fetch more supplies. If we're to leave here now, there's yet more we'll need to bring with us."

Both boys immediately rushed to do as they were told. While Marco led the horses out of their stalls one at a time, Amelio stood by the door and watched for any signs of the creature, stealing occasional glances at their still-mysterious benefactor each time he bent down to put more supplies into his pack.

Finally regrouping alongside the saddled horses, Aziz put a hand on both boys' shoulders and said, "Now, pay attention." Both of them listened closely as Aziz explained their escape plan.

"Abarimon rarely travel alone—if you saw one in there, there are bound to be others close by. Now that it's come into contact with you directly, that thing and its allies will go on the hunt. Our plan is to get as far away from them as we can, as soon as possible. Here's what we're going to do.

"In a moment I'm going to open the back door to the stable. When I do, you both need to ride back the way you came, all the way to the front of the house. Go out the front gates and take the forest path to the right. A hundred yards in that path will zigzag three times down a hill before arriving at a shallow river. I'm hoping we can avoid the Abarimon, but if they're anywhere in sight, you'll need to charge into that river and ride straight through to the other side—the water will be knee-deep to your horse. If they're after us, I'll be at your rear and divert their attention so you'll have enough time to ride through. Then I'll meet you on the other end of the river once it's safe. You got that?"

"We do," Amelio said, starting to breathe heavily.

"Go back the way we came, out the gate, and take a right. Go three zigzags down the hill, then across the water if they're after us," Marco rattled off quickly. "Got it."

"Good—one last thing. If you hear the Abarimon, at any point, *do not look back.* Just keep your head forward, do what I said, and ride as fast as you can. Understood?"

Both boys nodded solemnly.

Aziz headed over to the stable's back door while the boys mounted their horses, Amelio climbing on the same black stallion that snuck up and scared him earlier.

"Wait," Marco said, getting onto a slightly larger horse. "There are two more horses still in the stalls. Should we let them go so the Abarimon can't use them to come after us?"

"If the Abarimon decide to come after us, they're not going to need any horses," Aziz said matter-of-factly, as he took the plank out of the stable's rear door.

"Now, on the count of three, you head through those doors and charge straight ahead. Ready?" Aziz said.

"Ready," Marco said, his hands tight on the reins of his horse.

"Ready," Amelio echoed.

Aziz jumped up on a mighty black horse of his own.

"One . . .

"Two . . ."

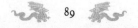

Chapter 22

...Three!"

Marco and Amelio's horses burst out of the gate. The cool night air whipped past them as their horses turned and charged, side by side, Aziz riding two lengths behind.

To reach their path, they had to gallop past the house they'd just escaped. They rode alongside the trees at the edge of the property, trying to keep as much distance between themselves and the house as possible. But it wasn't long before they heard a piercing noise. The Abarimon, sniffing the air outside the garden, saw them rush past, pointed its finger, and let out another horrible shriek.

"I was afraid of this—I can hold it off!" Aziz yelled. "Keep riding and don't look back!"

Aziz slowed his horse as the boys charged further ahead. He drew his sword and put himself directly between the creature and the boys.

Rushing toward the gate, Marco peered over his shoulder

to see Aziz falling back, with the Abarimon illuminated by the moonlight just behind him. As Marco watched, the Abarimon began a sudden and monstrous transformation. With the sound of crackling bone, both of the Abarimon's feet twisted around entirely on its ankles, until they faced the opposite direction. Its knees began to twitch, and in seconds they popped inward and inverted entirely. Its fingers grew and sharpened until its hands were jagged, deadly claws. Finally, its eyes grew glassy, then reflective, then fully white. Seeing it now—looking like the creature that killed Marco's uncle—it was hard to believe it ever passed for human at all.

Marco was so transfixed by the scene unfolding before him, he didn't notice the low-hanging branch in front of him until it smashed across his head.

CRACK!

Marco fell off his horse and onto the ground, disoriented, seeing colors swirling all around him. His horse continued riding into the distance.

"Marco!" Amelio yelled, hearing his friend fall and stopping his horse.

Seeing Marco hit the ground at the same time, both the Abarimon and Aziz started toward him.

"Keep riding!" Aziz yelled to Amelio as he rushed ferociously toward the fallen boy. "I have Marco, go, go, go!" Amelio kicked his horse and did as he was told.

Still behind Aziz, the transformed Abarimon had broken into a full-force run, stronger and faster than any creature should be. In no time at all it nearly caught up with him.

Without slowing, Aziz put out his arm, grabbed Marco off the ground by his shirt, and, with a jerk, swung him across the back of his surging horse. "Grab on to my waist, Marco! Now!" Marco clung to Aziz for dear life.

Approaching the front of the house, Aziz saw Amelio already galloping through the front gate and onto the forest path to the right. Then Marco started to shout. "Aziz, it's behind us! It's only twenty feet away!"

Soon it was fifteen feet away, impossibly fast, its white eyes gleaming as it clenched and unclenched its sharpened claws.

"We're not going to make it!" Marco screamed.

"Then I'll buy us some time!" Aziz yelled. Reaching down, he unfastened a long, coiled whip he'd slung to his waist. As they approached the swinging iron front gate, Aziz snapped the whip forward. It wound around one of the iron bars.

Five feet away.

"It's right on top of us!" Marco shouted.

With a powerful surge the creature sprang forward, extending its claws and baring its hideously pointed teeth. It soared through the air toward them, so close Marco could see the drool dangling from its mouth.

But, with a snap of the taut whip and the rusty squeal of iron hinges, the bars of the gate swung closed the instant Aziz and Marco rode through it.

BOOOM! The creature's head hit the iron gate, and the metal vibrated with a deep ringing. It collapsed to the ground as their horse continued on ahead.

"Ouch!" Marco said.

"We're not out of this yet," Aziz barked, charging sharply down the path to their right.

Continuing at breakneck speed, they shot forward until

Marco could see the hill with the three bending zigzags, the riverbed at the bottom, and the wide blue ribbon of water just beyond. "Hold on tight, we're nearing the hill!" Aziz yelled.

No sooner did they make it down the hill's first bend than Marco saw the Abarimon, recovered, bounding furiously after them. By the time they hit the second bend, the Abarimon was already at the first.

"It's back! It's gaining on us!" Marco shouted.

"We're almost there!" Aziz yelled.

They reached the third zigzag in the road and saw Amelio on his horse riding straight into the river in front of them. They were only thirty yards away from joining him.

Bounding behind them, the Abarimon crouched down on its haunches, compressed itself like a spring, then—with an unbelievable surge of power—leaped high into the night air and landed immediately in front of Aziz and Marco, cutting them off from the river. Aziz's horse screeched to a halt in terror.

Without a word, Aziz climbed off his horse and drew his sword. "Stay there, Marco." With the *swoosh* of claws slicing the air, the creature went straight for Aziz, who was able to jump backward just in time. The Abarimon slashed again, two more times, almost impossibly fast. Narrowly sidestepping each blow, Aziz swung his own sword as hard as he could and gashed the Abarimon across its exposed stomach. The creature looked down at the blood leaking from its torso, then angrily up at Aziz.

With a deafening shriek, the Abarimon charged, grabbed Aziz by his shirt, then threw him forward, sending him hurtling down the remainder of the trail toward the water. Before

Aziz could stand up again the Abarimon jumped through the air and crashed down on top of him. Snarling, it raised its enormous claws above its head and prepared to deliver a fatal blow.

Crack!

The creature let out a terrible wail as a heavy rock struck it square in the back of the head. Still on top of Aziz, it whipped around.

"You . . . *Polo's son* . . . ," it snarled, seeing Marco standing on the path, two more rocks at the ready. It began to salivate.

This brief distraction was all the time Aziz needed—he held tight to his sword and plunged it directly into the Abarimon's chest. The creature made no sound. It turned to look quizzically at the sword going through it. It didn't move for several seconds. Then it collapsed, slumping all the way forward on the blade—and on top of Aziz—with a lifeless *thud.* Aziz pushed the creature off of him, stood up, and ripped his blade from its chest.

Before Aziz or Marco could say a word to each other they heard another Abarimon's screech, echoed by the wails of two others, and the sound of more large creatures heading their way.

"The others!" Marco yelled, remembering the dead Abarimon's warning.

Aziz and Marco quickly mounted their horses and rode into the water. Though the river was wide, the current wasn't particularly strong, and they made it quickly to the other side where Amelio and his horse stood waiting.

Moments after they reached the opposite bank, three more transformed Abarimon crashed down the zigzag of the hill and burst out onto the riverbank. But they each slowed as they neared the water, snarling with a mix of anger and fear. Though Aziz, Marco, and Amelio prepared themselves to fight, it seemed these Abarimon did not intend to follow them across.

"What . . . what are they?" Amelio asked in stunned disbelief, staring at the Abarimon once they made no further efforts to chase them. "Men, or some kind of—"

"They were men, for a time. Until Arghun got hold of them," Aziz replied cryptically.

"But we're safe now? They're not going to come after us?" Marco asked.

"It looks that way. Something about the water seems to be holding them off," Aziz said.

As if it had heard them, the largest of the three Abarimon turned its head slowly from left to right, surveying the three humans with a merciless gaze. It sniffed at the air—two short snorts and one deep breath.

"It's taking in our scent, isn't it?" Marco said. Aziz silently nodded *yes*.

Raising a hand, the creature pointed at the boys across the river and let out a scream. Amelio felt as if they'd all been marked for life.

Then, without another word, the largest creature turned around and headed back up the zigzag path. The two other creatures followed silently behind it.

Chapter 23

For a long while the three sat wordlessly by the edge of the river, catching their breath and trying to make sense of what they'd just seen. Then Amelio broke the silence.

"Just one question," he said. "*What just happened? I mean, what was that?*" Clearly shaken, he got up and paced nervously along the riverbank, talking like a dam had broken inside of him. "This was a bad situation to start with—*what are we doing here?*—but an even better question is *what are they doing here?*, because there's *no such thing as monsters*, so what just happened exactly? If this is some kind—"

"Amelio," Marco cut in, attempting to calm his friend while trying his best to stay calm himself. "Amelio, stop!"

"You want *me* to stop?" Amelio said, turning on Marco. "No, *you* need to stop! *You've* been getting us into trouble since we were old enough to walk, and *this* is the biggest mess of our lives! So *you* stop—this is happening, it's not some crazy adventure story!" With that, Amelio whipped around and stomped over to a large tree several feet away. He leaned against its trunk and crossed his arms in front of his chest.

Marco turned to Aziz, still breathing heavily. "He'll calm down," Marco said. "Amelio didn't intend to be here—it's a long story."

"I see," Aziz replied, sizing up the boys now that the immediate danger had passed.

"But he's right. I mean, what were those Abari-men?" Marco said.

"Abari*mon*," Aziz corrected him. "Myths come to life."

"Huh?" Marco said.

"I grew up in Bukhara, the city that divides the world into East and West via the great Iron Gates at its border," Aziz said. "When I was a child, my grandmother told me stories of the West you know. But the East . . . in her telling the East was another place entirely, a land of Mongols and mystics, still wild and untamed. A place where ancient dragons ruled the skies, creatures mixed with common men, and some men had power over the elements of earth, water, wind, or fire that made them anything but common.

"I heard these stories until I was old enough to travel some distance to the East myself, to the border of the Insurmountable Mountains. Once there, travelers who knew more of the world than I told me my grandmother had exaggerated. The East was indeed a far different place, where some forms of magic still exist. But my grandmother took things too far, telling me about serpents that lived beneath the desert, or creatures called Abarimon that split the difference between man and beast. Abarimon were numerous and deadly, she had said, man's animal nature brought to flesh, and they were twice as strong and five times faster than any human could be. But traveler after traveler had never heard of such creatures come to life. Eventually I dismissed all her tales as the creative imaginings of an old woman, told to a receptive grandson hungry for adventure.

"Until, that is, your father brought that map, and we journeyed through to the Unknown Lands ourselves. That's when I heard of the fire mage Arghun and the fear he inspired. And when we all faced creatures under his reign that could be nothing other than what my grandmother had once described. Man's animal nature brought to flesh.

"Even in Eastern lands of magic, Arghun is spoken of as something new. His power brings back a darker past. Those Abarimon we just faced—I no longer think they never were. I just think they long ago ceased to be. Until Arghun found a way to summon them back to flesh."

"If Arghun summoned these . . . Abarimon," Marco said, "and they're the ones who attacked my father's caravan, who killed my uncle in Venice, and ransacked our Constantinople estate . . . why is he doing this to our family? What does he want?"

"If I only knew," Aziz said, shaking his head.

"And if Arghun and his Abarimon are this powerful . . . how are we going to rescue my father from Mount Dragoian?"

"We?" Aziz said.

"We're going to rescue my father together," Marco said. "Isn't that what you've been waiting for?"

"I was waiting for your uncle, a skilled warrior. He was to bring with him a hundred Venetian men," Aziz said, readjusting the saddle on his horse. "It will prove difficult, but things can be done to save Niccolo . . . even without soldiers from Venice. However, taking an inexperienced boy with me would make the task infinitely more dangerous. Your intentions are good, but you could only be a liability."

"Liability?" Marco said defensively. "If I remember correctly, you were about to get your throat slashed open by an Abarimon not two minutes ago, until I provided the distraction that gave you the upper hand. I just saved your life."

"No," Aziz said. "I just saved yours. Once when I rescued you from the garden, and again when you got knocked off your horse. If you'd only listened to my instructions, that fight with the Abarimon never would have occurred."

"He's right, Marco," Amelio said. "When you looked back and that tree branch whacked you in the head . . ."

Marco clenched his jaw, his face turning red. "I don't care. I'm a better warrior than you realize, and I didn't come all this way to turn back now."

"Listen," Aziz continued in a gentler tone. "Even if you *can* fight, you have no experience in the lands of the East. I've only just learned many of its rules. For a boy like you . . . if I led you into danger, your father would never forgive me. And if anything happened to you, I would never forgive myself."

"You can't lead me into danger if I was heading there anyway. You're being unreasonable," Marco said.

"I think he's being more reasonable than anyone I've spoken to in weeks," Amelio said. "And I couldn't agree with him more. So, Aziz, why don't you put us on the next ship from Constantinople to Venice, and we'll both be out of your hair once and for all."

Aziz's brow furrowed. "As much as I wish it otherwise, I'm

afraid that's not an option either. The next ship for Venice won't set off for another week, and now that those Abarimon have your scent, Constantinople won't be safe. We're going to have to keep moving forward. In the morning we'll depart for Bukhara, a city several days journey to the East. I'm an old friend of an innkeeper there—he can put you up until I return with Niccolo Polo, or with news of his fate. You'll be safe with him."

"I don't like that the sound of that at all," Amelio said, looking defeated.

"I'm afraid neither of you is in a position to argue," Aziz said.

"And what makes you think I'll just sit at an inn hoping my father will be rescued?" Marco said. "If I wouldn't wait back in Venice, why Bukhara?"

"Because I'm also old friends with Bukhara's head prison guard," Aziz said with a hint of menace. "If you keep this up, I'll get you a room there instead of the inn. The food is terrible, but you'll both make plenty of interesting friends."

"You—" Marco sputtered. "But I came all this—what about—"

Marco wanted to continue in protest, but he didn't know what else to argue. He stared at the ground beneath his feet and took a deep breath.

"Fine. You're right. Both of you," Marco finally said. "I'm not a finely trained warrior, and I don't know anything about the Unknown Lands. But what I do know is, I'm terrified for my father. And if anything happened to him, and I didn't do something to prevent it . . . I could never forgive myself. Maybe I can aid you in battle. Maybe I can only fetch you meals and clear brush along the way. I don't care what it is, but I need to know I'm doing something to ensure my father's return. Going back home and waiting . . . it just isn't an option."

As Aziz listened, his expression slowly gave way to something that suggested pride. He thought for a long moment, noticing Maffeo's pack around Marco's shoulders and seeing, if he took after his elders, who Marco might one day become. When Aziz continued, his voice was gentler. "All right, both of you. I'm not making any promises. But for now—let's start moving. You may have the chance to prove yourselves yet, but in the meantime there's plenty of ground to cover. Let's see how we feel once we arrive in Bukhara."

Chapter 24

They had been traveling east for less than an hour when they finally found Marco's runaway steed. She was galloping through a moonlit briar patch, wild-eyed and whinnying hysterically. Even after Aziz managed to wrangle her with a long coil of rope, it took several minutes of soothing and stroking to calm the horse completely.

"The Abarimon really frightened her," Aziz explained.

"I can relate," Amelio muttered.

With everything they needed, they rode for another hour before stopping to camp at the mouth of a nearby cave. Only a few minutes after they settled inside their rocky shelter, it began to rain outside.

The long day's journey and their life-or-death struggle had left Marco and Amelio on the brink of exhaustion. Marco quickly scribbled everything they'd encountered in his uncle's notebook. Then—although they had no blankets, and only their balled-up shirts for pillows—each quickly drifted into a deep sleep, lulled by the patter of rain echoing musically throughout the cave.

When Marco and Amelio next opened their eyes, it was light out. Aziz had already risen and was tending to a small fire outside.

The two boys dressed, grabbed their packs, and joined him.

"Sleep well?" Aziz said as they drew closer.

"As well as can be expected," Marco said, sitting next to Amelio on the ground. Azia handed Marco one of the rolls that had been warming by the fire, and Marco bit off a steaming piece. "You brought food with you?" Marco asked.

"I had everything I needed already in my pack back at the stable, so we could set off as soon as your uncle arrived. Or so I could set off on my own, if I had to."

"You really would have gone on your own to rescue my father? If my uncle never came?"

"You look just like him, you know," Aziz said, dodging the question. "Smaller. And a little less sure. But it's hard not to see your father when I look at you."

"What did he do?" Marco asked. "That you're prepared to risk your life to save him?"

Aziz offered up a slight smile. "I've known your father for many years. And when the time came, he always did what was right. That's all I'm doing now. From our talk yesterday, it sounds like that's what you're doing too." Marco seemed to accept this, for the moment, and Aziz nodded in Amelio's direction.

"It's good you're both awake. We still have a few days' ride before we reach Bukhara—we should get going."

"Bukhara . . . ," Amelio said, playing with the word in his mouth.

"And what happens after Bukhara?" Marco asked. "Whether you take us with you or not . . ."

Aziz looked at Marco with a hint of suspicion, then decided not to hold back. "After Bukhara . . . the trek to rescue your father begins in earnest. Every day that passes is another he's in danger; the sooner we return to the Unknown Lands, the better."

"If that's the journey, I may have something that can help," Marco said, taking off his pack and rustling around inside. He took out a rolled piece of parchment. "It's my uncle's map. It shows the path through to the Unknown Lands."

"I have my own," Aziz said. "Everyone on our first expedition made a copy. Not that I need one any longer—I don't think I could forget a word on that map if I tried."

"Oh. I see," Marco said, clearly disappointed. But before he could put the pack away, it caught Aziz's eye.

"That's your uncle's pack, isn't it? I recognized it earlier. What else do you have in there?"

"Some of my clothes. Some money. But mostly things my uncle left me—the map, an empty notebook. A blue pearl."

"A pearl . . . can I see it?

Marco reached into the pack and dug around until he found the light blue pearl glowing softly and small enough to fit in the palm of his hand. Its surface was cold to the touch, but there seemed to be an odd heat radiating from its center.

"Strange," Aziz said. "Your father had a red pearl just like this, acquired in trade from a fellow merchant. We had never seen a red pearl before; your father thought it would bring him luck, and when we were traveling he brought it along with him in his pocket. I didn't realize there was a blue pearl as well. Your uncle and father must have gotten them both together.

"You can put it back in your bag," Aziz said in a new tone, his eyes growing somewhat glassy as he spoke about the Polo family. "If we want to get to Bukhara in time, we should start moving."

"'If we want to get to Bukhara in time'? In time for what?" Amelio said.

"In time to hire a nomad," Aziz continued, his voice growing stronger. "Past Bukhara are the Insurmountable Mountains, with a narrow path between them and a harsh desert beyond. We'll need a nomad to guide us through."

"But I thought the map—" Amelio went on.

"There's a map, and it points to the narrow path we'll need to take. But surviving the path and the desert beyond is another thing entirely, and for that we'll need a nomad guide. Nomads are in Bukhara for three days of the month, but no longer—if you miss them, you have no choice but to attempt the journey on your own. And, after my first experience, without a nomad I don't have much hope any of us would live to tell the tale. Now come, gather up your things. Let's cover as much ground as we can while the light is still with us."

Chapter 25

Over the course of the following days they rode along a forest path. As they progressed, the terrain grew more dangerous, and slowly but steadily the forested mountains gave way to the sand and desert regions of Persia, which led to the great city of Bukhara.

"Both of you. Before we go farther, take these," Aziz said, slowing his horse to a halt, reaching into his pack, and removing three thin, flat, gray stones, each about the size of a small coin.

"What do we do with these?" Marco asked, taking one and marveling over how thin it was between his fingers.

"I grew up in Bukhara, learning a wide range of languages as a boy. But there are many words spoken here that you won't understand, and as we travel farther East that will go for me as well. These stones, when placed in your outer ear"—Aziz illustrated by placing a thin stone in his own—"have an enchantment of some kind. They can bend words from even the most foreign tongues and make them sound just like our own."

"So . . . when you stick this in your ear, you can understand any language?" Amelio asked, carefully placing the stone.

"Like much we'll soon find, I can't explain how it works. But once it's in place you'll have no problem understanding others. Employing methods of their own, most will be able to understand you as well."

Aziz's expression was somber, befitting the seriousness of their task. But, especially with Bukhara just ahead, Marco couldn't help himself. With an enormous grin, he slipped the thin stone into his ear.

A short time later the three came to the top of a small sand dune and found they had arrived. Where only a moment before they could see nothing but desert and cloudless skies, now a majestic city was spread out below them. Shimmering in the heat of the midday sun were the fortified walls, towering turrets, and dome-capped temples of Bukhara.

"I've never seen anything like it," Amelio whispered, mouth agape.

Aziz put a hand on Amelio's shoulder. "Wait until you get inside and see the Iron Gates."

"Who can wait?" Marco yelled, running past the two of them. "Let's go!"

Within moments they found themselves entering the busiest city Marco and Amelio had ever seen.

Bukharans were coming and going in all directions. Old men bounced along on gray-faced donkeys, whipping the animals with thin riding crops. Younger ones rode atop horse-drawn carts, carrying food and merchandise to the marketplace. One princely-looking man with a ruby-studded sword rode by on a Persian steed; four bodyguards followed just behind him on coal-black stallions.

Marco, Amelio, and Aziz headed into the city, winding their way down narrow streets lined with two- and three-story buildings. Canvas awnings jutted out everywhere, providing a patchwork pattern of shade for the vendors whose booths lined the streets. Everyone wore colorful wraps on their head and shoulders to block out the desert sun. The densely packed crowds became an ocean of surging colors, a sight made all the more fantastic juxtaposed with the gray sands of the desert.

Turning a corner, they came upon the bustling central marketplace. Aziz couldn't help but smile at the expression of wonder on Marco's and Amelio's faces. "Surely some parts of Venice aren't too far off from this."

"Venice gets pretty busy," Marco said. "But the water and canals divide everything into pieces. You can't fit too many people in one place at a time. Whereas this . . ."

Marco looked in wonder at the enormous Bukharan market, stretching from where they stood as far as the eye could see. Every inch of dusty earth had a makeshift structure thrown on top of it, and every structure was there to show off the strangest, most dazzling array of goods Marco had ever seen.

And filling every free inch between the structures were more people—people of every shape and size in the world. Men who were broad and tall, women who were squat and fat, those with skin of every shade and color, dressed in everything from long, flowing, beautifully colored dresses exposed at the legs, stomach, and back, to those entirely obscured in black shrouds, every one of their features hidden from view.

The only thing all of these people had in common that Marco could see was the hunger with which they lusted over the items on every counter, each stand's offerings as different as could be from what was coming up next. As Marco and Amelio watched, a woman bending over a table nearby picked up a strange yellow frog by the skin of its back, dangling it up and down as its merchant stared at her with small, greedy eyes. A man caressed a small wooden elephant at a neighboring table, admiring its smoothness and detail, while his wife stole a glance at the next table's goods, a combination of green jade and pungent, powdered spices.

"Venice is lots of things. But Venice is nothing like this," Marco said, desperate to take it all in. "My father . . . now I know why he . . . Once you've seen things like this, you can't live your life in just one city anymore."

Aziz grinned, amused to see Marco almost unable to finish a sentence.

"I can't wait to tell him everything I've seen. He always wanted to take me to places like this—it was only my grandfather who held him back. Hey, what is that thing? *Is that a camel?*"

Without another word Marco dashed down a dirt road after a man who was leading a humped brown animal on a red leash.

"You know, he really does believe all that," Amelio said to Aziz as Marco ran off. "The stuff about his father wanting to take him along on his journeys, but his grandfather not allowing it. I mean, he knows it's not true. His father doesn't take him because he's too young and not yet prepared. But Marco still tells his stories. Isn't that strange?"

"No, it's not strange at all," Aziz said, looking ahead.

"One time Marco got in trouble in Venice—I mean, Marco was always getting in trouble in Venice—but this time, he got in a fistfight with another local boy. The boy said the reason Marco's father is always traveling is so he'd always have an excuse to get away from Marco. I've never seen Marco get so upset."

"Speaking of Marco getting into trouble and people getting upset," Aziz said, "where in the world did that boy just disappear to?"

Chapter 26

One block up and around a corner, Marco was having a discussion with the owner of the camel. "My father told me all about them," he rambled, "but I've never seen one in real life." The man smiled and nodded, laughing as Marco looked straight into the camel's face. The camel looked back at Marco with two strange, almost alien eyes. Then it turned its head to the side and spat onto the ground.

"There are many wonderful sights to behold in Bukhara, aren't there?" a voice intoned smoothly over Marco's shoulder. Turning around, Marco found himself face-to-face with a short, stout merchant in colorful flowing robes.

"*Hello*, young sir!" the merchant said, performing a deep, exaggerated bow. "Allow me to introduce myself: I am Theron, known far and wide as the most respected jewel merchant in all of Bukhara. African diamonds, Chinese pearls, I have them all. Can I convince you to take a look? Take a gander at this, perhaps?" he said.

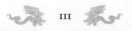

With a magician's sleight of hand, from Theron's finger-tips there suddenly dangled a metal chain with a polished dark stone hanging at its end. "Note the rich layers of color in the grain," the man said softly, swinging the stone hypnotically like a pendulum. "Look deep into its mysteries."

"No thanks," Marco said mechanically, his eyes nonetheless following the stone's rhythmic path back and forth. "I . . . I really should be getting back to my friends."

"Why, your friends are right here!" Theron said, as he stepped backward into an alleyway and drew Marco along with him. "They were just down this alley and in my shop looking for you!"

Marco barely registered the man's words, so instantly transfixed by the dangling stone. As he stared into it, the grains inside seemed to swirl and deepen, until he could see, in the tiny rock, an entire churning universe. Marco began to feel light-headed.

"We buy and we sell," Theron said soothingly, leading Marco farther into the alley and, finally, through a beaded-curtain doorway that led into his shop at its end. "Do you have money to buy? Do you have jewelry to sell?" As the man spoke, his voice both seemed to grow louder and sounded farther away, as if it were echoing from the end of a long, empty hallway.

"Yes," Marco said in a monotone. "Yes, I do have some things to sell. All of my things are in my pack."

Inside the shop—a cordoned-off section of the alley piled high with Theron's belonging and wares—Theron dropped the stone and chain into Marco's open palm. As Marco held it and stared into its depths, he felt like he was drifting forward. The shapes and colors of the room, already dim, now faded completely into darkness as swirling, cosmic clouds from the stone engulfed him. He floated pleasantly along. After another moment, he had the distinct sensation of growing even lighter than before.

The merchant had slipped Marco's pack off his shoulders.

"Now let's see what goodies you have for Theron," the merchant said to the deeply hypnotized boy. He rooted around in Marco's bag. "Clothes, food . . . some kind of map . . . and what's this?"

Theron's hands darted into the pack and removed a round object carefully wrapped in a scarf. In his eagerness, Theron fumbled with the fabric and the object inside slipped out, rolling across the floor and into a puddle of water.

"Wonder of wonders," Theron gasped.

Sitting in the dirty water was the softly glowing pearl.

"The blue pearl! What they've all been looking for—and it's mine!"

Chapter 27

The blue pearl they've all been looking for?" intoned a deep, steady voice at the front of the alley, repeating Theron's words.

"The shop is closed!" Theron barked. But as he turned, the sight of the man standing there stopped him short.

"Aziz!" he exclaimed nervously.

"Theron," Aziz replied as he stepped inside, Amelio following closely behind.

Theron began laughing strangely and forced a wide but unconvincing smile. "My, what a sight for sore eyes! My good old friend Aziz," he said unctuously. "Why, I haven't seen you in years!"

"No, not since the time that you sold me that horse. You know," Aziz said, bending over to pick up the blue pearl from the dirty puddle of water, "that horse that never belonged to you to begin with."

"Oh, I tried to find you!" Theron said theatrically. "It was all a huge mix-up!"

"Of course," Aziz repeated flatly. He held the blue pearl in front of him. "What about this? Is this a mix-up as well?"

"What about it? What is that? Your friend is the one who brought it here and dropped it, why aren't you asking him?" Theron laughed nervously.

Aziz looked over at Marco, still staring at the dangling stone, locked in a trance. "My friend appears a little preoccupied right now."

"What, him?" Theron replied. He passed his hands over Marco's and quickly palmed the dangling stone, slipping it back in his pocket.

As the stone disappeared from view, Marco, who had been drifting comfortably through the cosmos, suddenly felt as though he were falling, and his vision returned in a rush. He would have lost his balance if a firm hand hadn't propped him up.

"You see, he's fine," Theron said amiably, holding Marco in place, patting him on the back, and brushing some dirt off his shoulder. "He was just checking out my merchandise."

Confused and slightly groggy, Marco felt as if he had just woken from a particularly vivid dream. "Aziz? What happened?" Marco looked around the unfamiliar room and at the short man in the colorful robes at his side. "Who's he?"

"He's an old acquaintance of mine," Aziz said. "Theron here used to be a first-class Bukharan pickpocket and con artist. But he's apparently graduated to hypnotism spells and larger stolen goods."

"Why, Aziz, you insult me!" Theron protested, pretending to be hurt. "I've graduated to nothing—my days of crime are behind me. I'm an honest businessman now!"

"So let's talk business," Aziz said, holding the blue pearl out in front of him. "How did you know about this?"

"I don't!" Theron repeated.

"Let me jog your memory. *It's the blue pearl they've been looking for.* Your own words. Tell me, Theron—who are *they* that are looking for the pearl?"

"I'm sorry," Theron said, straightening up. "All customer transactions are private and confidential. As a respected businessman—"

Theron was cut short when Aziz grabbed him by the scruff of his shirt and roughly hoisted him high over his head and against the wall. Theron gasped for breath as he struggled with his collar.

"Please, please put me down," he said, his short legs kicking wildly.

"Boys," Aziz began, looking at Marco and Amelio without lowering Theron. "When you're dealing with a scoundrel on this level, there are only two things they respond to—brute force and handsome rewards. First, brute force—"

In one swift move, Aziz whipped his sword out of its sheath, pointed it at Theron's jugular, and thrust it forward—fast. For a jaw-dropping moment, Amelio and Marco thought Aziz had stuck his blade through Theron's throat.

Instead, the edge of the blade sailed just past Theron's neck, poking through the fabric of his shirt and burying itself in the wooden beam behind him.

"And now, the prospect of a handsome reward." Aziz dangled a small sack of coins in front of Theron's face. "Why don't we let Theron decide which method of persuasion he prefers?"

"The reward, definitely the handsome reward," Theron said in a hoarse voice.

Hearing this, Aziz pulled his sword from the wall and put Theron back on the ground. The short man immediately began smoothing out his ruffled clothes.

"Start talking."

"I only saw them once," Theron explained, his tone sounding much closer to the truth. "Hooded men, going around the marketplace from one jewelry merchant to the next, saying they were looking for a blue pearl and they thought one might arrive here shortly. 'A blue pearl?' I said. 'I've got red rubies, green emeralds, white diamonds. But I've never even *heard* of a blue pearl.' So they told me to keep an eye out—it's worth serious money to whoever finds it. At the time I thought they were crazy. But what do you know—two days later a blue pearl rolls across my path."

"And who were these men exactly?" Aziz asked.

"I don't know," Theron answered. "Like I said, this was the first time I'd ever seen them. They were strange-looking under their hoods though; really stood out in a crowd. Must have been six feet tall, rail thin, pale—and what crazy voices!"

Amelio and Marco looked at each other from across the room.

"Remember when that Abarimon said it was looking for something, something it thought we had . . . maybe it was right," Marco whispered.

"And it sounds like a new pack of Abarimon are combing the entire city to find us—and the pearl—as we speak," Amelio said.

"The Abarimon seem to want the pearl for Arghun. Why?" Marco said.

"You heard the boy," Aziz said, turning the question over to Theron. "What do you know about Arghun, and why do his men want the pearl so badly?"

"How would I know?" Theron said.

Aziz jingled the bag of coins in front of Theron's face, pulling it away just as Theron went to snatch it. "Start with Arghun. Tell me everything."

"All right, all right! In the Unknown Lands, Arghun was a sorcerer—a sorcerer in the inner circle of Kublai Khan, who rules over all the Mongols from the Forbidden City in Peking.

"But from what I've heard, unlike most of the inner circle, Arghun began as an outsider. He had talent, some comprehension of the more complex magical arts. After hearing of his abilities, the khan wanted to meet him for himself, so Arghun was invited to the seat of the khan's empire, to travel to Peking.

"When the khan met Arghun, he was quickly impressed. He granted the young sorcerer access to the Forbidden City and, in it, tomes of spells unknown to the outside world. After that, it didn't take long for Arghun's ambition to take hold. He made quick work seducing everyone around him, as skilled a politician as he was a sorcerer. And in time," Theron continued, "his impressive skills and growing influence made Arghun known, then famous, then the most celebrated man in all the East.

"But some time after Arghun was named chief magician, several members of the khan's court began to disappear. Many among the missing were sorcerers, particularly powerful sorcerers—including one who was betrothed to the khan's own daughter. The khan ordered a full investigation. When black deeds were uncovered and evidence started pointing to Arghun, the khan sent troops to question him. But Arghun was gone as well. When they searched his chambers they found bodies of half the missing sorcerers, coupled with remnants of unspeakable acts and tomes of forbidden spells no mortal should ever see.

"After that, the khan sent every man in his empire to find Arghun, swearing none who betrayed him in such a way could live. But they didn't find a thing. After months the khan declared Arghun captured, quartered, and killed, but there wasn't a single witness and ever fewer citizens who believed his claims. The khan rules with too strong a hand; he could never afford to admit a rogue sorcerer escaped him. Of late even the khan's own daughter hasn't been seen for weeks. According to rumor she's been taken by Arghun as well, the 'dead man's' taunt to an arrogant ruler.

"Since Arghun was 'killed,' all sorts of creatures have begun appearing throughout the Lands, all acting in his name. And Arghun has become the boogeyman. If you believe what you hear, he continues to be behind any number of dark deeds. No one knows where he is, and no one knows how to stop him.

"The more excitable folks around these parts have been scared out of their minds. But for the criminal component it's been a godsend. The thieves love it—no matter what happens, everyone blames it on Arghun. Thieves wipe out a caravan in the desert, it's said to be Arghun's minions and they get off scot-free. Crime is higher than it's ever been, and criminals are happier than ever."

Aziz glared at Theron suspiciously. "And how does all this come back to the pearl? What do the Abarimon want with it?"

"The blue pearl, let's see . . . well, if those hooded men

are whatever you keep calling them, and they're working for Arghun . . . if they want the pearl, it must be enchanted, right? It can't just be a pretty stone. Wait! I may have just what you need." Theron went to the back of the alley and began rifling through dusty trunks and wicker baskets stacked along the walls. "A few months ago, an old man died who sold rare objects and artifacts in the central market. I found this in the trash along with the rest of his things." Theron came up with an old, leather-bound book and brought it to Aziz.

The spine of the book was broken, and though the front and back covers were still intact, it was clear a large number of pages had fallen out. Those that remained were written in a foreign and exotic penmanship, and several diagrams and illustrations had been added in the margins. On the inside of the front cover a detailed map of the East had been drawn, and a small red square with a triangle cap marked the location of the Shrine of the Eternal Order, where the book had been compiled and transcribed by an order of monks. Aziz ran his finger over the title of the book, gilded in gold lettering. He translated slowly: "'On Magical Herbs and Enchanted Objects.'" He looked at Marco. "It's an encyclopedia of magic."

"It is?" Marco said, his eyes growing wide with excitement.

"And yours for a very reasonable price," Theron cut in.

"Except less than half of the book is here," Aziz continued as he flipped through the tome, quickly reaching the end of the bound pages. "And if I know you as well as I think, if any of these pages mentioned pearls you would have read them the second you heard a blue pearl could earn you money, and I would have seen that a moment ago all over your face. Nonetheless, what's here might prove useful, and I've heard of the Eternal Order. We'll take it just the same."

"And at a discounted price available only to my old friends!" Theron said.

"How does four hundred dinars sound?" Aziz said.

"Make it five hundred," Theron said greedily.

"All right," Aziz said, smiling. "Five hundred dinars."

"Aziz," Theron gushed. "It's so good to see you, my friend!"

"That's five hundred dinars," Aziz repeated. "We'll take that out of the thirty-five hundred dinars you still owe me for that horse I had to return to its owner, so now you'll only have to repay me three thousand."

Theron looked crushed.

"Don't worry," Aziz said, patting Theron on the back. "I'm not going to take any of your money. Instead, I'll just take some of your time."

"My time?" Theron repeated.

"Your time. You see, since I can't trust you not to sell us out before we leave Bukhara, I'm going to have to make sure you're preoccupied for the next few hours. After that, you and I will be even." Aziz lifted the clay top off a nearby tall earthen jug. It was filled with red wine and he took a deep breath. "Hmm, smell those spices. Fermenting your own wine, eh?"

"It's a hobby," Theron said nervously, wondering what Aziz was planning.

Before Theron knew what was happening, Aziz lifted him quickly off the ground and dropped him unceremoniously inside the jug, which was taller than Theron. Theron slashed around, up to his shoulders in wine, as Aziz replaced the heavy lid.

"Aziz! Aziz!" Theron called out from inside the jug. "Please don't do this to me—I'm afraid of the dark!"

"Don't worry," Aziz said reassuringly as he stacked several heavy stones on top of the lid. "I'm sure one of your, uh, business associates will be by in a few hours to let you out."

Aziz turned to Marco and Amelio.

"Come on, you two, let's get out of here. I think I have a plan."

Chapter 28

Stepping out of the alley and into the warm Bukharan after-noon, it took Marco more than a few moments to adjust to the light. He felt disoriented in every sense—everything was happening so quickly. The idea that the pearl from his uncle's pack might be more than just a trinket was competing with thoughts of the spell he'd just been under, coupled with the knowledge that Abarimon were in Bukhara and the frenetic sights and sounds of the marketplace all around them. It was dizzying.

"At least we now know what the Abarimon were looking for in the house," Aziz said. As he pushed his way through the crowd Marco and Amelio scrambled to keep up. "I'll hold on to the pearl for now," Aziz said, slipping it into his pocket.

"But we still don't know why they want the pearl," Amelio said, trying to match Aziz's pace.

"That's what we're going to find out. And that book Theron sold us is going to help."

"Even if we don't have any of the pages we need?" Marco said, his head finally starting to clear.

Aziz stopped them in front of a small tavern called The Thirsty Camel.

"Let me show you something," he said, opening the inside cover of the book. He held out the two-page map of the East for the boys to inspect. "We're here," Aziz began, pointing to the small black dot that represented Bukhara. "And those creatures took your father to Arghun . . . here," he continued, pointing to an ominous shape on the map representing Mt. Dragoian. "That means the path we'll take will look something like this. . . ." He traced an invisible line connecting Bukhara to Mt. Dragoian, and his fingertip went past the picture of the small red house. "This house symbol here represents the monks who compiled this book, in the Shrine of the Eternal Order. I've heard of them before—they're learned men, as wise as any we could hope to discover. If anyone could tell us more about the pearl, it's them."

"And if the map is correct, the shrine is right in our path—we can ask them!" Amelio exclaimed.

"Exactly," Aziz said. "But before we get to the shrine we'll need to pass the Insurmountable Mountains, and there's a desert to traverse after that. This tavern is where we'll find a nomad who will provide safe passage for a fee. Both of you, stay here and keep an eye out for anything suspicious. I'll be out in fifteen minutes. Keep each other company, but do not—*do not*—wander off."

"You're going to leave us?" Marco asked. "After what happened earlier?"

"The tavern can be dangerous, and I should negotiate with the nomads alone. Just wait."

"But . . ."

Aziz retreated into the tavern, planting the book in Marco's hand to keep him occupied. "Stay outside. Play lookout."

Resigned, Marco and Amelio kept themselves busy. Amelio thought of all the incredible objects he'd seen back at the marketplace. Marco thumbed through the pages of the encyclopedia, not understanding the strange symbols but marveling at the illustrations and diagrams inside. Aziz said this was a book of magic. Soon they'd be past Bukhara's gates, and from that point forward anything could happen. . . .

Just as Marco's thoughts began to wander, a drunk nomad stumbled loudly out of The Thirsty Camel's front door. His clothes were dirty and unkempt, and his face was grizzled with a graying beard. Looking around for someone to talk to, his eyes landed on Marco and Amelio.

"Listen to me," he said matter-of-factly, as if they were old friends in the middle of a conversation. "I told him flat out. I said, 'You're crazy!' It's too dangerous out there. With all the mysterious attacks, with Arghun on the loose—"

"Arghun?" Amelio cut in.

"Don't tell me you haven't heard," the man said impatiently. "Arghun, the fire mage! Most dangerous kind of sorcerer you can be. The khan says Arghun is dead, but we all know those are lies. If he's dead, what's with all this black magic, caravans disappearing, creatures in the night? What's going on in those Insurmountable Mountains? Arghun's alive, and until he's found I'll tell you this—I'm not guiding anyone nowhere.

As far as I'm concerned, I'll stay here and drink, and those Mountains and those Lands can both stay unknown forever!

"It's crazy," the man repeated as he turned away from Marco and Amelio. "Insane!" Both boys watched as he sauntered drunkenly away, taking the path of least resistance and stumbling down a gently sloping hill. He slowly disappeared from view, barely able to keep from hurting himself.

Though the hill the man vanished down sloped gently, it went on for quite some time. The Thirsty Camel, in fact, sat on the large hilly divide between the two halves of the city. To their left was the winding, busy, eye-popping marketplace that gave the city its fame. The long hill to their right led to rows upon rows of square houses, alongside Bukhara's still-bustling fairground.

All the way to their right, on the far end of the residential district and fairground was the Eastern border of Bukhara itself—a towering stone wall that encompassed the city, including the enormous and famed Iron Gates. From where Marco and Amelio stood, though the gates were easily a mile away, they could still see the huge systems of gears and pulleys at its edges. Marco couldn't help but stare at them in awe, wondering about all the people the gates had let into—or out of—the Insurmountable Mountains and Far East.

"Don't look now," Amelio said, tapping Marco on the shoulder and snapping him out of his thoughts. "But I think our friend Theron just showed up."

"What?"

"Over there," Amelio whispered, nodding toward the far end of the street.

Theron, dyed purple as a grape from the neck down, stood out clearly from the crowd. He was joined by a taller man, well dressed, steely-eyed, and impassive. The taller man walked quickly and deliberatively while Theron, gesticulating wildly, struggled to keep up. Just behind them were two large, astonishingly muscular men who were identical in every respect— builds, faces, and wardrobes. And, ten feet or so behind the muscles, a half-dozen dirty-faced thieves followed anxiously.

"This is trouble—we've got to tell Aziz," Marco said.

The boys turned back toward The Thirsty Camel—"We can make it through this," Amelio half-whispered, to himself as much as Marco—and slipped casually through the entrance. As the door swung closed behind them, Amelio glanced back over his shoulder. And, out of the corner of his eye, he saw Theron, still some distance away, pointing in the direction of the tavern.

Chapter 29

The tavern was bigger than it looked from the outside.

The long central room was dimly and unevenly lit by two rows of hanging lights. Each row held three rusting iron candelabra, suspended from the ceiling by a series of pulley systems that were anchored to wooden cleats on the wall.

Under the left row of hanging lights a long, polished counter stretched to the rear of the room. The faces of several unsavory-looking patrons, spaced evenly on its barstools, were visible in the long mirror behind the bar: a gray-haired woman with an eye patch across her face and a pointed dagger on her hip; a short, squat man with greasy hair and a bushy beard covered in small pieces of food; and a man at the very end of the bar whose thin body was entirely covered by a hooded gray robe, only his pale, bony hands exposed to the light.

Under the right row of hanging lights, Marco and Amelio saw a dozen or more scattered tables. They walked through this section, scanning the patrons for Aziz, but they only found grim mouths and hard, unfriendly eyes.

"Excuse me. Pardon me," Amelio apologized to the unhappy-looking patrons. "I really like your tattoo," he mumbled nervously to a huge man whose bald head was inked with a spiderweb pattern. Though the tattooed giant said nothing, his eye twitched twice in response.

"There he is," Marco said, pointing to a table in the corner.

Aziz was in the rear of the room, directly beneath the final candelabra. Across from him was one empty chair, then another chair holding a small, lithe nomad whose body and face were shrouded in black—only his eyes could be seen. As the boys approached the table, those eyes fixed directly on them, moving from Marco to Amelio, then back to Marco again and lingering.

"Aziz," Amelio cut in.

"I thought I told you boys to wait—" Aziz began, but the expression on Marco's face cut him short.

"We've got trouble," Marco said. "Theron's on his way—and he's got company."

No sooner had Marco said the words than the front door of the tavern swung open. The two musclemen entered first, flanking the doorway on either side. Then the tall, well-dressed man followed. He stopped at the entrance and carefully surveyed the room.

Under the tall man's gaze, much of the laughter in the tavern died down. Sentences trailed off and silverware stopped clinking on plates. A bearded man at the bar fumbled with his metal tankard. Others sat frozen and stared into the froth of their beer.

The tall man quickly identified his targets, then walked steadily alongside the length of the bar counter. As he passed beneath each of the candelabra, the light from above cast his face into shadow, and two deep black ovals made his gaunt face look like a human skull.

Then he turned and made his way toward them, his hard eyes gleaming in the light.

"Theron tried to tell me, but I couldn't believe him." The tall man came right to the edge of their table. "Now I've seen it with my own eyes."

A thin smile spread across the tall man's lips.

"It's been a long time, Aziz."

Chapter 30

When the tall man sat down in their table's only empty seat, the other patrons of the bar—relieved the tall man hadn't come looking for them—began speaking again, though not as loudly as before.

"How many years has it been since we've seen each other, Aziz?" the man continued. "Two? Three?"

"Four," Aziz said dryly.

"Four!" the man repeated, staring at Aziz and smiling strangely. His musclemen came up behind him, crossing their bulky arms in front of their bulkier chests. "Have you met Aala and Ailani yet?" the man continued. "Twins—even I can't tell them apart." He turned and gave one of the twins a playful punch on the arm. Then the tall man looked over at Marco and Amelio. He broke into a wide grin. "I see you've got two impressive bodyguards yourself!"

"I don't know who you are, but if you think we're afraid of

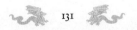

your henchmen—," Marco began defiantly, eyeing the muscle-men up.

But Aziz cut him off. "Marco, shut up and stand in the corner."

Marco was taken aback. "What?"

"Both of you, shut up," Aziz repeated, "and stand in the corner." Aziz's eyes narrowed and his eyebrows arched in a strange way: He looked from Marco to the nearest corner, then back at Marco again.

Marco followed Aziz's gaze—then he saw it and understood. "Come on," Marco said, grabbing Amelio's arm in mock-anger for the benefit of the others. "Let's go." Though the tall man and his two bodyguards ignored the boys as they walked away, the man shrouded in black followed them closely with his eyes.

Amelio was bewildered but followed along. "The hanging lights," Marco whispered into Amelio's ear as they moved closer to the corner. Looking around, Amelio saw it and finally understood—the cleat for the pulley that supported the heavy iron candelabra was mounted on the corner wall, now directly in front of them.

"Let's get to the point," the tall man said matter-of-factly once the boys left the table. "Theron tells me you have something valuable—a blue pearl, is that right? Theron says he purchased it from your little friend. Fair and square."

"You know Theron never gets anything *fair and square*," Aziz said.

"Hmm, he does have a reputation," the tall man said, as if carefully weighing Aziz's words. "But then again, here in Bukhara, so do you."

Aziz didn't say a word.

"You say the blue pearl belongs to you," the tall man continued. "Theron says it belongs to him. And some strange gentlemen have been going around Bukhara saying they'd like it to belong to them. In light of all this, the only fair thing to do, it seems, is to give the blue pearl to *me*."

Chapter 31

Marco stood in front of the wooden cleat to which the pulley and iron candelabra was anchored, and slowly unwound the rope that connected them all.

The tall man at the table picked up Aziz's mug and took a long, deep sip.

"Ahh," he said, smacking his lips. "Now, here's the deal: Either you walk out of here without the blue pearl, or you don't walk out of here at all."

Aziz stared across the table, steely eyed and silent.

"In addition to my friends here," the man continued, gesturing to the twins, "I've got a few other *associates* waiting outside." He pointed to the windows at the front of the tavern, where the thieves Marco had seen earlier were watching them vigilantly through the dirty glass panes.

Theron was outside peering into the window too. Except he was also gesturing wildly, pointing to someone at the bar counter on the other side of the room.

The tall man laughed when he saw Theron, still dyed purple from his neck to his toes.

"You would think Theron soaked up enough wine for one day, eh, Aziz?"

But Aziz's face remained impassive. After a pause, Aziz reached into his pocket, put the pearl down on the tabletop and rolled it toward the man.

Marco and Amelio saw this and felt their hearts skip a beat.

"What do ya know?" the man said. "A blue pearl after all. How strange!"

"It's a piece of costume jewelry. Not worth anything."

"I'll be the judge of that," the man said suspiciously. "Flawless, is it?" His eyes squinted as he scrutinized the pearl, turning it in his fingers. "Hard to tell in this light."

For the first time, a hint of a grin appeared at the corners of Aziz's mouth.

"Hey, Marco," Aziz called out. "How about a little light for our friend?"

Marco knew that must be the signal—he let go of the rope that he had, by now, fully unwound. Pulleys whirred loudly, and in an instant the candelabra above the table came crashing down.

Aziz and the man in black pushed away just in time. The heavy iron frame of the candelabra hammered both of the twins on the head, then came crashing down on the table, knocking the muscles out and pinning the tall man's arms.

Before the tall man could scream in pain, Aziz's shrouded nomad placed one hand on the edge of the table and delivered a graceful roundhouse kick to the man's face, knocking him unconscious. Then the nomad reached over, took the pearl from his limp hands, and presented the stone to Aziz.

"All right," Aziz said, impressed. "I don't know much about you, but you're officially hired. Boys, meet the nomad Kokachin. Kokachin, meet the boys. Now let's all get out of here."

No sooner had Aziz said this than the tall man's thieves poured in through the tavern's front door. Drawing swords and knives, they fanned out and advanced toward the back of the room.

"How are we going to get out of this?" Amelio said.

"This way," Kokachin instructed confidently in a muffled voice. He headed to the tavern's back wall, then reached down and grabbed a metal ring bolted to the floor. When he lifted it up, a trapdoor revealed a series of stairs leading down to the basement. "If we climb down, we'll find a door that leads out onto a back alley. Let's go!"

Kokachin jumped down, then Amelio and Aziz quickly followed. Marco lowered himself last and reached up to close the trapdoor behind him. But before he got it all the way shut he felt a cold and bony hand grab on to his wrist. Looking through the narrow crack, he saw what was holding him. It was the thin man who had been sitting at the end of the bar the entire time, his body fully covered by a hooded gray robe.

It was an Abarimon.

Chapter 32

The Abarimon held tightly to Marco's wrist, oblivious to the band of thieves that was advancing. But, to the thieves, this hooded figure was nothing but an obstacle, preventing them from getting to their targets. One anxious thief raised his blade above his head and brought it down hard, slashing the Abarimon across its arm. The creature let loose an ear-piercing scream and, just for a moment, released its grip.

In that second Marco pulled away his hand, quickly slammed the trapdoor shut and bolted it securely.

Aziz was waiting anxiously at the door to the back alley when Marco charged down the basement steps and joined him.

"Did I just hear—"

"—an Abarimon's shriek?" Marco said, finishing Aziz's sentence. "Yes."

"That must have been what Theron was trying to signal from the window," Aziz said as he and Marco bolted out the exit and into the alley. "One of the hooded men who'd come to him about the pearl."

Kokachin and Amelio were already halfway down the long alleyway, and Marco and Aziz sprinted ahead to catch up with them at the end.

"Things just went from bad to worse," Aziz explained quickly. "We've been found by the Abarimon."

"The figure from the bar wearing gray robes," Kokachin said. "It was watching us in the mirror behind the counter. Its shape—I knew something wasn't right."

When they reached the end of the alley the road forked in two. "It's time for us to leave Bukhara, and both of these paths will lead to the Iron Gates," Aziz said. "Those thugs and the Abarimon will try to find us soon enough, but if we split up we can get lost in the crowds and it'll be harder for them to follow. Marco, you come with me. Amelio, go with Kokachin."

Amelio looked from Aziz and Marco to the strange nomad draped in black.

"It's fine," Aziz said. "You can trust him. Take the path to the right, which will cut through the rest of the city. Marco and I will take the market side streets to the left. We'll meet again when we reach the gates."

"All right," Kokachin said.

"All right," the two boys echoed, nervously.

Aziz nodded. "Let's go."

After several moments of charging to the left with Aziz down a dirt road toward the markets, Marco saw the great Iron Gates of Bukhara looming farther up ahead. Earlier, the massive structure stood out as the doorway to a mysterious new world. Now, as they ran toward them, the Gates represented something far more immediate: escape from the deadly Abarimon.

Plunging deep into the market side streets, they hit a patch of merchants, and Aziz slowed at a table selling short swords. He grabbed two swords and handed one to Marco. "If you need it." The shopkeeper, a fat, slovenly man in stained clothes, immediately jumped to his feet. "Hey! You better pay for those! Hey!" he shouted as Aziz and Marco ran off.

"Keep going," Aziz said. "There's no time!"

"Hey!" the merchant yelled as they disappeared into the crowds of the market. "Get back here! Thieves! Those—"

Before he could say another word, the heavyset shopkeeper was cut off by a loud, inhuman screech.

"The Abarimon! Run!" Aziz shouted.

Marco couldn't help but look behind him and he saw the Abarimon turn left at the back alley path, before charging after them down the market side streets. The Abarimon's robes had been discarded, and fully transformed, its inverted legs, gaping jaws, and enormous claws filled Marco with terror. It also had the same pale skin, milky-white eyes, and wispy hair as the other Abarimon they'd encountered.

"Don't stop!" Aziz shouted. "Keep going!" Then, seeing a three-story building bordering the markets up ahead, Aziz pulled Marco sharply in its direction. "I have an idea—this way!" When they reached the building Aziz plowed open the door, then started sprinting up the building's steps with Marco close on his heels.

Quickly reaching the roof and climbing outside, they ran to the building's edge and took in the scene down below. The Abarimon was shrieking and charging down the street as merchants scrambled to escape the market's narrow aisles. In a moment of fury the Abarimon flexed its legs, leaped high into the air . . . and came crashing down on the table of the heavyset shopkeeper. The man stumbled backward in horror. "Please . . . please . . ."

Suddenly, the Abarimon jerked its head around, sniffed the air, then—with a snarl—it whipped its head up toward Marco and Aziz on the rooftop.

"It's on to us," Aziz yelled. "Let's go!"

By the time the Abarimon crashed toward the steps of the building, Aziz and Marco were already jumping from the far edge of that rooftop to the near edge of the next one.

"Keep going," Aziz shouted without slowing down. "The houses bordering the marketplace were built along the downward slope of a hill. Each roof is higher than the following one. We should be able to keep jumping from one rooftop to the next in the direction of the Iron Gates!" The two charged and leaped from one building to another, desperately trying to keep away from the deadly Abarimon.

Chapter 33

At the same time, Kokachin and Amelio ran as fast as they could down the path to the right. Desert sands blew through the windy Bukharan streets, and Amelio covered his eyes with his sleeve to keep the dirt out, running half-blindly as the vibrant displays of street vendors whizzed past.

Halfway to the gate Amelio mistakenly ran ahead of Kokachin through a busy intersection, only to be nearly trampled by a racing steed. He skidded to a stop as the braying horse reared back and kicked out its front legs. Amelio had to dive to avoid being struck and he crashed hard into the ground.

Looking up at the horse from the dust, he was horrified to realize its rider was one of the dirty-faced thieves from the tavern.

"You can't escape!" the thief yelled, raising his curved blade high above his head.

A black whip snapped forward just in time to wrap around the man's wrist. With a sharp yank Kokachin's whip pulled the thief's arm backward, causing him to lose balance and fall from the steed. As the man hit the ground and rolled onto his knees, Kokachin sprang forward, used his back like a stepping stool and leaped onto his horse. Reaching down, Kokachin grabbed Amelio by the wrist and swung him up onto the horse in one fluid motion.

"*Keeyah!*" Kokachin yelled, spurring the animal with his heels. The steed took off, bounding ahead in a cloud of dust and leaving the wounded thief behind.

"Thanks," Amelio said.

Amelio turned his head, only to see five more thieves riding toward them side by side in an unbroken line.

"There are more of them behind us!" Amelio yelled over Kokachin's shoulder.

"Not for long," he answered.

Kokachin turned their horse sharply from the main road into a narrow alleyway that cut between two rows of houses. The pursuing thieves were forced to enter the alley one at a time, spacing them apart and slowing them down.

When Kokachin and Amelio burst out of the alley they cut hard to the right, turning out onto another wide road. The tall man's henchmen eventually galloped after them, popping out of the alleyway one after the other.

"*Keeyah! Keeyah!*" Kokachin yelled, spurring their horse faster and faster. As they blasted through a busy crossroads, they charged past a rickety wooden cart pulled by an old horse and stacked high with cages of loudly clucking chickens.

When the first and second of the thieves bolted through the same crossroads a few moments later, the elderly merchant driving the cart was startled out of a daydream.

When the third thief nearly hit the merchant when he whizzed by, the old man did his best to turn his cart sideways and leave the intersection behind.

Suddenly the fourth and fifth of the thieves charged ahead, moving far too quickly to change their course. The merchant saw them coming and jumped just in time, as both henchmen's horses crashed headlong into the cart. The thieves were thrown to the ground and stacks of cages crashed into the road, full of desperate, scrambling chickens flapping wildly.

"Two down, three to go," Amelio yelled.

Kokachin and Amelio raced ahead toward another open square market. Instead of cutting to the side roads that bordered the square, Kokachin charged straight into the busy marketplace and rode through the narrow lanes between merchant tents. Merchants leaped out of their way and screamed loudly as they blasted their way down the zigzagging path. Amelio was afraid they would get tripped up in the narrow lanes, but Kokachin was a skilled rider, adept at navigating all the tight turns.

But after turning a final corner, it became clear they'd run out of road.

"It's a dead end!" Amelio screamed as he saw their path intersected by the square tent of a carpet salesman, blocking the exit.

"Not for us, it isn't!" Kokachin screamed as they rushed forward. "*Keeyah!*"

Without stopping or slowing down, Kokachin rode their horse straight into the large tent. The carpet merchant was standing next to the tent beating a hanging rug, and his hands flew up in a panic when he saw their horse ride roughshod over his merchandise, trailing a cloud of dirt in its wake.

"My carpets!" he screamed as they charged away.

"Sorry!" Amelio yelled as they came out the other side of the tent and rode into the next square.

The salesman shook his head in stunned disbelief when, moments later, another horseman charged through his tent.

Seeing two more on their way, the merchant stood in front of the tent to block their path. "No, no, no!" the merchant screamed, frantically waving his arms. "Go another way!" But the riders didn't slow. Realizing he was about to be trampled, the merchant leaped away at the last minute. But the second and third thieves, unable to aim straight through the tent, instead crashed into the supporting poles to the left and right of the entrance. As the poles tipped over the heavy canvas tent came crashing down all around them, trapping both men beneath it.

"Two more down!" Amelio yelled over Kokachin's shoulder. "There's just one left."

"Just one?" Kokachin repeated.

To Amelio's great confusion, Kokachin slowed the horse to a standstill and turned around completely, facing straight toward the last thief.

"You know how to ride a horse, right?" Kokachin asked Amelio.

"I can ride well enough," Amelio said nervously.

The remaining thief was still some distance away, but he drew his sword as he charged directly toward them.

"You'll have to do better than well enough," Kokachin said, handing Amelio the reins, then swinging around behind him on the horse. "Do what I say, ride!"

"But—"

"Ride!"

Amelio kicked off, charging in the direction of the thief. As both horses drew closer, Kokachin squatted on his front legs. Even closer, the thief aimed his blade straight for Kokachin's heart. Finally, in the split second before impact Kokachin leaped high into the air, sailed above the attacker's blade, swung himself off the man's extended arm and landed in the saddle behind him. With one quick karate chop to the back of the head, Kokachin knocked the thief unconscious, watching his body slump forward in the saddle.

After slowing his new horse to a trot, Kokachin pulled over next to a watery basin where mules and horses drank. Then he pushed the stunned thief's body into the water. After a moment the man sprung awake, his head bursting out of the basin gasping for breath, and his hands wiping wet hair out of his eyes.

"Thanks for the ride," Kokachin said as he took off on the horse. He rode over to an amazed Amelio, and the two of them continued on horseback toward the Iron Gates of Bukhara.

Chapter 34

Several streets over and a few stories up, Marco and Aziz continued running and leaping from one rooftop to the next. Marco's lungs burned and his heart felt like it was about to explode, but the thought of the Abarimon kept him going farther. Marco was running so hard he almost didn't notice an extra-wide street that cut like a canyon between the next set of rooftops; he stopped short but nearly lost his balance, teetering on the building's edge. Seeing the drop to the road below, he felt a dizzying sense of vertigo and might have pitched helplessly forward if Aziz hadn't been there to grab his shirt and yank him back.

"This way!" Aziz said without pausing, pointing to the entrance to the rooftop's stairwell.

But before the two of them could take another step, a dark mass soared high above, momentarily eclipsing the midday sun before landing hard in front of their only escape route.

The Abarimon had found them, and it had them cornered.

Aziz quickly placed himself between Marco and the creature, then drew both his sword and the short sword he'd taken from the merchant. The Abarimon toyed with them from a distance, moving slowly and furtively, sizing up its prey.

"We don't want to hurt you," the creature said in a high-pitched voice. "We only want what we must have."

"The pearl?" Aziz asked.

"The *other* pearl," the creature said, growing excited. "The dragon's pearl. We thought the first one had them both, but we were wrong. And one's no good without the other."

"The dragon's pearl?" Aziz repeated. "What does that mean?"

"Give it to us!"

"Give me back my father!" Marco shouted from behind Aziz. "Give me Niccolo Polo!"

"Nic-co-lo," the creature repeated strangely. "Yes. Arghun will gladly trade, boy. His life for the pearl."

"What?" Marco said, shocked.

"You have our word. Give us the pearl and *Nic-co-lo* is yours again. He waits at Mount Dragoian. We will bring him to you, Polo."

Marco stared at the Abarimon and said nothing for a long while. Then he narrowed his eyes. "I have a better idea," he said. He spit on the ground. "How about we keep the pearl, kill you, destroy your master, then rescue my father ourselves?"

The creature's eyes filled with rage and locked on Marco, a low, ominous growl coming from deep within its chest.

In that split second Aziz made his move. He ran forward and swung his blade at the creature, who barely jumped away as the sword whizzed past its shoulder. The Abarimon readied itself and fought back, its claw whizzing toward Aziz's throat, but Aziz dodged it, then slammed his elbow into the creature's face.

The Abarimon screamed, then leaped quickly backward, flipping through the air until it landed on the roof of the previous building. Its taloned feet clung to the roof's edge as it reared back on its haunches. Aziz assumed a battle stance, anticipating the creature would try to pounce on him from above.

Instead, the Abarimon leaped high into the air, sailed directly over Aziz's head, and landed behind him, just feet away from Marco. In a split second, the creature had grabbed the boy by the scruff of his shirt and forcefully picked him up—and suddenly Marco, his feet kicking in wild panic, was dangling over the edge of the building from the Abarimon's claw.

Chapter 35

Don't hurt him!" Aziz yelled. "We'll make a deal!"

"Yes," the Abarimon snarled. "We like this better. Disarm, human. Now."

As the Abarimon watched, Aziz laid both his swords on the ground.

"Put Marco down and I'll give you whatever you want."

"Don't do it!" Marco yelled.

The creature's angry eyes turned on the boy. Marco felt its grip on his shirt tighten and his collar constricted around his throat.

"The dragon's pearl for the boy's life," the Abarimon snarled.

"All right," Aziz said. "You'll get what you want."

Marco glanced around wildly, trying to figure out a plan. He could try and strike the creature, but if it let him go he'd fall over the edge. He looked straight down. Three stories below him was a busy Bukharan street. Marco saw a group of school-boys playing tag, an old man bouncing along on a donkey, and a rug merchant standing next to a stack of carpets piled twice as high as he was tall, each happily oblivious to the life-or-death situation occurring just above.

Looking at them all, Marco had an idea. . . . It was risky, but he had to do something to stop the Abarimon. Without stopping to think, he moved his hand stealthily toward the waistband of his pants, where he'd tucked the short sword from the merchant's table.

"Here," Aziz said, taking the softly glowing blue pearl from his pocket. "Now give me the boy."

"Place it on the roof, next to your weapon," the Abarimon said.

Aziz did as he was told, slowly and without sudden moves.

Aziz and the Abarimon had their eyes locked on each other in a death stare. And neither noticed Marco carefully withdrawing his short sword. As they spoke Marco's eyes darted back down to the street.

"Now walk away from the pearl," the Abarimon hissed. "Walk away slowly."

If Marco was going to act on his plan, he should do it now.

"Aziz, I'll meet you at the gate!" he screamed.

The Abarimon turned just as Marco lifted his sword, plunging it deep into the center of the creature's chest. The Abarimon shrieked in agony and covered its injury with its hands.

Immediately, Marco felt himself falling. He thought back to the advice his father once gave him, bent his knees, relaxed his body, and aimed for the stack of carpets piled down below.

Marco's aim was good. He smacked into the carpet at the

top of the stack feetfirst, his legs absorbing most of the impact. Then his balance faltered and he fell from the stack, tumbling and crashing hard against the street. For a moment everything went black. Marco vaguely heard the rug merchant yelling, his voice an odd mix of anger and confusion. "My carpets . . . Where did you come from? What have you done?"

Marco opened his eyes slowly, his entire body throbbing. He was in a lot of pain, but he was alive.

Up on the rooftop the Abarimon was still shrieking, Marco's blade sunk entirely through its body. It spun blindly in agony, then pitched onto the roof in front of Aziz.

"You will suffer and you will die!" the beast choked out. "You cannot escape Arghun—he will come for you!"

As Aziz watched, the Abarimon's mouth foamed and it twitched several times, then it lay still. Aziz, horrified, snatched up the pearl, grabbed his sword, and ran headlong downstairs, terrified of what he might find when he reached the bottom.

Outside Aziz prepared himself to search for a lifeless body. But Marco quickly snapped Aziz out of his misery. "Aziz! I'm over here!" Aziz's head whipped around, and Marco forced himself to stand and limp out from behind the stack of piled carpets.

Aziz's body trembled with relief. "You're all right."

"Did I kill it?" Marco said. "Is it over?"

"You took down an Abarimon," Aziz said. "You're a warrior after all."

"I don't know what an Abarimon is, but I saw him take down my carpet!" the rug merchant said. "The carpet at the top of my stack is ruined!"

Aziz and Marco, exhausted, paid off the rug merchant

then got supplies for their journey ahead. Finally, they headed straight for Bukhara's eastern border, arriving shortly after Amelio and Kokachin showed up on their horses. Doubling up on the steeds—Kokachin and Amelio on one horse, Marco and Aziz on the other—the four of them rode toward the massive Iron Gates. As they passed through the gates Marco felt a shudder of fear and excitement travel through his still-throbbing body. The sensation only grew when they came out the other side.

"Unknown Lands, here we come."

Chapter 36

Within hours, Kokachin, Amelio, Marco, and Aziz found themselves in the shadows of the great Insurmountable Mountains. They looked up in awe at the rocky peaks that jutted thousands of feet into the air, gray and lifeless, effortlessly dominating the land and the skies.

Back home Marco imagined these mountains countless times, picturing himself standing among them; nothing compared to their reality. They were enormous and unmovable, beautiful and terrifying. For the first time in his life he felt utterly small. He touched his hand to the raw stone, astonished.

And, turning his head, the mountains continued as far as his eyes could see. Now Marco understood why they were called the Insurmountable Mountains—why, for hundreds of years, not a single Westerner ever made it past them. The barrier was unrivaled in its majesty and power.

Aziz looked up as well, his face difficult to read. "From here on out, there's nothing else for hundreds of miles. Only stone. Many have tried to map these mountains, but if you track them too far—if you keep pushing ahead—at some point, you don't have enough food and water to make it back again. You're found dead weeks, months, sometimes years after you've gone."

"But that's if you don't know what you're doing—not something we have to worry about with a map and a nomad as our guide. Right?" Amelio said nervously.

Aziz offered a slight smile. "If you have a map, and a nomad as your guide . . . then, instead of the certainty of death, it's only a high probability."

Amelio shook his head. "I can see why they call them Insurmountable." He sighed.

"But it's only in the West that they're called Insurmountable," Kokachin said, drawing everyone's attention. "In the East, where people have been crossing for centuries, they are called something else entirely. In their completion, they are the Himalayas. In their parts they are the Hindu Kush, the Tian Shan, the Tannu-Ola, the Pamir Mountains, and the Karakoram Range. They are majestic and deadly, and they are conquerable. As we shall conquer them. Now come, follow me. We have some ways to go before we reach our path between the mountains."

They all dutifully followed their new, shrouded companion.

As they rode Aziz whispered to Marco, who sat behind him on their mare. "Before my old friends showed up in the tavern in Bukhara, I told several nomads we were looking for a guide. I said our path would be more dangerous than most—in addition to mountains and deserts, we might also face powerful forces trying to stop us. Many guides passed me by without another word, but Kokachin stayed and listened to our story. He was silent for a time . . . then he said he was not afraid of any human or earthly danger, before agreeing to take us on our way."

"And what about the Shrine of the Eternal Order? Does he know how to take us there, too?" Marco asked, remembering the encyclopedia of magic in his pack.

"He said he can. And, after that, he's willing to take us through the Unknown Lands to the very path toward Mount Dragoian. We were lucky Kokachin agreed to join us, Marco. I don't know what motives he has in all this—but for now, and until he proves otherwise, for the services he provides we should be grateful."

Marco let the information sink in as they continued riding, mountains alongside them and the ground rising steadily beneath their feet.

Chapter 37

Some time later, all four dismounted by a narrow mountain passage marked off by two enormous boulders on either side of a trail. Marco didn't know who—or what—was strong enough to have first maneuvered those boulders, but he hoped they wouldn't have to find out.

"This is our mountain pass," Kokachin said, placing his hand on the larger of the two boulders. "From here on out we travel on foot through the heart of the Hindu Kush."

"This path doesn't look too bad," Amelio said, gazing just past the boulders.

"It won't be, at first. It's a mountain road like any other," Kokachin said. "But, as we continue, the mountain will rise to great heights on our left, and the land will drop off entirely to our right. The path will grow narrow, and you'll be unable to fit two feet together. We'll have no choice but to keep going, holding tight to the side of the mountain and praying our footing is sure. We can take no breaks, and we can make no errors."

The look of pleasant surprise on Amelio's face gave way to terror in record time. "You're serious? That's what we'll have to do? But what if . . ." Amelio gasped.

"What if one of us falls?" Kokachin finished. "Let's try not to find out."

Amelio turned to his friend. "Marco? Are we ready for this?"

"I don't know," Marco said, tightening his fingers around the straps of his pack. Both boys gazed at the path, mountains looming all around them and making them feel dwarfed and foolish, little specks on an impossible mission, creeping into the heart of an eternal beast.

But it was time to begin. Following Kokachin and Aziz's lead, they took their first steps along the path.

The ground was just as it had been at first, providing plenty of room to walk on either side. Marco and Amelio felt like they were climbing a gentle slope. But when the passage started growing steeper the floor of the mountain quickly receded to their right, and sooner than any of them would have liked they were forced to walk one in front of the other, where one misplaced move could send them tumbling to their death.

They each continued on, not talking much. Concentrating on holding on to the rock wall, putting foot over foot with each successive step. The only sounds were their breathing, footsteps, and the occasional scatter of pebbles kicked off the path. Amelio tried, only once, to watch the pebbles as they fell into the crevice to his right, but his first glance left his head spinning and his stomach began to churn. He'd never felt that sort of vertigo before, and from that point on he kept his eyes focused on his friends just ahead of him, and the steady rhythms of their careful feet.

Chapter 38

After hours of ascent, they almost grew accustomed to the peculiar form of walking the passage required.

Kokachin had been leading them at a steady pace, but he slowed when a heavy fog rolled down from the mountain peaks. The fog was thick and it smelled somewhat piney. Marco tried to enjoy the scent as he continued until Kokachin brought their progress to a complete halt.

At first Marco thought Kokachin stopped them because the fog was growing too thick to see, but up ahead it had already started clearing. He followed Kokachin and Aziz's line of vision to the right . . . and he saw what had given them pause. There was a ledge, only fifty feet below them, entirely covered in bones.

Marco had never seen so many skeletons in one place—in fact, he'd never really seen any skeletons at all. But even if he had, this impromptu graveyard would have stopped him in his tracks. Marco shuddered, imagining those who had fallen and met their end on that ledge. At the very bottom of the crevasse, similar piles of bones likely extended the entire length of the mountain path.

Marco forced his eyes away from the gruesome sight. Kokachin, Amelio, and Aziz took one last look at the skeletons as well, then continued along their way.

Many hours later the path came to an end. Without fanfare, the narrow road opened onto a wide swath of land. Spent from their nerve-racking journey, the group gratefully fell to their knees and Kokachin pointed into the distance. "Welcome to the edge of what your people call the Unknown Lands. Tonight, we set up camp in a nearby cave. Tomorrow, we'll continue to our next destination—the Shrine of the Eternal Order. But for now, let us rest and eat."

Promptly, Amelio laid out blankets, Marco found brush in the clearing they could use as firewood, and Aziz expertly arranged the kindling before sparking a small blaze. Kokachin added more wood, and soon they had a roaring fire. They all sat in a circle, and everyone took water and dried meat from their packs.

As they ate, Aziz looked at the mountains all around them with peaks that tore through the sky. "I wasn't sure I'd survive my first expedition through these mountains. I must say, I'm humbled to have survived my second."

"Once you passed the mountains . . . how far into the Unknown Lands did you get the first time?" Marco asked, the flames throwing shadows across his face. "When you were with my father. Before you were attacked."

Aziz chewed his meat slowly. "We traveled some distance. Our goal was to meet with the leaders of the Unknown Lands, in the interest of opening new routes of trade. And we made our way through the majority of the Mongol territories, to the very palace of the great Kublai Khan."

All three of the others turned to Aziz. "You did?" Amelio said, the first to speak.

"But my uncle, neither he nor you ever said anything about—"

"We didn't want to scare you. Or give you any ideas. But after we crossed these mountains, with your father's map in hand, we journeyed through the Lands for some time."

"Tell us about the Mongols," Amelio said, fear still plain in his voice despite everything they'd just been through.

"Understand, the Mongols are far from the savages they've been made out to be. When provoked, of course, they can be fierce and deadly warriors, every inch befitting their legend. But when treated with respect we found them to be a strong and noble race. Their language and customs are foreign, and they are suited to a way of life that is far more dangerous than our own. But our men, for the brief time we knew them, were proud to call some of them our allies."

"Tell us how you came to travel to the palace of Kublai Khan," Marco said.

"It started in a town called Bascia," Aziz said, "where we happened upon an envoy to the great khan. When we told him of our journey, he presented us with a golden tablet and said, should we ever reach the Forbidden Palace, presenting it would grant us an audience with the khan himself.

"The envoy was true to his word. When, some weeks later, we did reach the outskirts of Peking, we presented the tablet and were brought directly inside."

Marco and Amelio looked at each other, speechless. Kokachin cocked his head in a way that suggested his surprise as well.

"By this time we had heard of the wizard Arghun, and of the terrible darkness growing in the Lands. Many would not speak of it outright, but we learned through whispers and hushed tones of fear. We knew a man named Arghun betrayed the khan, amassing great power along the way. We knew the khan said Arghun had been captured and killed, and—though none believed his words—to contradict the khan in his presence was immediately punishable by death. We even heard the princess herself had gone missing, though the khan would never admit it was true; and the only ones willing to say it to him were those prepared to go missing too.

"However, on the day when we entered the khan's palace all of this seemed like lore. The palace is magnificent. They took our golden tablet and treated us as visiting dignitaries. We met with the khan's senior advisors before being granted an introduction to the khan himself, a fierce and noble man like few others I've had the privilege of meeting. When the khan presented the jewels of his kingdom we displayed our most expensive wares—a gesture of mutual respect. Then we explained we came in hopes of opening a new route of trade, a route between the East and the West. The following morning the khan said we could remain in his palace as long as we wished, and—when we ventured home—we could inform our council that he found our proposal of interest. He would strongly consider it."

Aziz stabbed at the fire, letting loose a spray of sparks that died out quickly in the wind.

"Before we left the khan's palace, one of his merchants took a particular interest in your father's wares," Aziz said, looking at Marco. "Especially the red pearl your father kept as a good-luck charm. At the time we thought nothing of it, and when the insistent merchant continued trying to buy it your father simply said that it wasn't for sale. But within a month of that day, as we were on our way to report news of our journey back to Venice, our caravan came under attack.

"It's only now, knowing it was the pearl they were after, that some pieces of our tale make sense. We heard that nowhere in the Lands was safe, that Arghun's spies infiltrated every quarter. It would not be a surprise to learn the khan's palace still hosted secret sympathizers of Arghun and his men. But we never imagined we had anything of interest to such fiends. The red pearl your father kept—and the blue pearl your uncle had mixed among his things—they were baubles received in trade. One of thousands of artifacts passed back and forth among merchants. Even now, I don't understand—"

"Which is why the Shrine of the Eternal Order is the next step in our journey," Kokachin said. "I've heard of their wisdom and you are right to go to them now. If Arghun is, indeed, behind your troubles, you must have a better understanding of what it is you possess."

The fire crackled and the four of them lapsed into silence.

As Marco looked at the faces all around him, framed by the enormous mountains and illuminated by the glow of the flames, he realized how far they had already come—and how very far they still had to go in their quest to save his father.

"There are few things, if any, more powerful than a dragon. In the wrong hands, a captive dragon could tear the world apart. . . . "

—FROM THE JOURNALS OF MARCO POLO

Unknown Lands

Insurmountable Mountains

Part Three

ECHOING

CAVES

and

THE

SHRINE

OF THE

ETERNAL ORDER

Chapter 39

As the skies grew dark Kokachin led Marco, Amelio, and Aziz into a nearby cave to set up camp. "We'll spend the night here," he said. "Tomorrow, we'll continue on our journey to the shrine."

Deep in thought, Marco sat down in a shadowy corner of the cave and quickly became lost in himself. Recognizing that Marco seemed to want to be alone, Amelio went off to explore, noting the cave's soaring heights and its surprising depth. When he shouted as much back to his friend, each one of his words were returned to him as endlessly repeating echoes.

Amelio doubled back to find Marco in much the same position, while Kokachin and Aziz were rustling through their packs on the ground. "If I were you, I'd find a spot to camp," Kokachin said. "We'll need all our energy in the morning."

Kokachin and Aziz found dark corners; in their exhaustion, they quickly drifted off to sleep. Amelio made his way over to Marco and the two boys huddled together.

"It just seems crazy," Marco said, trying to take everything in. "We've heard all our lives about the Unknown Lands, and now we're nearly in them. We've been warned since we were children about the Mongols, and my father was greeted by their king. And these pearls . . . the red trinket my father kept as a good-luck charm . . . It sounds like Arghun's spies knew they wanted it from the second they saw it. They just never knew my uncle had one as well."

Marco sighed. "If only my father hadn't taken that pearl out of his pocket. If he'd kept it hidden away, he would have come safely home. And my family wouldn't have been hunted by a madman one by one. But you know what, Amelio? Now that we are where we are, I won't just sit back. *I'm* the one with the pearl now. If Arghun wants it so bad . . . he's just going to have to go through *me*."

Chapter 40

Once Marco recorded their travels in his journal, and the boys lay down to sleep, the cave turned into a buzz of industrious activity.

Only minutes after the last of them closed their eyes, wave upon wave of small creatures swarmed everywhere. Each creature walked upright, was colored bright red, and was no larger in height or girth than a man's outstretched hand. They numbered in the thousands and quickly filled the cavern in a carpet of trembling, frenzied motion.

As they went about their task, for each sound made by Marco, Aziz, Amelio, or Kokachin—whether a snore or a dream-addled shriek—the creatures all responded, half a second later, in high-pitched, collective mimicry. What Amelio earlier assumed to be the natural echo of the cavern had been these creatures all along, now rifling through each one of their packs in search of scraps of food.

Working quickly, within minutes their bellies were full with the supplies the travelers brought with them from Bukhara. Once sated, they promptly and noiselessly retreated into the depths of the cave.

Chapter 41

Hours later, Aziz was the first to wake.

He rolled up his sleeping mat and tucked it in his pack, before rummaging for some bread. When he found nothing, he looked through Kokachin's, Marco's, and Amelio's packs in turn. Then he cried out, waking the rest of them from their sleep.

"What kind of a trick is this?"

"What are you talking about?" Marco said, rubbing at his eyes.

"Check your packs, our food is gone!"

Amelio looked in his pack while Kokachin did the same. Then—seeing a trail of bright pink goo along his pack's interior—Kokachin cursed himself.

"What is it?" Aziz said.

"I should have known...."

Before any of them could stop him, Kokachin cupped his hands in front of his covered mouth and yelled as loud as he could. His voice echoed back a thousand times, shaking the walls of the cavern.

"What did you do that for?" Amelio said, clutching his ears.

"The echoes," Kokachin said. "They're not created by the cave. Look at that sliver of daylight against the cavern wall."

When Aziz, Marco, and Amelio looked, Kokachin whistled loudly. In an instant a dozen tiny red heads poked into the light to repeat the sound. "They're called Yamabiko," Kokachin said, shaking his head. "And they stole our food while we slept. Our rations from Bukhara were probably the finest meal they've had in years. You're welcome!" Kokachin shouted angrily.

And they were all treated to a thousand echoed "You're welcome!"s in return.

Marco, Amelio, and Aziz quickly grabbed their weapons, steeling themselves against the need to hack through a thousand Yamabiko that had somehow surrounded them throughout the cave.

"There's no need for weapons," Kokachin said. "Yamabiko are scavengers who live in the mountains and hide from the light, avoiding other creatures. As a rule they're nocturnal. Now that there's daylight they're likely getting ready to go to sleep."

"If they avoid other creatures, why do they keep echoing everything we say? Shouldn't they just shut up and hide?" Marco asked.

"It's how they communicate. When one of them hears a sound they mimic the noise, and every Yamabiko in earshot mimics in turn. Within minutes the sound can travel miles, alerting any Yamabiko in the area to the presence of food. Then, when you fall asleep . . . you wake up without any rations."

Amelio looked concerned. "But if all our food is gone . . . what will we *eat*?"

For the sake of the boys, Aziz forced back his frustration and attempted good cheer. "We'll improvise. This is how legends are born—in twenty years, travelers from Venice to the Unknown Lands will tell the story of Marco, Amelio, and Aziz, who took down the sorcerer Arghun on nothing but a diet of weeds."

Marco and Amelio offered up slight smiles, then everyone gathered up their things—each fighting back the thought that, if their rations really were gone, they ran the risk of collapsing if they didn't find more food.

Once they had everything they needed, a strange rumbling noise abruptly called their attention to the darkness farther inside the cavern.

"Is that . . . ?" Amelio asked.

"More Yamabiko? No," Kokachin said, suddenly alert. "It sounds more like someone approaching."

"Someone approaching from *inside* the cavern?" Marco asked.

"This isn't just a cavern. It's—"

"Shh!" Aziz said, his put-on cheer instantly forgotten as he rose and drew his sword. "We weren't looking for more company. And," Aziz said, looking at Kokachin somewhat sharply, "after you just led us into a den of Yamabiko—we're going to handle this one my way."

"You don't understand, this is—"

"Quiet!" Marco and Amelio said, grabbing their daggers and preparing for the worst.

"But—"

"On my count . . . ," Aziz said.

As Aziz started counting, the rumbling grew closer, plunging the entire cavern into a cacophony of echoing Yamabiko.

Then, before Aziz could finish counting or any of them could react, a figure slipped out of the darkness and stepped into view.

Chapter 42

The figure stood half-covered in shadows, staring at them, and—for what seemed like minutes—the only sound they could hear was the *drip-drip* of their nervous sweat hitting the floor.

Then the figure spoke. At first its voice was drowned out by the Yamabiko's echoes, but, when the chorus died down, they all heard the words: "... It ... it is ... it is me ..."

Amelio thought of all the horrible creatures they'd recently come upon that could identify themselves as *me*.

Then the figure waddled out and came fully into view. Rather than an enemy, this was a very short man wearing a thick pair of glasses. His clothes consisted of simple wooden sandals and a snug-fitting orange robe, and his round stomach was echoed in the smooth curve of his bald head. When he neared them, he smiled.

"I'm sorry, I didn't mean to scare you. But it's only me."

"Me?" Aziz said, dumbfounded.

"That's right, me. And you can put down your weapons, you know—no need for weapons when you're in the presence of a monk. My name is Kar-wai. I knew you'd be coming."

"You're a monk?" Amelio said.

"That's what I was trying to tell you," Kokachin said. "But you wouldn't let me speak. I told you, when we woke, we'd continue toward the Shrine of the Eternal Order. We have a bit farther to go—but the only way to reach the shrine is trekking through this cave."

"It does go on for quite a while," Kar-wai said, pointing into the darkness from which he came, before the others had time to react. "And there are particularly aggressive tribes of Yamabiko who make this cave their home by either entrance. But positioning our shrine in the middle of the cave has thus far kept us safe. And we tend to have only visitors of the purposeful kind. As I said, my name is Kar-wai; I knew you'd be coming," the small man repeated, waddling toward them.

Aziz sized him up, before slowly lowering his sword. "I'm Aziz."

"Marco." He put away his dagger.

"I'm Amelio. If this leads to your shrine—do you have food? All of our rations were stolen by Yamabiko."

"We have more food than we can eat," Kar-wai said. "And the Yamabiko are what they are—let go of your anger. What they've taken we will gladly replenish."

"My name is Kokachin. My companions and I have come to—"

Kar-wai stopped Kokachin with a quick wave of his hand.

"No need, no need to explain," he said. "I'm sure there are things to discuss, but all will be revealed in due time. For now, follow me—we're flanked by Yamabiko, and they've been keeping quiet out of respect. But it's daylight now, so I believe, more than anything, we should leave them alone and let them drift to sleep."

Chapter 43

Kar-wai led Marco, Amelio, Kokachin, and Aziz further into
the blackness of the cave. For a brief while it was so dark none
of them could see, and they were forced to follow the monk
based solely on the sound of his footsteps. Then, bit by bit, the
darkness was punctured by light from candles mounted on the
cavern's walls.

Finally, they stepped into the cavern's largest chamber and
were shocked to find candles everywhere, from the ceiling to
the floor, illuminating every inch so brightly they might as well
have been outdoors. All of their eyes went wide with amazement. Here, inside this cave, the world was green and lush.
They had stepped into an artfully arranged, landscaped, and
beautifully serene oasis.

In the middle of the chamber there was a two-story shrine,
made from polished wood and capped with a burnished bronze
roof. Something about it projected a powerful aura of tranquil-
ity. On either side of the shrine there were smaller buildings: a
rectangular wooden dormitory for the monks to sleep in to the

left, and a modest clay hut housing their kitchen and dining area to the right.

In a shape vaguely like a circle around the three structures, a stone path drifted lazily here and there. As it rambled, it connected everything in an utterly roundabout way. Inside the circle-shape there were grassy lawns, flower beds, shade-providing trees and a man-made fish pond, all defiant, seeming not to care that they had no right to exist within the belly of a gargantuan cave.

"This is impossible," Marco said, looking around with wide eyes as Kar-wai led them farther into the heart of the cavern.

"Oh, it's quite possible, I assure you," Kar-wai said casually, as if he'd grown used to this reaction. "It's not likely, I'll give you that—not unless you've been trained in the proper arts and meditated for months on end. But with the right knowledge to draw upon, and the right conditions in place, grass will always find a way to grow, and even a stone can be convinced to spout water."

As they drew closer to the central shrine Aziz and Amelio began to see animals all around them. Lovebirds flew through the air and squirrels jumped from tree to tree. In the pond, different species of fish swam quickly past. Rabbits hopped around their feet. And, just as they reached the shrine's steps, Marco saw it.

"A peacock!" he exclaimed. The iridescent, blue-green bird looked at them strangely before spreading out its tail feathers, which rose up behind it like a giant painted fan. "Check out the 'eyes' on the end of the feathers!" Marco said. As soon as the words left Marco's lips the bird turned and ran, as if doing its best to deny its guests a closer look.

"If this is your shrine," Amelio said, taking in the finely pol-ished wood, "then where . . . where are all the other monks?"

"Ah, yes—the brothers of the eternal order. Most of them aren't here at the moment," Kar-wai said, leading them up to the central shrine's sliding rice-paper entrance. "You see, on one end of this cave you'll find what Westerners call the 'Insur-mountable Mountains.' And at the other there is the 'Endless Desert.' Whether at one end, the other, or here in between, we live in a world unique for its solitude and insularity.

"For the most part our place in this world is our shrine. But every six moons we live among the sands or the rocks, to reestablish our close link with nature. Right now, most of my brothers are doing just this. But a few must always stay behind to tend to the animals and the garden. . . . And I'm quite fond of all the trees and peacocks," Kar-wai said.

"And how *do* you take care of them?" Marco asked, looking around. "I mean, we're in a cave. How do you keep everything so alive?"

"I wasn't joking earlier when I said even a stone can sprout water," Kar-wai said. With that, he reached down and grabbed a small glass basin sitting by the shrine's paper door. Inside were three stones submerged in a clear liquid. "Each of these rocks has been soaked in the waters of enchanted springs, and blessed by our order for a period of years. Now each of them is a water stone." With that, he tipped the basin and let all the liquid inside spill out, splashing at their feet. As soon as Kar-wai held the basin upright again—miraculously—water squeezed out from the pores of each stone, and the basin immediately grew full.

"That's amazing!" Amelio said, with both Marco and Aziz too shocked to speak.

"You haven't seen anything yet. Do you think we created that fish pond back there one basin of water at a time?"

Kar-wai took one of the rocks from the basin and squeezed it in his hand.

Without any further warning, a jet of water blasted from the bottom of the stone. The jet pushed the stone up, entirely free from Kar-wai's hand, up and up again, high up into the air toward the very roof of the cavern.

Then, when it was as high as it could go, the rock began spinning madly, shooting hundreds of jets of water, raining endless torrents over every creature and blade of grass in the cavern. Marco, Amelio, Aziz, and Kokachin looked on in absolute amazement as the stone spun faster, water completely drenching their clothes and skin.

Once they were all sufficiently wet, Kar-wai smiled and snapped his fingers, and the water immediately ceased. The stone stopped spinning, fell from the sky, and landed with a satisfying *plop* in Kar-wai's wet, outstretched hand. "As I said, with the right knowledge to draw upon, and the right conditions in place . . ."

Seeing Marco's clear and continuing awe, Kar-wai tossed him the stone. "Keep it. It's a gift."

"What? No, I couldn't—"

"Come inside the shrine. You'll see, we have hundreds of them. Thousands. No need for us to keep one more."

"Go ahead, take it," Aziz said, a smile on his face. "It'll be your very first artifact. Found on your first adventure."

Kar-wai bowed and slid open the shrine's rice-paper door. Aziz and Kokachin stepped inside, and Amelio watched Marco slip the stone into his pocket.

Chapter 44

The center of the shrine was a modest, elegantly simple room. The walls were polished wood, and there was little in the way of furniture besides a few low-to-the-ground tables, a series of straw mats and floor pillows.

"So," Kar-wai said, squeezing the water from his clothes. "Every traveler comes to the shrine for a reason, and each reason is answered as best we can. Now that we've been introduced, would you like to give voice to yours?"

"We're in possession of a pearl that seems to have attracted attention," Aziz said. "We'd like to understand why."

"Along the way we found this," Marco said. From his pack he took out the tattered copy of the encyclopedia of magic they received from Theron in Bukhara.

"Ah, yes," Kar-wai said, wiping off his wet glasses on his wet shirt. "That's one of ours, isn't it?" He took the book in his hand and flipped through its pages. Then he frowned. "It appears more than a few chapters are missing. It's very hard to use without them."

"Exactly," Aziz said. "We were hoping you might have another copy. Or some other text that could help us understand what we need to know."

"Yes, of course," Kar-wai said. "Come with me." They all followed as Kar-wai led them into a small, plain room to their immediate right.

Chapter 45

To their surprise, the room was immaculately clean and entirely empty aside from two wooden shelves holding vials of strangely colored liquid, and a particularly dusty spot on the floor just beneath.

"This way, this way," Kar-wai said, leading them over to the two shelves, both adjusted for men of Kar-wai's height. On each shelf there were thirty or forty vials, each one long and narrow. Every vial was corked at the top and flat at the bottom so it could stand upright, and the liquid was a strange and different color inside each.

"Our shrine is rather open on the whole," Kar-wai said. "But, for the good of all, some of our knowledge remains more hidden than the rest. The knowledge in this particular tome requires the assistance of a liquid drink. Please, pick one of the vials and drink it to find what you seek."

"But . . . there's different-colored liquid in every vial. How do you know what to pick?" Amelio said, looking from one vial to the next. There was light green liquid, dark yellow liquid, thick orange liquid, blue liquid with small brown dots floating inside . . .

"Ah, yes. And some of the vials do the exact same thing, regardless of their color. Others, something altogether different. Some will be refreshing, others entirely deadly."

"Excuse me?" Marco said. "Did you just say 'deadly'?"

"I'm afraid that's just what I said," Kar-wai continued in the same tone. "You see, as a monk, it is not my duty to decide who does and does not receive the knowledge in our tomes. I can direct anyone arriving here, with an idea of what they need, to the proper location. But some of our more sensitive tomes can only be found with liquid assistance. And the liquids in these vials . . . self-select."

"What do you mean?" Aziz said with a slight hint of menace.

"By that I mean, if you're meant to see a particular tome, the vial you choose will help you do so. And if your intentions are sinister, you may find the vial you drink from to be the same. I have no bearing on what you do or don't drink—the vial you choose is entirely up to you."

Marco, Amelio, Aziz, and Kokachin looked at one another with suddenly worried glances. Kar-wai had gone from helpful to dangerous in only a matter of moments.

"Please, if you seek our knowledge, choose from the vials and drink," Kar-wai said. "Amelio, you first."

Amelio stared at the differently colored vials on the shelf.

"We can find the information we need some other way. There are other books—" Aziz said.

"No. It's fine," Amelio said, his expression resolute. "We've come this far to rescue Marco's father. And it's time for me to take some risks. For the good of Niccolo Polo, we're meant to see what's in those books."

As the rest of them looked on, and before they could stop him, Amelio grabbed a vial with light green liquid from the shelf. No sooner was it in his hands than the glass began to vibrate madly. "Hey, what's this?"

"Oh, my," Kar-wai said, looking concerned.

"Oh, my?" Aziz repeated, his hand shooting over to the sword still at his waist.

"What is this? What's going on?" Amelio said, the vial vibrating faster and faster, so quickly he could barely hold on to it.

"Why, that shouldn't be happening—that shouldn't be happening at all! My, I would drop that if I were you. I would drop it right away!"

Amelio immediately let go of the vial and watched it crash onto the ground. It exploded in a tiny puff of odorless green smoke.

And, as soon as the smoke cleared, in the midst of the glass from the shattered vial they all saw a tiny green creature.

The creature, in a bit of a daze, climbed to its feet. It looked something like a small person if the person were green, covered in scales, and the size of two fingers side-by-side. There were also two tiny wings on its back, just barely large enough to support its weight.

"Ohhh, Sarap is so sore!" the creature said. "Stuck in that bottle for so long, eating nothing but air! Who let me out?" The creature looked around wildly until it found Amelio standing above him. "Greetings! Are you my new master, to whom I am now saluting humbly?"

Amelio stifled a laugh. Compared to some of the horrors they'd just been through, and the real threat of death from drinking the wrong liquid, this creature seemed like one of the funnier things he'd ever seen.

"Oh, dear," Kar-wai said. "This has never been drawn from these liquids before." Then he paused, speaking almost to himself. "But the liquids do have a mind of their own. If this is what you drew, this is what was meant to be."

"Then you are my new master!" Sarap said, staring up at Amelio with a wide green grin. "The monk just said it, you were meant to have me! I am Sarap, your new bottle sprite. And for freeing me, I owe you three boons!"

"This is most unusual, but Sarap is yours now," Kar-wai said. "And this means he owes you three favors. Three wishes."

"Yes!" Sarap said. "Most correct. Though favors, not wishes—Sarap does what he can, but he knows no magic. At your service, the forever powers of my hands and feet." Quickly, Sarap cleaned up the broken shards of glass from the vial and stacked them one on top of the other. Then Sarap leaped into the air and, propelled by his tiny wings, landed on Amelio's shoulder.

"I'll just sit up here," Sarap said. "Don't worry!" he yelled in Amelio's ear. "I'll make myself scarce. You won't even know I'm around!"

Amelio winced at the sound in his ear, but once he saw Sarap's face up close, he couldn't help laughing again.

"Amelio has chosen. Aziz, it is now your turn. To receive our knowledge, choose your liquid."

Aziz was apprehensive, but he followed Amelio's lead and grabbed an orange vial. Giving Kar-wai a somewhat menacing look, Aziz uncorked the vial, put it to his lips, and drank deeply.

Within seconds, Aziz's entire body started to tremble. Then he simply disappeared.

Chapter 46

When Aziz next opened his eyes, he was standing alongside an enormous glass tower shooting hundreds of stories up into the air. Light refracted into and through the glass madly, making the entire structure appear as though it were charged with explosive energy.

Before Aziz could try to figure out where he was, he felt an enormous burst of wind, then Marco appeared beside him. Two more gusts and they were joined by Kokachin and Kar-wai.

Aziz had his sword out and pointed at Kar-wai's chest before the small man could even clean off his glasses.

"What have you done? Where have you taken us?"

"Taken you? I haven't taken you anywhere at all," he said, removing his glasses from his face and wiping them off on his shirt.

"I'm in no mood for games, little man," Aziz growled. "If you don't start talking, and I mean quick—"

"Aziz, I think he's telling the truth!" Marco said, inserting himself between Aziz and the small man. "Look up!"

"At that glass tower? I've never seen anything like it in my life. It's some kind of—"

"No, look *farther* up. Straight up, as far as you can."

Aziz did as he was told without loosening his grip on his sword—and cried out in absolute horror.

"What is that? What is that massive beast?"

"That beast is your friend Amelio," Kar-wai said as he put his glasses back on his face, calm as ever.

"What? What have you done to him? He's enormous!"

"I'm afraid Amelio is the same size he ever was. We're the ones who have shrunk."

"Shrunk?" Aziz said, finally starting to understand what just happened.

"A fiftieth of the size of the nail on your finger. Things look quite a bit different from this height. The glass from Amelio's broken vial, for example, looks quite beautiful when it's stacked just like that."

One by one, Marco, Aziz, and Kokachin took in the glass tower and understood.

"Of course, there are quite a few new dangers when you're this height—for example, if Amelio took one wrong step, we'd all be crushed—but I explained what was happening and instructed him to stay quite still before I drank the liquid in my own vial. Let's just hope he listens."

As Aziz began to relax, Marco looked around until he saw

what he'd earlier mistaken as a spot of dust in the otherwise immaculate room, just beneath the two shelves.

From this height, it wasn't a spot of dust at all. Instead, they were shelves of books. Millions upon millions of shelves of books, one row after the other, going on as far as the eye could see.

"All of you, welcome," Kar-wai said, "to the Grand Library of the Shrine of the Eternal Order."

Chapter 47

"Let's see, let us see," Kar-wai said, quickly thumbing his way through a particular set of shelves. "It's a pearl you're hoping to learn about, is it?"

"Exactly," Aziz said, feeling better but still shooting nervous glances at the now enormous Amelio.

"And what kind of pearl might it be?" Kar-wai said.

"Kind?" Aziz asked, confused.

"There are many kinds of pearls, and different ones will have very different names and stories."

"Aziz," Marco said, remembering something. "That Abarimon we faced in Bukhara. He called it a name we hadn't heard before, didn't he? Not just a pearl—a *dragon's pearl*."

As soon as Marco said those words Kar-wai froze. "Did you just say a dragon's pearl? Why would you want to know about a dragon's pearl?" he said, apprehensive.

"The Abarimon told us we had one—it's here with me now. A blue pearl, and my father had a red pearl as well."

All of the color immediately drained from Kar-wai's face.

Kokachin, too, seemed shocked. "Could it be . . . the Abarimon said it was a dragon's pearl?" he whispered.

"What does that even mean?" Marco asked.

Kar-wai slipped a particular book off the shelf, heavy and large, then turned toward them, far more solemn than he'd been before. "If that's the case, the book you had would have done you no good," he said. "To understand what it means to have a dragon's pearl, *this* is the proper tome." Kar-wai squeezed the book tightly between his fingers.

Kar-wai said nothing for several moments. When he continued, it was with an entirely new sense of gravity.

"Dragons, my dear boys," Kar-wai explained, "are the ultimate source of magic in this world. Think of them like the sun—the sun provides us with energy, light, and heat. A tree, for example, absorbs the sun's energy to grow. A human, in turn, might cut down that tree and burn its wood, turning the wood into light and heat. So the light and heat from a fire ultimately found its source in the sun.

"The same is true of magic and dragons—all sorcerers and mystical creatures ultimately draw their energy from a dragon. Dragons fuel all magic in this world.

"Of the four great dragons, the first lived in the West and fueled spells of water. The second lived in the West and fueled spells of wind. The third lives in the East and fuels spells of the earth. And the fourth lives in the East and fuels spells of flame. When a human becomes a mage, it is because he is born with a connection to one of the four great dragons. And the dragon he connects with determines the kind of mage he is and the types of spells he can cast."

"But what do dragons have to do with pearls?" Marco asked, not entirely sure he wanted to know the answer.

"For every Eastern and Western dragon, there are two indestructible pearls. The pearls contain the essence of the dragon—the dragon's soul, an essential part of the world itself. When a dragon is flesh, two pearls are embedded in the center of each dragon's brow." Kar-wai tapped on the center of his forehead. "But when a dragon's physical body is slain . . . its spirit lives on eternally in the pearls."

"Dragons can be slain?" Marco asked.

"Dragons can never be killed . . . but their physical bodies can be slain like any other. When this happens, the entirety of their essence is forced into their pearls. Over time, a slain dragon's connection with the world grows weaker, and the magic that dragon fueled eventually disappears. In the West, for example, some time ago, you came to fear your dragons. You viewed them as dangerous beasts, and the wind and water dragons were mercilessly hunted and eventually slain until only their legends remained. As a result, magic has disappeared entirely from the Western lands.

"In the East, on the other hand, dragons are revered as wise and noble creatures. Statues of dragons can be found in the most holy places, and the dragon of fire and dragon of earth still exist among us. As you travel these lands you will no doubt find mages with strong connections to each. These strong, proud dragons are the reason Eastern magic continues to thrive."

As he listened it was all Marco could do to keep his mouth from falling open. He was hearing there had once been magic in the West! Spells of wind and water!

"The two slain Western dragons . . . what became of their pearls?" Aziz asked.

"Exactly. What did become of their pearls?" Kar-wai opened the book in his hands, flipping to a particular section. "If you do indeed have what you claim—those blue and red pearls could contain the essence of the slain wind dragon, Shen Lung."

"Long ago in the west, Sir George the Dragonslayer—by order of his sovereign king—assembled a team of warriors and alchemists to find, capture, and kill the wind dragon. They believed the dragon posed a threat to the empire, and they could only be safe once it was slain. Driven by fear, Sir George and his men spent years doing everything they could to vanquish the dragon—and when they finally succeeded in their task, only the blue and red pearls remained. In time, half of the West's mystical creatures faded to human forms, and half of the West's great magicians felt their skills reduced to nothing more than parlor tricks.

"As for Sir George—after slaying the dragon, he presented the pearls to his king as proof. The king did not understand the pearls' purpose and wasted no time mounting them upon his staff as symbols of progress and the triumph of reason. It is known the king went on to carry his staff with him into battle, and died himself—a casualty of the Crusades—but further whereabouts of the pearls have remained a mystery. While the exact tale is different, in the case of the slain water dragon the results remain the same. Neither dragon's pearls have been seen in recent history."

Kar-wai closed the book and looked very seriously at his guests. "All of you. If you have what you say, you must know a dragon can still be resurrected from its pearls. In the hands of a powerful sorcerer, a slain dragon might still rise again.

"Now, if its pearls are freely given, a dragon can go among the living. But if a dragon is resurrected and its pearls are kept, so long as the pearls remain in your possession the dragon is bound to do your bidding. There are few things, if any, more powerful than a dragon. A captive dragon in the wrong hands could tear this world apart."

Kar-wai turned toward Marco and Aziz. "If you were to have Shen Lung's pearls, where might they have been found? After all these years, where would one come across them?"

"Marco's father and uncle received them in trade," Aziz said. "In the course of their dealings as merchants. They were items mixed among many, passed along thousands of times before, and no one could have known they had any further value than that."

"Arghun's spies in the khan's palace must have had some idea," Marco said, still trying to comprehend everything he'd just been told. "Once my father arrived with the pearl, it was only a matter of time before Arghun and his Abarimon came after us all."

"No . . . ," Kar-wai said, his face turning pale. "Arghun is involved in this as well? Oh, this is very bad indeed."

"You've had dealings with Arghun?" Kokachin said.

Kar-wai bowed his head solemnly. "I have. Arghun came to our shrine once, many years ago. An ambitious young fire mage, as powerful as any we'd seen, he was traveling the Lands in an insatiable quest for knowledge. In our library there are spells undreamed of anywhere else in the world, and when Arghun arrived he quickly demanded them all.

"As with all guests, it is not our duty to decide who receives the knowledge in our tomes. The liquid in our vials self-select.

But when Arghun drank from the vial he'd chosen, he fell badly ill. For a week he was with us, in terrible shape, tended to by all of our brothers. And the instant he was well enough to walk again he grabbed another vial, drank, and fell twice as ill as before.

"It was not long after he left our shrine empty-handed that Arghun's skills and wanderings drew notice, and he soon came to the attention of the king of the Mongols, Kublai Khan. In the bowels of the Forbidden Palace the khan has tomes that even we do not, and when Arghun learned of this he set every ounce of his being toward acquiring them. He charmed everyone in the palace, stayed close to the khan, and was eventually named chief magician. It was only a matter of time, with the access that followed, before Arghun found his way to dark knowledge he was not ready to receive.

"You must understand—for every spell cast by a mage, they tap into their connection with their dragon. Simple spells require little connection; sophisticated spells require far more. But dragons are beings beyond men, and the connection required to cast the most powerful spells takes a serious toll. It requires time to learn how one can draw deeply from their dragon without growing distorted from the experience.

"On the path to chief magician, Arghun attempted far too much, and he quickly began to lose himself. Later, learning the summoning spells in the hidden tomes of the Forbidden Palace, he twisted himself entirely. For to cast a summoning spell is to force the essence of your dragon onto someone else, to reshape their body and will in your dragon's image. No other spells require a deeper connection with your dragon. And the summoning spells have long been forbidden because they are always too much for a human to bear."

"Is that . . . is that what happened to all the mages that went missing in the Forbidden Palace? Arghun used them to practice the summoning spells?" Marco asked.

"Many wizards disappeared. The wizards whose bodies were found, who died—those were the ones Arghun used to practice."

"And the rest?" Aziz asked.

"At a certain point, Arghun learned to create Abarimon—men remade in his image, infused with the essence of the fire dragon. Because of this essence of fire dragon, Abarimon cannot tolerate water. But they are otherwise a vicious and monstrous force from ages past, deadly and unrelenting. In packs, they are thought to be unstoppable."

"They can't tolerate water. That must be why the Abarimon didn't chase us through that river," Marco murmured to himself.

"Once Arghun's Abarimon forces grew, he fled the Forbidden Palace to create an army of his own. And he's been a danger to all ever since. If he is now after the wind dragon's pearl, we are all in the gravest of danger."

"Then we'll need to do everything we can to ensure he won't get his hands on it," Aziz said, strengthening his resolve and resting his fingers on his sword.

"Arghun is still a man of flesh and blood. He will fall before he reaches the pearl," Kokachin said, his hand on his dagger.

"I think it's time that we join Amelio and continue on our way," Marco said, more determined than ever.

"Then close your eyes and wish it so," Kar-wai said, his tone once again serene. "You have learned what you needed—as each of us wish, we all shall grow."

Chapter 48

"Amelio? Amelio, where are you?"

Marco's eyes quickly scanned the room while Aziz and Kokachin looked themselves over to ensure they were at their full size again.

"I don't see him," Marco said as Kar-wai shot up to his normal height, then calmly cleaned off his glasses. "Do you? He's not the type to wander off."

"No, he's not," Aziz said, growing worried.

"And we weren't away very long," Kokachin said.

Kar-wai closed his eyes and listened carefully without saying a word.

"Where would he have gone?" Aziz asked Kar-wai, who appeared to be ignoring him.

Marco's eyes landed on the two shelves of vials against the wall. "Weren't there more of those vials a few moments ago?"

"Why?" Kokachin said.

"We left him on his own out here. What if he grabbed another vial to try and shrink down to join us?"

"Nobody move!" Aziz said, beginning to panic. "If he shrank himself, one misstep and we could crush him!"

Kar-wai slowly opened his eyes. "Your friend is just outside the shrine. He seems to have been found by my colleague. Come with me, and I will introduce you to Kai-shek."

Chapter 49

In the shade of an enormous tree, just along the stone path, Amelio sat by a small but comforting fire with Sarap perched on his shoulder. Next to them the monk Kai-shek—nearly identical in appearance to Kar-wai, but lacking glasses—was feeding twigs and branches into the flame to keep it going.

"Brother Kai-shek, I see you've found Amelio and his new bottle sprite. Please meet Marco, Aziz, and Kokachin as well. I told you they would be coming," Kar-wai said as he led his companions to their friend.

"Yes, yes. I knew you would be here. I kept Amelio company while you were rather small."

"It's a good thing you left me behind," Amelio said, standing up and dusting himself off. "Kai-shek came inside the shrine and nearly stepped on you. If I hadn't yelled out in time . . ."

"I'm grateful that you did. I usually wear glasses like Brother Kar-wai, but today I don't have them on me. Your eyes served to augment my own."

"Thanks for keeping me company either way!" Amelio said, jumping up to join his friends, Sarap holding tightly to his shirt while he ran.

"And thank you," Aziz said, turning to Kar-wai. "For everything."

"It is why I am here," Kar-wai said. "This was a trial you all have passed. But your next trial lies not in this cave, but through it." Kar-wai pointed in the direction opposite that from which they had first come. "Just past this shrine, you'll find the entrance to the other end of the cavern. You'll need to head down that path for some time, and in the darkest black. Unlike your journey here, when you pass through the cave there will be no candles to guide you. But when you see the blazing sun and the great desert beyond, you'll know you've found your way.

"Good luck. If you have what you say, keep it safe. Good luck to us all."

Chapter 50

When Kar-wai guided the four from the cavern, Kai-shek returned to sit alone by his fire.

As he peered deeply into its red and orange center, the cave around him fell away. There was only the heat and the light.

"They are coming," Kai-shek whispered into the flame. "And they have the dragon's pearl on them. Master Arghun, in the heat of the desert may your will be done."

Chapter 51

In no time at all, as Kar-wai had warned, Kokachin, Amelio, Sarap, Aziz, and Marco were swallowed by a seemingly impenetrable black.

While this cavern was high and wide enough that they could walk freely, their eyes were instantly useless. Sarap, fearful of getting lost, buried himself inside Amelio's shirt. The rest of them stayed together by touch, and by following the footstep, the stumble, the measured breath just ahead.

"Aziz?" Marco said in the darkness at the end of the pack.

"I'm here."

"We're never going to let Arghun get his hands on that pearl. And we're going to get my father back."

"Don't you ever doubt that," Aziz said with genuine emotion. "Don't." Aziz slowed until he was closer to Marco. "Are you all right back there in the dark?"

"Yes," Marco said. "In Venice, at night, when no one else was around, my father and I used to play hide-and-seek in the canals. Sometimes when I'd hide in the alleys, on cloudy nights, it was almost like this. Not quite this dark—but almost."

"And on those nights—did your father always find you?"

"Whenever I was sure, for once, I'd gotten away—that's just when he'd sneak up behind me."

"Your father was always good at finding things." He paused. "Even things better left unfound."

"You never told me. How did my father find you?" Marco asked.

Aziz hesitated before responding. "It was many years ago. I was working as . . . as a thief," he said. "I never knew my parents, and my grandmother raised me in Bukhara. She died in debt to local men; her house was taken, and I was left with nothing. Not knowing what else to do, but relying on my size and strength, I turned to local thieves—Theron and his tall companion we met back at The Thirsty Camel." Aziz paused. "I joined their ranks for pay, protection, and shelter. We lived together as thugs, not caring for any man or law, robbing and stealing from anyone we saw."

It was a good thing the cave was pitch-black, as Marco was unable to stop his mouth from dropping open in surprise.

"One day our band spotted some merchants traveling just outside Bukhara. They looked helpless so we . . . we attacked them, hoping to steal their wares. But this time we misjudged, and the merchants were far stronger than they appeared. When they fought back they overpowered us to a man. Theron and the rest broke free and ran, but I struck them first, and I was the first they retaliated against in turn. One of the merchants stabbed me deeply—I still have the scar—and when my companions ran off, they left me with the merchants to die.

"Most of the merchants were content to let me do just that. I was a thief and I'd brought this upon myself. Why shouldn't they let me bleed and take pleasure in my death?

"But your father was among those merchants, and he insisted they help me. Under his strict instructions they put me on their cart and took me to a local inn. He found a nearby doctor, paid for my care, and watched over me as I recovered."

Marco tried to take this in, the idea of Aziz attacking his father in the night. It was almost impossible to imagine—the Aziz he knew today was an entirely different man.

"Before then, for some time, I'd been without purpose," Aziz continued. "But your father saved me. He asked for my story, spoke to me as his equal and eventually offered something better than the life I'd known. He told me about his caravan that traded in every town, relishing the adventures they found along the way. As soon as I was well he insisted I join them, and over the following years we saw many wondrous things. Today I owe my life to your father. So it's only fitting that I'm prepared to lay my life down if that's what it takes to save him now."

Somehow in the spongy black it was easier for Aziz to say these things, things he truly felt but he had never spoken aloud. He could say them and mean them, let them propel him forward, as they all continued on their quest through the darkness.

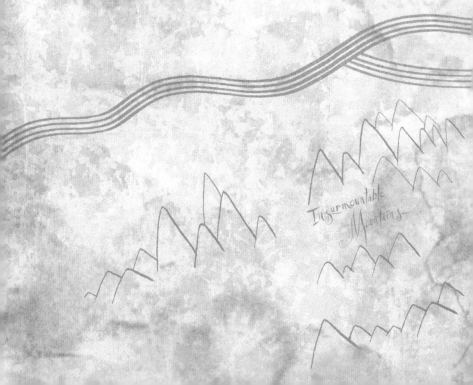

"I turned to see a giant serpent exploding from the ground—just like the worm but thousands of times larger. Dirt and sand flew in clumps as the creature pulled its enormous body from the earth. With a belly as wide as a small ship, it was the largest living thing I had ever seen. . . ."

—FROM THE JOURNALS OF MARCO POLO

Part Four

ENDLESS

DESERTS

and

UNKNOWN

LANDS

Chapter 52

It was several hours before they saw their next glimpse of light. When they did, it seemed almost impossibly bright, as though the sun itself had disappeared and grown stronger with their travels, coming back twice as powerful as before.

"Is that . . . ," Amelio said, squinting at the light up ahead.

"Shh," Kokachin said, continuing toward it. "Don't let your energy flag. It may look close, but we still have some ways to go."

However—whether the hint of light made time go faster, or they were closer than Kokachin thought—it wasn't long before the cave seemed to grow wider, more light crept in, and fine grains of sand appeared under their feet. Darkness gave way to vague silhouettes, then shapes, then each of them were able to see the others' features for the first time in what felt like days. By the time they came to the end of the path and the cavern opened completely, they each felt more exhausted, and invigorated, than they had in some time.

"We made it . . . ," Marco said as they grew closer, almost not believing it could be true.

"It felt like it would go on forever," Amelio said.

"It was just like being stuck in that bottle all over again!" Sarap said, poking his head out of Amelio's sleeve.

With Marco, Amelio, and Aziz following, Kokachin stepped up to the very mouth of the cave.

"Welcome to the desert," he said, eyes fixed on the open landscape ahead. "Here in the East we call it the Taklamakan, which joins with the Gobi. Not far is the Hanhai desert, which means 'endless sea.' This desert is our final natural barrier before we reach the land of China in the Mongol territories, home of Kublai Khan. And from there, straight on to Mount Dragoian."

"And is that where you leave us? On the path to Mount Dragoian?" Marco said.

"No," Kokachin said, shaking his head solemnly. "I'm afraid I took this assignment for reasons of my own. I have . . . history with Arghun. If your goal is to put an end to the fire mage to rescue your father, then I'll continue on to Mount Dragoian as well."

"What's your history with Arghun?" Amelio asked.

"I'm afraid that's mine and mine alone. But I think you'll find my help to be as invaluable going forward as it has been in the past."

Marco, Amelio, and Aziz let Kokachin's words sink in. Kokachin's tone made it clear the matter would not be up for discussion.

Then Kokachin continued. "All of you. Though we've been through much, the desert ahead is just as deadly as the mountains behind. The sands here can shift suddenly under your feet. Each step will feel like many, and you'll have to keep going no matter how tired you feel—without cover, in the time it takes to rest, the heat of the sun will sap twice as much energy as you've gained. Many travelers have rested too long and never moved again. But this desert, like the mountains, can be conquered. If you follow me, and do just what I say, we will find ourselves safely through it."

Without saying another word, Kokachin left the cave and took his first steps on the hot sands. Marco, Amelio, and Aziz followed after a moment's hesitation, with nothing else around in any direction but endless sand, blue skies, and the merciless blazing sun.

Chapter 53

The sun grew higher and brighter in the sky, pushing wave upon wave of heat across the desert. As they pushed onward Marco and Amelio felt a constant stream of sweat bubbling on their foreheads and trickling down their faces. No matter how quickly they wiped it away, a new layer was already there, waiting to take the last one's place. Their cheeks grew red and burned in the heat.

"Are you sure we're going the right way?" Amelio asked Kokachin after some time. "There's nothing around but sand. If we got lost, how could you even tell?"

"I've been through this desert many times," Kokachin said, squinting at a mound in the distance. "I know it better than you can imagine. Have faith that we're traveling along the right path."

"If you say so," Amelio said, sighing as he fell back alongside Marco.

"Hey, you heard Kokachin," Marco whispered earnestly. "Have faith."

"After all this heat," Sarap chimed in, flying on his tiny wings, "the only thing I'm starting to have faith in is that we're lost."

"Though I suppose it could be worse," Amelio grinned, looking at Marco. "Instead of following Kokachin we could be following you. Then we'd be lost for sure."

Marco shoved his friend playfully, and Amelio teetered briefly on one foot.

Before Amelio could retaliate, Kokachin squinted up at the sky, breathed in deeply, then motioned for all of them to stop in their tracks. "From this point forward, things are going to get far more dangerous." Kokachin set his pack on the ground and removed several handkerchiefs made of a nearly transparent white material, and a length of rope. "All of you, use these to cover your faces," he said, handing out the material. "Then take a section of rope and tie it around your waist. We're going to have to connect ourselves to one another."

"What good is tying ourselves together going to do?" Marco said, as Sarap tucked himself safely inside Amelio's shirt.

"In this area, ferocious sandstorms can kick up suddenly within seconds, and we won't be able to see more than a few inches ahead of us. This will make sure no one gets lost. But there's more to it than that. This desert is home to bands of specters, and in the midst of a storm you may see figures in the sand. Though they may look familiar, ignore them all. They can shift their shapes and they mean you only harm.

"Most importantly, no matter what the specters do or say, no matter what they offer you, even if they touch you first—never reach out and touch them in return. Specters live in the space between our world and the next, and active physical contact gives them strength. If you ignore them, they're harmless. But a specter touched can turn to flesh. And, depending on the specter, against some creatures come to life we'd have little hope of survival."

All of them nodded solemnly as they tied the rope into firm knots, then looked around, feeling a bit strange, the rope hanging from their waists like a shared umbilical cord.

But despite their skepticism, no sooner were they tied together than Amelio noticed something in the distance.

"Hey, over there—something's kicking up sand. . . ."

Everyone looked down the sight of Amelio's outstretched arm. A huge funnel of sand was moving toward them.

"Travelers on horseback?" Marco asked.

"No," Kokachin said, his eyes sliding closed. "No one rides horses through this desert. We prepared ourselves just in time—this is how it begins."

"To our left!" Aziz said, and everyone save for Kokachin turned to look. Another whirling cone of sand, this one twice as large as the first, was blowing quickly toward them.

"Remember what I said. Hold tight to the rope. Do not listen to anything. Do not reach out and touch anything, even *if what you see looks exactly like one of us.* What hides within these sands can take any form. Even if it touches you, *do not touch it back.* If you just keep moving, I will guide us all through this to safety."

At that exact moment the group was engulfed completely in a column of howling and whirling sands. The last thing they heard was Kokachin's voice: *"Don't worry,"* it said. *"Remember my words and we'll all be fine!"*

Chapter 54

And then there was nothing but sand, a blinding wall blocking out the world. An incredible roar filled Marco's ears, almost deafening. Through the material covering his face Marco could see individual grains that made up the massive yellow barrier, but Aziz, Amelio, and Kokachin were lost to him.

Suddenly, moving toward him through the sand, Marco saw a face. It was somehow visible through the storm, emerging like someone walking through a waterfall, or a dense fog. The face was immediately familiar. It was his father, Niccolo Polo.

"Father!" Marco shouted, ignoring what Kokachin warned them about only minutes earlier as his father's entire body pushed toward him through the sand. Niccolo's mouth was moving, his face contorted in distress, but Marco couldn't hear anything he was saying over the howling winds.

It's not my father. It's not my father. It's not my father, Marco told himself, as he was tugged forward by the taut rope around his waist. But when his father was standing right there it was hard to treat this as some trick of the sands. Marco and his father always bore an uncanny resemblance to each other—they both had the same piercing blue eyes, thick, curly hair, and strong, noble features—and the man who approached matched Niccolo Polo to the finest detail.

As Marco's father continued toward him, closer and closer, Marco couldn't help but strain against the rope, to reach out his hand to touch him. But he withdrew his hand just as quickly when he heard Amelio's voice, directly behind him in the maelstrom, screaming out, "No! No! No! You're not her! She died! She died!"

Marco could hear Amelio's screams. He checked the rope behind him, and it was taut—still connected to Amelio.

"Amelio! Amelio, it's all right," Marco yelled, craning his neck around to try and get a glimpse of his friend. All he saw were millions upon millions of sand particles swirling around. The coarse sand scoured Marco's skin, and on his face sweat mixed with several splotches of blood.

Niccolo was still hovering just out of Marco's reach, but his friend's cries made it easier for Marco to strengthen his resolve and keep focused. He repeated the words in his head over and over again. *It's not my father. It's not my father. It's not my father.*

To combat the apparition, Marco let his mind wander into the past, to memories of his *real* father. The first memory that came was a day when he was eight years old, and his father had just returned from a trading expedition.

"*Son!*" *Niccolo Polo swooped into the foyer of the Polo residence, whisking Marco into his arms. "You've grown since I saw you last! How old are you now? Ten?"*

"*Father, I'm eight!*"

"Well then, you're the heartiest eight-year-old I've ever laid eyes on! Have you been getting yourself into any trouble while I've been gone?"

"No!" Marco gazed up at his father. His body was hidden behind sumptuous, flowing robes, but his face, weathered and tan from months of travel, grinned warmly at his son.

"You've gotten into no trouble at all? We'll need to do something about that right away! I'll not have my son growing up to be a nontroublemaker!"

Marco's grandfather Lorenzo looked on with visible disapproval. "Niccolo, enough. Don't get the boy too excited. He still has accounting lessons to complete for his tutor tomorrow. He's in training for a very important task, and misunderstanding even one element—"

"Accounting lessons? A tutor? Marco, listen to me," Niccolo said, giving his son his undivided attention. "Son, the world is the only tutor you need. From now on, no matter what your grandfather says, I order you to get out of this house for at least one hour every day. I know you're still young, but you're a Polo! You need to scrape your knees, mess your hair, break a bone or two!"

Marco's grandfather huffed and stormed from the room. "Just what this family needs, another vagabond," he muttered angrily. "I give up, really I do. You're lucky your and your brother's adventures are so profitable, Niccolo. Otherwise I'd consider both my sons to be a complete disgrace. If I wasn't the responsible one, staying here in Venice to keep this end of our operation running . . . if I didn't have hope that my grandson could be trained to keep things going once I'm gone . . . but this impossible mindset of yours, it's going to get you and *your* brother killed one day."

At that, Lorenzo disappeared downstairs.

Marco turned back to his father. "Father, now that you're home, *can you tell me everything you saw while you were gone?"*

Niccolo Polo looked at his son. "Marco, I just got back only moments ago. I'm very tired, and any minute now the porters will be delivering all of my things to unpack. There's plenty of stories I can tell you later."

Marco held his hands behind his back and looked sheepishly to the floor. "But maybe just one or two?"

Niccolo pulled a roll of parchment from his robe and looked it over quickly. "Later, Marco. For now, why don't you go run around with a friend of yours? You have friends, don't you?"

"I have Amelio," Marco said quietly.

"The servant boy? Giuseppe's son? Sure, sure. Why don't you go play with Amelio, and I'll be waiting here when you get back. I'll tell you a few stories then. I have more than a few stories to tell. . . ."

At that, Marco felt a tug on the rope at his waist, and he jolted himself back to the present. That seemed to stand in for many memories Marco had of his father—Niccolo Polo would descend on his life in a whirlwind of treasure and adventure stories, showing Marco exactly what he could aspire to be. Then, just as abruptly, Niccolo would disappear, lost inside his business dealings or going miles away to partake in some new and epic quest.

Marco looked into the sandstorm, and the image of his father had begun to fade. His mouth was still moving, but his body had already started growing vague and indistinct. Eventually, it disappeared entirely into the sand.

Chapter 55

It wasn't my father anyway, Marco thought, trying without much luck to keep tears from welling up in his eyes.

Marco took a deep breath, then listened for Amelio's voice. Hearing nothing, he hoped Amelio had conquered whatever it was that was menacing him as well.

Suddenly, Marco heard another strange noise, this time seeming to come from all around him.

Shhhhhhhhh . . . Shhhh . . . Shhhhhhh . . .

The noise was loud, rising above the wind, seeping into his ears. It sounded like a steel blade scraping hard against stone, but extending on and on, and amplified a thousand times. It was a horrific and unsettling sound, making Marco's entire body cringe.

Shhhhhhh . . . Shhh . . . Shhhh . . . Shhhhhhhh . . .

"Amelio! Aziz! Can you hear that? What's that noise?"

Shhh . . . Shhhh . . . Shhhhhhhhhhhhhhhhhhhhh . . .

It buzzed in Marco's ears, so loud it was the only thing he could hear. The noise was almost alive, taking root in Marco's head and blasting, ceaseless and unending, making his insides swish and churn.

"What it that? Make it stop! Make it stop!"

Until, without warning, it did.

And, to Marco's left, he saw the silhouette of another man walking calmly alongside him in the sand, seemingly unbothered by the whirling and whipping storm that, if anything, had only picked up speed. He strolled along as if without purpose. Then, as Marco watched, the man turned his head to face him. Marco wrapped both his hands as tightly as he could around the rope.

The apparition was in the shape of the most beautiful man Marco had ever seen. His eyes were closed but he kept exact pace with Marco, smiling serenely all the while. His skin was pale and unlined. His short dark hair hung loosely around his ears. He wore a comfortable black robe, but even through the fabric Marco could tell he was strong and athletic.

Just keep walking, Marco thought. *Keep walking.*

The man turned toward Marco and his face twisted into a grotesque smile. He blinked once, twice, then opened his eyes—

They were entirely black, the darkest black Marco had ever seen. Looking into them, Marco felt a sharp twisting in his gut, like his insides were being pulled in every direction, like he was on the verge of being torn apart. Marco grabbed at his stomach in incredible pain.

The sand continued blowing all around them but the man

seemed unbothered, and Marco, even through his pain, found he couldn't turn his head away. As he continued staring, the man calmly held up both of his hands, and in the center of each palm—like possessed stigmata, torn, hungry, and bloodied—Marco saw angry mouths filled with sharp and gleaming teeth. They began to snarl and gnash, slowly at first but rapidly picking up speed, until each one foamed like the jaws of a rabid animal.

The man, his black eyes calm and unblinking, now started walking toward Marco, and Marco felt as though his entire body were being sucked into a bottomless pit. He didn't understand what was happening, but he knew one thing with absolute certainty—if he didn't do something, this man was going to kill him.

"Aziz! Kokachin! Help me!" Marco screamed.

As the man continued toward him a sucking whistle came out of the gnashing mouths, a shrill slurping that, in time, crystallized into a single word said again and again and again.

"*Arghun.*"

"*Arghun.*"

"*Arghun.*"

The wind picked up speed, spitting sharp crystallized sand in every direction, trapping Marco as though he were in the center of a tornado.

"*Arghun.*"

"*Arghun.*"

"*Arghun.*"

Each grain of sand was like a tiny dagger being dragged across his face. Marco grabbed on to the rope around his waist and held it tighter than ever, letting it pull him forward. The wind howled relentlessly in his ears, this time shaping into a new, solitary phrase:

"Give us the dragon's pearl."

"Give me back my father!" Marco screamed with all the rage that had been building up inside him. "Give me back my father or I'll hunt you down; I'll hunt you down and kill you and take him back myself!

At that the mouths begin foaming and twitching again, spasming with—laughter? Marco shut his eyes tightly and told himself none of this was real. He didn't have to do a thing. If he concentrated, the specter would disappear like a bad dream upon waking.

"It's fine," Marco said. "It's not rea—"

But before Marco could complete the sentence, an endless stream of thick, wriggling, fiery red worms began to stream from the man's palms, crawling out of the mouths and over the jagged teeth, flooding onto the sand in a gushing torrent that wriggled feverishly on the ground.

More and more worms poured out of the man's palms until there was a pool of worms on the ground at Marco's feet. And, as Marco watched, the pool of red worms spread quickly toward him, flopping and wriggling around.

"Kokachin! Aziz!" Marco cried out. Within seconds there were already too many worms to avoid, all underfoot. Marco's eyes grew wide as they started to crawl on top of his feet, streaming onto him without hesitation. They began to crawl up his legs, on top of his clothing and underneath, until he soon felt entire masses of their moist, spongy bodies against his skin.

He did all he could not to scream, not to react or touch them back in any way. The worms covered him, moved quickly up his torso as he closed his eyes and thought only of moving ahead, of taking step after step, of pushing his way through the desert. None of this was real, none of it. They couldn't hurt him—

Until one long, particularly thick and oozing red worm crawled up Marco's pant leg, across his bare stomach and chest, and came out the top of his shirt at the neck, covering him in a dripping trail of slime. The worm reared sharply and fiercely back as though it was about to strike hard at Marco's neck, as though it was going to bite him—

And, almost involuntarily, Marco grabbed at the worm and tore it away from him.

He stared at it, nearly a foot long and wriggling in his hand, dumbfounded. He scraped at it with his fingernail and the red skin peeled back, beginning to bleed. It wasn't an apparition at all. It was an enormous worm, in the flesh. Marco reared back and threw the worm as hard as he could, watching its body disappear fifty yards into the distance.

When Marco turned back toward the man—who he could only assume was the image of Arghun—there was no one there. Marco looked at his feet, but the rest of the worms were nowhere to be found . . .

. . . and then the sandstorm faded completely away as abruptly as it began, leaving the travelers alone in the center of the silent, windswept desert.

Chapter 56

"Is it over?" Amelio said, wiping the sand from his eyes and looking around in a daze.

"For now," Kokachin said, clearly shaken.

"I was so happy to be free, but staying with you people is far worse than being stuck in that bottle," Sarap said, poking his head out from the collar of Amelio's shirt.

All around them the sand had settled. Before the storm the desert was a flat surface, constant and unending as far as the eye could see. Now there were dunes of varying shapes and sizes undulating toward the horizon.

Heart still racing, Marco patted furiously at his clothes, looking for some sign of the worms that had been crawling on his body. He shuddered uncontrollably in disgust, but they were gone. There didn't seem to be any trace of even a single worm.

Kokachin began solemnly untying the thick rope from his waist and each of them followed his lead. They were all completely silent, processing what they'd seen. But no sooner did they free themselves from the rope than the ground beneath them again started to rumble.

"No...," Aziz said, looking pale and drained from whatever he encountered in the sandstorm. He felt vibrations all over his body, and his teeth began to clatter.

"Not again. I can't go through that again," Amelio said, grabbing for the rope nonetheless to retie it around his waist.

Kokachin put his hand on Amelio's shoulder. "No, not again. This is something else. Did any of you—did any of you touch anything in the sandstorm? Did any of you put your hands on—"

The rumbling escalated until the ground felt as if it were going to crack in two.

Then they heard a splitting noise in the distance to their right, followed by a terrible, inhuman shriek.

Chapter 57

In the exact direction Marco had thrown the wriggling phantom worm, he turned to see a giant serpent exploding from the ground—just like the worm but thousands of times larger, dwarfing even the most massive sand dunes they'd been climbing. Dirt and sand flew in clumps as the creature pulled its enormous body from the depths of the earth. With a belly as wide as a small ship, it was the largest living thing Marco had ever seen. Its ringed flesh was slathered with a thick mucus that dripped in puddles all around it.

"No, please, what is that?" Amelio yelled, tying the remainder of the rope needlessly around himself.

The creature was free from the earth now, only fifty yards away and slithering closer. It coiled its entire body into an enormous circular pile, around and around and around again, with its long neck and eyeless head extending upward to stand as tall as the palazzo back in Venice. Its head was pink, dripping with goo and capped by a mouth of jagged teeth.

"It's a Naga," Kokachin spat, eyeing it with a mix of anger, terror, and dread. "Ancient demon of serpents. They're in our books, but never in this desert—they shouldn't be here, unless—" Kokachin surveyed Marco, Amelio, and Aziz accusingly.

But before he could continue, the Naga sized them up, and moving faster than any of them imagined it could, it smashed its enormous head directly into Kokachin's chest, sending his body flying across the sand.

Kokachin rolled with the blow but landed hard against the ground. Seeing Kokachin was clearly hurt and having trouble climbing to his feet, the Naga swiveled its head over to him, bared its teeth, and started to salivate.

Marco and Amelio froze in horror, but Aziz already had his blade out and was quickly climbing the coiled rear of the serpent. "Over here! The creature seems to have some kind of wound; we have to distract it from Kokachin!" Marco turned toward Aziz's voice and saw a raw and exposed area of flesh in the Naga's side—exactly where he'd scraped at the phantom worm with his thumb.

Kokachin had warned them not to interact with anything they saw in the sandstorm. Somehow, *he* had done this. His actions had summoned the Naga—this was all his fault.

As Marco watched, Aziz climbed his way to the Naga's wounded area, steadied himself, then plunged his sword as deeply as he could into the worm's oozing flesh. There was no response. The Naga's head continued observing the wounded Kokachin, saliva pouring from its gigantic mouth as it cast a dark shadow over its prey.

Aziz hacked at the same spot over and over again. "Get over here!" he shouted at Marco and Amelio, snapping them to attention. "We all have to focus on its wound and hope it can be killed!"

A few more blows and Aziz pierced through to the next layer of the Naga's viscous skin.

That got the creature's attention. It swung its head around, trying to grab Aziz in its teeth.

"Aziz, run!" Marco shouted, drawing his sword. Amelio drew his own weapon alongside him.

Aziz didn't stop, continuing to slash away at the same spot with his blade, creating an ever-deeper gash in the Naga. "We have to keep going! If we can't stop this thing, it'll kill us all!"

"Aziz!"

As Aziz sliced, the creature's head angrily swooped in toward him.

"Boys, take the lead! Hurry!"

Just as the Naga's mouth approached him, Aziz whipped around and slashed his blade across its jaws. He slashed again, aiming his blow lower, and cut the flesh right under its head. It let out a furious *hiss*.

With incredible force, and its teeth fully bared, the Naga threw its head toward Aziz; just as Aziz flexed his legs and leaped off the Naga, landing hard on the sand below. The creature roared, its own head smashing into itself where Aziz had just stood, incredibly sharp teeth tearing straight into its wound.

"We have a chance . . . ," Marco said with breathless amazement as the Naga's wound bled, Aziz scrambled to his feet, and Amelio tightened his hand on his weapon.

But before they could act, the Naga's entire body began to quiver and its flesh began to shift. As all of them watched it rolled the damaged area in on itself. Its wound disappeared inside the coiled serpent foundation that was supporting the creature's neck and head.

"You mean, we *had* a chance," Amelio croaked, seeing their only hope vanish.

"It's not over yet," Aziz said forcefully. "We're going to have to—" he continued, before the Naga's head came at him again, teeth bared, and this time met its mark.

The Naga's enormous jaws sunk into Aziz's chest. He screamed as the Naga lifted him high off the ground in its teeth—then, with a sharp flick of its head, sent Aziz's body flying across the desert.

"Aziz!" Marco screamed.

"We have to help him!" Amelio shouted, readying himself to run off in Aziz's direction.

Marco tried to think clearly. "No—there's nothing we can do for him right now. You heard Aziz a moment ago, we have to stop this thing before it kills us all. There'll be time to help our friends once the creature is dead."

Marco looked at the Naga, its body still in the huge circular pile, its head turning back to the now-recovered Kokachin. "That wound in its flesh. It rolled it to the inside of the pile. We're going to have to scale the Naga and jump inside. We'll find that wound and finish what Aziz started."

"That's crazy!" Amelio said.

"It's our only chance," Marco said. "We won't last long at this rate. No time for thinking; let's go!"

And with that, a yell starting deep in his throat, Marco charged straight for the serpent, Amelio running and shouting just behind him.

Throwing themselves entirely into their task, the two boys climbed up the gooey flesh of the serpent. Their hands sunk easily into its spongy body, creating instant hand- and footholds as they climbed.

Kokachin tried to distract the beast. "Is that the best you can do?" he shouted, grabbing at his injured chest with one hand, parrying and slicing at the Naga's chomping head with the other. A hundred yards away Aziz lay motionless, his blood leaking into the sand.

That image was the last thing Marco and Amelio saw as they reached the top of the serpent's coiled body and, without hesitating, took a blind leap into the interior below.

Chapter 58

The inside of the coiled serpent was surprisingly calm.

With bloodied elbows and knees, Marco and Amelio stumbled to their feet in the sand, the light from above just barely illuminating the living chamber. If they hadn't known better, it would have been easy to think the perfect, concentric coils all around them were built and stacked together by an architect. It was only the occasional, slight quivers of movement that gave away that this was, in fact, a serpent all around them, capable of constricting its body and crushing them at any moment.

"That's the wound," Amelio said, seeing a bright pink gash with something large and pulsing just beneath it in a coil that was eye-level and immediately ahead.

"We're going to have to do this together," Marco said, both boys gripping the handles of their swords until their knuckles turned white from the pressure. "Slice as hard and as deep as you can, and don't stop cutting, no matter what happens. We can't stop. It's now or never."

Outside the Naga, Marco and Amelio heard Kokachin scream in pain. Amelio raised his blade. "Now!"

Both of them charged and, as soon as they reached it, buried themselves in the Naga's wound, stabbing again and again, hacking at its flesh. Its body quivered all around them.

Kokachin, bleeding from where the Naga's teeth tore at his arm moments earlier, was barely holding its mouth at bay when the Naga started jerking its head from side to side in terrible, confused pain. Kokachin redoubled his efforts and kept up his attack, trying to buy Marco and Amelio time while keeping the demon worm away from Aziz.

Inside, pieces of viscera flew out of the creature's wound, caking on the boys' clothes and sticking to the mucus on their arms. With each strike it got easier to pull out their blades. Marco found himself picturing the Abarimon—*slice*—the deceitful merchant Theron—*slash*—the apparition of his father, of Arghun, of everyone in the world who had ever made him feel helpless and hurt. As the Naga's trembling grew more pronounced, the walls of its body began to close in.

"Marco! The coils, they're constricting! The Naga knows we're in here; it's trying to crush us!"

"It doesn't matter! Don't stop! Keep slicing!"

Ignoring what was happening all around them, Marco continued stabbing with a constant rhythm, joined by Amelio. The two boys attacked together, over and over again as one, and—finally—an essential membrane gave, engulfing both boys in a powerful torrent of liquid, drenching them and pushing them back to the other end of the chamber.

Outside, the Naga jerked stiffly upright, emitted a single, ear-piercing shriek from its horrible mouth, then its entire body uncoiled and collapsed onto the ground with a deafening crash.

With the serpent walls suddenly no longer around them, Amelio blinked up at the light. "We . . . we did it," Amelio said. "Marco, we're alive! We actually did it!"

Marco was hunched over, breathing heavily, red-faced and gripping his sword. The dead serpent, unspooled in every direction, dominated the desert floor.

Then, as if it were only a dream, the serpent's body lost all of its color, turned entirely white, and in an instant became nothing but smoke and steam, dissipating out across the desert.

Before Marco and Amelio could react to this, both boys heard Kokachin's desperate cry.

"Aziz! No, Aziz!"

Chapter 59

When the boys arrived at Aziz's fallen body, Amelio saw Kokachin crouched in the sand and gripping his arm, blood dripping between his fingers.

He locked his eyes on them. "You did it," Kokachin huffed between breaths. For a second Marco thought he meant *You did it—you summoned the Naga. And the Naga killed Aziz.*

"I didn't know—I couldn't stop myself—," Marco began, something terrible crumpling and giving way inside him.

Then Kokachin continued, his eyes softening. "You killed it. You . . . both of you. You saved us."

"But Aziz . . . ," Marco said, his eyes welling up with tears as he looked at the warrior's body sprawled on the sand, his eyes closed, gashes where the Naga had sunk its teeth into his chest.

"No, please," Aziz said without opening his eyes, his voice raspy and just above a whisper. "Don't cry on me, you'll just make my wounds sting." He attempted a laugh, but only a pained wheeze escaped.

"You're alive!"

"It takes more than a snake bite to put me down," he coughed, blood still leaking from his chest. "And look at you two, killed the snake without a bite on you. The apprentices have surpassed the teacher." Through his pain, Aziz did his best to smile.

"Stop talking for now, and stay very still," Kokachin said, suddenly all business as he quickly removed supplies from his pack to help with Aziz's wounds. "If we treat you quickly, we can prevent infection from setting in."

"What about yourself?" Aziz rasped, looking at Kokachin's still bleeding arm.

"I asked you not to talk for now. Boys, I'm going to need your help cleaning and dressing his injuries. They're deep, but Aziz is tough. I think he's going to be all right."

Chapter 60

"Take my arm ... that's it ... slowly now, slowly ..."

Under Kokachin's guidance, after a short period of rest, Aziz was able to lift himself off the ground and continue walking. He and Kokachin each had an arm wrapped around the other's neck, and they moved slowly in tandem. Kokachin warned that Aziz would be lacking in energy for some time.

Alongside them, Marco, Amelio, and Sarap moved through the desert and held their own counsel.

"If he hadn't been able to walk, I don't know what we would have done," Amelio said.

"We would have stayed with him until he got better," Marco said.

Both boys nodded their heads, knowing full well that this was a comforting thing to say, but if they had needed to stay with Aziz in the sun, with no protection from the elements, none of them would have lasted long.

Luckily, Aziz was doing fine. Nonetheless, Marco looked at

his friend limping along with Kokachin and tears welled up in his eyes. Aziz had said, early on, that Marco and Amelio would be a liability. That taking them along could get them all killed. What if Aziz had been right?

"Sarap," Amelio said, oblivious to his friend's anguish. "You owe me all these boons. Why can't you just make Aziz well again? Or fly us right to Mount Dragoian? For that matter, can't you just take care of Arghun, snap your fingers and have that be that?"

"Master Amelio," Sarap said from Amelio's shoulder, "I've told you, a boon is not a spell but a physical gift. Anything within the power of my small frame is yours. Anything I can get, push, or move. But I have no connection to the great dragons. I cannot—"

But before Sarap could say more, a great rumbling descended on the desert.

"What?" Amelio said, shocked.

Next to Kokachin, Aziz's eyes grew wide—while he would never say it, he was in no shape for another confrontation.

"What is it? Another sandstorm?" Marco said, his terrified voice nearly drowned out by the increasingly deafening rumble.

Kokachin studied the sky. "No. Not a sandstorm," he said.

"A Naga?" Amelio asked, horrified by the thought of facing another demonic sand worm.

"Not a Naga, either," Kokachin said. "Look."

With his free arm Kokachin pointed into the distance, where the rest of them saw a fast-approaching procession of men on horseback. They were all covered in strange armor from head to toe and, though the dust kicked up by their horses did resemble another sandstorm, when they slowed, the sand quickly dissipated into the dry desert air.

"Who are they?" Amelio asked, not sure whether he should still be terrified or could begin to feel relieved.

Kokachin looked to Aziz, who was trying to stay strong, though he was still clearly in pain. Kokachin breathed in deeply, gritted his teeth, then committed himself to a course of action.

"Marco, Amelio, I'll remain standing to assist Aziz. Both of you, get down on your knees and put your hands in the air. *Now*," Kokachin said quickly but assertively. "Sarap, make yourself hidden."

All three did exactly as Kokachin said. They felt their hearts begin to pound and their stomachs churn at the sight of the fast-approaching soldiers.

"What's happening?" Aziz said gently.

"This area of the desert is considered part of the Mongol Lands, and the khan's soldiers sometimes patrol it. Without permission to enter, we're guilty of trespass. Those soldiers look keen to enforce it."

"The khan's soldiers?" Amelio said.

"What should we do?" Aziz asked.

"In our present state we're in no position to run away or fight them. If we tried and failed it would be our end. For the moment, we'd do best to comply with anything they say."

"For the moment?" Marco asked.

"We're all heading in the same direction, and I've escaped from Mongol soldiers in the past. I promise you, this will only be a temporary delay. As soon as the time comes and our strength returns, you'll know what to do when I give the sign. Understood?" Kokachin said, looking to Marco and Amelio.

"Yes," they both said.

"Also, should the subject arise," Kokachin whispered, "according to the khan, Arghun has long ago been put to death. To say otherwise near his soldiers is to invite a death of your own. As we travel in the land of the Mongols, for all of us, we'd be wise to watch our tongues."

"Understood," they said in unison as the soldiers drew increasingly near.

Twelve riders approached, each dressed much the same. They wore helmets made of the finest wrought iron with blood-red tassles that flared as they rode. They were armored in thick sections of leather hide reinforced by iron studs. Each had a quiver of arrows and a bow just over their shoulders, and each rode forward with a curved metal saber in hand.

Even if Kokachin hadn't identified these riders, Marco and Amelio would have known who they were. These were the legendary armies of the khan in the flesh. The Mongol warriors of lore. Amelio strengthened his nerve and tried to remember all that he'd recently learned. For his part, Marco was torn between fear and excitement.

When the soldiers came within yards they broke their tight formation and circled around the outsiders on horseback. Marco, Amelio, Aziz, and Kokachin were quickly surrounded on all sides. A dozen steel blades were pointed at their throats, and in no time the circle began to tighten.

The leader of the men dismounted and stared at them forcefully. His eyes were dark and humorless, his cheeks and forehead pockmarked from years of riding through the elements, and his mouth was half-hidden under a severe black mustache and goatee.

"You are trespassers in the land of the khan," he said in a deep and gravelly voice. "To trespass in these lands is a crime. Two of you sit prostrate in surrender, which I acknowledge as a sign of respect. So we will not kill you here and now. But two remain standing in defiance. What have you to say for yourself?"

"My friend is injured, and I stand only to offer him support. Otherwise we, too, would be down on the ground before you," Kokachin said in a flat, unwavering voice, as though these words were a ritual he had gone through before. "We are friends of the Mongol people. We come bearing gifts in homage to—"

"Enough," their leader said, cutting Kokachin off in a definitive tone. "The courts of the Mongols will decide."

"Decide what?" Marco asked.

"Whether your paltry gifts are enough to save your lives. We do not take trespassers lightly."

With that their leader turned and signaled to his men.

"Take them. We shall continue on our path to the Forbidden City immediately. These trespassers will have their fates decided there as well."

Marco began to stand up. "We're fortunate to have met you, as my father and Aziz were recently guests of Kublai Khan in the Forbidden City. The khan may even remember—"

Mid-sentence, Marco was knocked off his feet and back onto the ground—the leader of the Mongol soldiers struck him squarely across the face with the back of his hand.

"Make no mistake, you are traveling to the Forbidden City as prisoners of the khan, not as guests."

In a moment two different Mongol soldiers approached with ropes to bind their hands and feet.

"A final question," Kokachin said loudly as his hands were bound behind his back. "I know the Mongols as fierce but honorable men. My companion Aziz is injured. Will he be cared for along the way?"

The leader of the Mongol soldiers turned to face Kokachin. "As you say, we are honorable men. I will personally see to it that your companion survives the journey. But whether he survives his trial after that is another matter entirely."

Each of the prisoners was soon tied up. One Mongol tethered a steed to the back of his horse using a short rope and had Marco and Amelio placed together upon it. Another Mongol did the same, his steed carrying Kokachin and Aziz.

As the rest of the Mongols prepared to continue onward, Marco and Amelio whispered to each other.

"Can you believe our luck?" Marco asked.

"Our luck has been bad before," Amelio said, "but it's never been quite *this* bad until now."

"Bad?" Marco repeated, sounding confused. "I was about to say things just took a turn for the better! Instead of hoping Aziz's injuries don't get worse, their leader is going to personally look after him. Instead of traveling for weeks on foot, these soldiers are going to ride us straight into the Forbidden City. On the way, what Abarimon or sand serpent would dare attack us in the midst of a small Mongol army? This is the safest we've ever been! And who knows, maybe the khan is ready to start facing facts about Arghun—with the information we have, if he becomes an ally, we'll be rescuing my father in no time. The more I think on it, the more this seems like the best thing that could ever have happened."

Amelio nearly lost his balance as their horse abruptly took

off, following the soldier up ahead as the Mongol pack continued on its way. As Amelio tried to remain steady he turned and held up his painfully bound hands.

"Yes, Marco," he muttered. "Best thing that could ever have happened, indeed."

"I cursed myself for being such a fool. These were the dreaded Mongols, after all, whose hands we had placed ourselves into. The vicious warriors who slaughtered hundreds of thousands of Europe's finest knights. The Mongols would think nothing of killing us all, and looked as if they might do so at any second. And for putting our trust in them, I could only blame myself."

—FROM THE JOURNALS OF MARCO POLO

Insurmountable Mountains

Part Five

FORBIDDEN

CITIES

and

DEADLY

SCHEMES

Chapter 61

The remainder of the Mongols' journey through China to the Forbidden City stretched across some of the most extreme terrain Marco, Amelio, and Aziz had ever seen.

The Mongols were willing to go out of their way, and take a much longer route, to avoid any further encounters with magic or mystical creatures. To do so, they first cut back briefly through the desert. Forced to ride on the backs of steeds with their hands tightly bound, all of the prisoners sizzled in the roasting heat. Conversations between the Mongols and their captives were forbidden by the Mongol captain, but he allowed those captured to speak with one another if they did so in quiet tones. And though the soldiers remained unfriendly, they did not prove to be unkind. Aziz had his injuries tended to several times each day. When Marco or Amelio would chafe from the ropes, their guard would wordlessly but carefully loosen the knots. And when Kokachin refused to remove his headdress, they allowed him to remain consumed by his shrouds.

After a time, the desert eventually gave way to the grasslands, wide expanses of dry earth dotted with scraggly shrubs. It was still a barren space, but after the heat and unending sameness of the desert it seemed almost like paradise. They rode past nomadic shepherds grazing sheep and tents made of animal skins, and Marco spotted entire packs of small, weasel-like creatures darting in and out of holes in the ground.

Before reaching the Mongol territories their path wound through a set of icy mountains, and they rode along a route that was dangerous, if well traveled. At times the trail became so narrow the Mongols would have to dismount, carefully guiding their skittering horses across narrow ledges. Yawning gorges surrounded them, quietly threatening death on all sides. And one afternoon, as they rode, the Mongols slowed their horses some distance away from an enormous catlike creature in their path, feasting on the carcass of a medium-size bird.

"It's a snow leopard," Kokachin whispered to Amelio, who was tied up behind him that day.

The leopard's fur was smoky gray and covered in black spots. Moving so silently the leopard didn't know they were there, several Mongols slipped off their horses and surrounded it from a distance on each side. As they began to close in, the leopard sensed their presence, turned away from its food, and lowered itself into a defensive crouch. Then it bared its sharp teeth, its heavy breathing pouring out like steam.

Quickly and calmly, half of the Mongols took out long spears, while the other half readied coils of long rope. Then the first soldier moved in toward the cat, his long spear sticking out in front of him.

As soon as the spear approached the leopard's face it let out an incredible roar, before swatting at the tip of the spear with a powerful claw. Its attention distracted, a Mongol behind the leopard threw a loop of rope over the creature's head, lassoing it. The cat whipped around, but before it could pounce, another loop ringed its neck from the other direction, pulling it backward. Finally, the leopard was forced back on its hind legs as the two ropes were pulled hard at once in opposite directions, locking it in place. With spears drawn, three more soldiers quickly approached the creature's unguarded belly. Marco couldn't help but be amazed at the speed and elegance with which a handful of men dispatched this mighty beast.

As they continued toward the Mongol territories the Mongol captain wore a leopard cloak and the rest of their band feasted on fresh meat for days.

Chapter 62

Over the course of their journey Marco had seen some incredible man-made locations, but none of them compared to what was coming next.

Some time after they passed the border into the Mongol territories, the soldier riding in front of Marco turned around and signaled for him to look up ahead. It was one of the first times they had ever communicated, and Marco sat up straight in front of Kokachin in their saddle.

They were riding toward the top of a rolling green hill, and suddenly Marco could see the turrets of a large stone wall. As his eyes scanned its length Marco blinked, unable to believe what was in front of him. The wall was stretching out in both directions as far as his eyes could see. The massive stone barrier zigzagged across the landscape, tracing every curve of the hilly region as it rose and fell. The wall stretched out into the far horizons of Marco's sight, tapering off as it disappeared into the distance.

Marco turned to Kokachin tied up just behind him. "That wall has got to be miles long!" he said in awe.

The soldier up ahead heard this and laughed.

"What's so funny?" Marco asked Kokachin.

"It's far, far longer than a few miles," Kokachin explained.

"A hundred miles?"

"More."

"Five hundred? *A thousand miles?*" Marco asked in disbelief.

"From what I have heard, the wall you see before you goes on for more than four thousand miles. It is called the Great Wall, and it is a testament to the ingenuity and might of the Chinese people."

"You're not joking," Marco said. "Amazing."

The group approached the wall, then turned to ride for some time along its base. Warriors similar in dress and build to those who had captured Marco prowled the walkways on the wall high above them, and watchtowers were spaced evenly along its length, ticking off the distance as they traveled.

After several hours riding along the wall's base, they came to a break in the structure they could ride through—a gateway with doors two stories tall, made of heavy wood and reinforced with metal plates. The Mongol soldiers transporting Marco signaled to guards above, who relayed a message to unseen guards on the other side. A moment later a weighted pulley system clanked and grinded, then the doors slowly opened in front of them.

As their group curved through the gateway, Marco realized they were now entering the main kingdom of the Mongol Empire. With only a few days' more travel through the countryside provinces they would find themselves in Peking, and then within the walls of the Forbidden City itself.

Chapter 63

The last leg of their journey through the provinces cut through giant paddy fields, rows and rows of rice planted in pastures flooded with water. Looking on from his horse, Marco saw small, one-room houses made of mud-brick and thatched roofs. The men who lived there were wearing large-brimmed hats to shield themselves from the sun while they waded through paddies, water past their ankles, bending down to cultivate their crop.

Moving steadily closer to Peking, Marco found their horses repeatedly passed by a number of identically dressed Mongols, sometimes jogging on foot and sometimes on horseback, all wearing tiny little bells that jingled softly as they moved. When he whispered to Kokachin, asking what they were, Kokachin explained they were part of the Mongols' elaborate messenger system. There were three levels of official Mongol dispatch— second class, first class, and top priority. Second-class messages were delivered on foot, by men who passed messages from one relay station to another three miles apart. Such handoffs ensured each message was delivered and continued moving along its route as quickly as possible, so what would take a single man ten days to deliver would instead arrive in less than one. First-class messages were handled in a similar manner, but on horseback and with relay stations twenty-five miles apart. And for top-priority messages, only the fastest of horses could be used. Their riders would gallop as hard as they could to the nearest station, and as soon as they grew close they would signal to the following rider using a brass horn. This was their cue to saddle up and prepare their steed so they would be ready to take off the very second the last messenger arrived.

Hearing this, Marco was awestruck—instead of mindless savages, the Mongols were ingenious and tightly organized. There was nothing in all of Europe comparable to this kind of system.

Before traveling much farther, they passed a first-class messenger by the side of the road who nodded at their horses wordlessly.

"That's the final messenger before Peking," Kokachin whispered.

"Which means we're almost there?"

"It's just over those distant foothills," Kokachin answered. He looked to Aziz, now fully recovered on the horse with Amelio just behind him. "This voyage served our purposes, as we're now far closer to Mount Dragoian, and in far less time than we would have been on foot. But if we intend to continue after Arghun we'll soon need to part from our Mongol guards. Stay alert, Marco, and keep an eye out for my signal."

Chapter 64

As Kokachin explained, a round stone wall formed a giant ring around the city of Peking. Inside the city, all the roads were a series of concentric circles, with smaller crossroads running back and forth between them. If you were to look at Peking from the sky, it would be organized in much the same pattern as a spider's web. Toward the center a second stone wall surrounded the palace of Kublai Khan, also known as the Forbidden City, which sat at the heart of Peking.

As they rode through Peking's first stone wall, Marco's eyes and ears hungrily devoured the sights and sounds. Previously the Mongol peasants they saw wore plain-looking clothing made from animal hides, wool, and stiff cotton. But those who dwelled inside Peking were among the wealthiest in the Mongol Empire, and this was reflected in their clothing. Marco marveled at men who wore robes with bright and vibrant patterns—images of flowers, sunbursts, and dragons embroidered on dyed silk fabric. Many women wore form-fitting dresses that came all the way down to their ankles, often carrying rice-paper fans as well.

The wealthiest citizens were attended to by a small army of servants, and Marco saw them running about everywhere dressed in plain robes of black or blue. Bustling through the noisy crowds, they saw to everyone's needs—pedaling manpowered carts that Kokachin called rickshaws, in which the wealthy cruised through the city streets; scooping steaming hot plates of food in the storefront windows of noodle bars; busily constructing grand new buildings ordered by the decree of the khan.

The buildings they constructed, in particular, were notable for their splendor. Marco saw houses being built of rich, polished wood, their roofs assembled from long pieces of bamboo that were lined one next to another in neat rows. Most houses had recessed entrances and elegant front porches, with perfectly landscaped gardens in the back.

But none of these buildings could compare to the incredible grandeur of the khan's palace, a truly massive structure that could be seen from every point in Peking. It was composed of gold-capped buildings and rich marble structures that glinted in the midday sun, opulent and almost overpoweringly beautiful.

"Listen carefully," Kokachin whispered to Marco as they made their way toward the second stone wall and the palace ahead. "When I rode two days back with Aziz and then Amelio, I prepared them for this as well. Very soon, we're going to find ourselves inside the palace walls. When first asked, I told our captors we trespassed to deliver a gift in homage to the khan; it's the most common excuse provided by those discovered in the Lands. They will consider us nonthreatening but liars, our case will be heard by a poorly armed guard, and he'll likely pronounce us guilty before attempting to mete out their punishment."

"Their punishment? What kind of punishment is that likely to be?" Marco asked, growing nervous.

"That's unimportant—they'll never get the chance to deliver it. Listen. The royal guardsmen are small and petty men, and when making pronouncements they are easily goaded into bouts of foolish rage. In their anger they grow sloppy, and that's all the opening we'll need. Watch what I do, keep an eye out for Sarap, and when the moment is right follow my lead. When it ends, be prepared to escape along the servants' alley to the left of the central route. Is that understood?"

"I . . . I guess so," Marco whispered. "But what do you intend to—"

"Shhh," Kokachin said, seeing several soldiers turn at the sound of their voices. "No more talking for now. From here on out it won't be long."

As Marco's steed rode closer and closer to the palace, he began to feel pangs of fear. Kokachin seemed certain he could help them escape, but Marco didn't understand the entire plan, and there was little opportunity to find out more with soldiers all around them. After such a long journey, what fate truly waited for them inside those inner city walls?

As they approached the stone gates of the khan's palace Marco knew he was about to find out.

Chapter 65

The Mongol soldiers led their prisoners inside the gates of the khan's palace. The soldier whose horse Marco and Kokachin's steed was tethered to, previously silent, now turned and spoke out of pride, explaining several of the sights as they passed them by.

"This is the Inner Golden Water River," the soldier said as they crossed a large and ornate bridge leading over a lazily flowing waterbed.

Just up ahead, through a lush field of grass, the soldier pointed to an immense and polished wooden platform. "This platform, in the shadow of the inner palace, is where judgment is met," he said. "The alley to its left allows servants to pass in and out, doing all they can to better service the khan."

The soldiers rode their horses on top of the wooden platform before dismounting. Then they hoisted their tied-up prisoners off their steeds and onto the wooden floor. "The marble structure before us is the Hall of Supreme Harmony," the soldier said, nodding to the massive building just ahead, "which leads to the inner palace of the khan. Unfortunately, most prisoners never go much farther than this."

As if in response, a tall and horribly pockmarked man with a shaved head, a thin black mustache, and a goatee marched out of the Hall of Supreme Harmony. He wore intricate and shining silver ceremonial armor, and his sword hung from his hip in a decoratively etched scabbard. "I am the newest member of the palace royal guard, and I shall hear your case. Kneel before me."

Marco, Kokachin, Amelio, and Aziz were pushed to their knees by four of the soldiers who transported them. As the royal guardsman approached, the soldiers all bowed in his direction. "We place our prisoners in your merciful care," they said before retreating to the far sides of the platform.

The guardsman paced expectantly in front of his four tied-up guests. He stopped in front of Marco, looking at him with his piercing brown eyes. "I have been informed you've been charged with trespassing on the borderlands of the khan. That you were armed when you did so, and freely admitted your trespass. Is this correct?"

"Yes," Marco said. "But we meant no harm—"

"Silence!" the guard shouted, his voice suddenly sharp and hard. "I asked you a simple question," the guard spat. "And it requires a simple answer. Was my statement correct—yes or no?"

Marco glowered at the guard. "Yes," he said.

"I thought as much. And were you aware how seriously the Mongol empire takes the crime of trespass? That, if convicted, it carries a penalty of death?"

"What?" Amelio gasped. "But we didn't know—we didn't even know going through the desert was considered trespass in the first place!" he blurted out, terrified. "We've never been to the Unknown—"

Without hesitation the guard drew his blade from his decoratively etched scabbard. Incredibly sharp, it gleamed in the light.

"Speak again without being addressed," the guard said, wielding his sword and looking at Amelio with honest menace, "and you can consider what you say to be your final words. So make sure they're quite well chosen. I will cut you down without a second glance."

The guard turned to Aziz, shifting his blade toward him. "I have also been informed our soldiers were told you've been a guest of the great khan. Is this true?"

"It is," Aziz said firmly.

"Lying dog. The khan would never meet with one such as you. Say it again in my presence and I'll have no choice but to cut off your head."

His hands tightly tied, Marco felt his heart beating faster and faster in his chest. He had been convinced—he had been positive—that being found in the desert by the khan's soldiers was the best thing that could have happened. Though he knew the khan forbid any talk of Arghun, perhaps in his palace they might find some form of assistance. And Kokachin seemed to know exactly what they should do if they needed to escape. But now, tied up in front of the fierce royal guardsman, Marco began to have doubts. What if Kokachin's plan fell through? These were the dreaded Mongols, after all, whose hands they had placed themselves into, the vicious warriors who had slaughtered hundreds of thousands of Europe's finest knights. If they tried something and had even one misstep, Marco thought, the Mongols would think nothing of killing them all.

Shifting his position, the guard stood in front of Kokachin. He bent down to get a better look.

"And what of you, hooded one? Do you, too, admit to horrid lies and illegal trespass? Do you humbly concede that you've broken our laws?"

Kokachin remained motionless and said nothing. The guard, waiting expectantly, appeared to grow angrier with each passing second.

Marco looked at the wooden floor all around him, trying to find something—anything—sharp enough to cut through his ropes so they'd have a fighting chance if Kokachin's plan went awry. But there was nothing at all within reach.

"I'll ask again, do you admit to your trespass?" the guard repeated. "Or can you not answer me because your mask is too tight for you to speak? Let me help you," the Guard said, reaching around to pull at Kokachin's head covering. As he did, Kokachin jerked his head away violently.

The Guard stepped back in anger and shock. "You dare?"

"What does a man like you want with my head scarf?" Kokachin said forcefully, addressing the guard for the first time. "Unless you desire to steal it to cover your hideous face? If you're the newest member of the royal guard, they must have fallen on hard times."

"You have nerve . . . ," the guard said.

"And you are the most horrible-looking creature I've seen in all my life. How can you even stay by the house of the khan? Are you not ashamed?"

"I am not ashamed, but I am impressed," the guard said in a low, menacing voice. "Most who come here look to hide their wicked nature, but you reveal your horrid spirit right away. Yelling at me, talking back to a guard." As the guard looked over Marco, Aziz, and Amelio, his face grew red with violence. "Your companions, though they have not all spoken, each stay by your side. In doing so they have spoken just the same. If you wanted your lives to end, you've taken the right course of action."

Marco looked to Kokachin. What was the rest of his plan? Now that he'd angered the guard, what did he intend to do?

Then Marco felt a tugging at the ropes on his wrists. He turned his head as much as he could without drawing attention.

"Sarap!" Marco whispered.

The small green creature made fast work of untying Marco's hands, while nodding his head in the direction of Kokachin, Aziz, and Amelio.

In a flash, Marco saw that Sarap had untied his friends' hands as well—and, in each, he'd placed a dagger stolen from the soldiers who had brought them in on their horses.

In front of Kokachin the guard continued talking, so worked up and absorbed in his anger he didn't notice as Sarap pressed a blade into Marco's palm.

"It is within my power to pass judgment," the guard said, pacing back and forth, "and there is no need to hear more from your doubly-forked tongues. For committing the crime of trespass, I sentence you all to death. Your burden will no longer be carried by our kingdom, or any other."

Marco saw Kokachin ready his weapon. As soon as the head guard came closer, he was prepared to strike.

Four of the Mongol soldiers who had brought them to the palace still stood oblivious at the other end of the platform, but Marco was confident his companions could take them on just the same. And the servants' pathway was to the left, cleared and empty, just as Kokachin said it would be, promising a swift and painless escape.

Unaware of the thoughts rushing through Marco's head, the guard turned and walked back in Kokachin's direction. With the plan now clear, Marco, Aziz, and Amelio prepared themselves to strike.

Chapter 66

Just then, a deep horn was blown three times in a row with the last note held for several seconds. Both the soldiers and the guard dropped immediately to their knees.

A tree full of sparrows scattered in fright, their desperate flapping echoing in the walled courtyard.

Kokachin, his body tense and prepared to attack, heard the calling of the horn and stiffened with a different emotion entirely. "What? He never comes to the trials. . . . He's not supposed to be here. . . ."

Marco looked up to see a tall and powerfully built warrior stepping out from the marble mouth of the Hall of Supreme Harmony, an older man with a thick but impeccably groomed black beard and the physique of someone half his age. He was armored in overlapping pieces of hardened leather that hugged his body like scales, each piece reinforced by shiny metal plates that reflected the white marble of the hall and the blue of the sky. A massive sword strapped to his back was the size of most men, and a belt of small daggers was fastened tightly around his waist. As Marco watched, the warrior moved slowly and with purpose, but his movements still carried the tension that he could spring into deadly action at any time.

And, fanning out just behind him—in a giant V formation—was a large and varied procession of ranking members of the Mongol royal court. Marco saw gray-bearded advisers, servant boys carrying trays of food and drink, beautiful girls waving giant ostrich-feather fans, musicians carrying all manner of instruments, elegantly dressed ladies of the court, bare-chested bodyguards carrying giant scimitars, and more.

After seeing the man, his followers, and the way the soldiers and royal guardsman reacted in his presence, there could be little doubt that this was anyone other than the great Kublai Khan himself, making his way across the palace grounds. Seeing a trial was in progress as he stepped free from the Hall of Supreme Harmony, the khan stopped to size up the proceedings. When he spoke his voice was deep and booming, and the twittering and noise made by his procession quickly died down to a murmur.

"I see your work is in progress," the khan said to the royal guardman, who remained kneeling in his presence on the ground. "In honor of your recent promotion, I shall grace you with my presence. Tell me, these people before you—what is their crime?"

"Trespass," the guard said, his tone suddenly humble. "They were each discovered trespassing in the sands, on the desert border of our kingdom."

"And their defense?" the khan said.

"The most common and baseless of the lot. When asked,

they say only that they are friends of the Empire, crossing over to bear gifts in homage to your glory."

"Ah, so they have come bearing gifts." The khan turned to his procession. "These men trespass not as enemies, but to shower gifts upon us!" he said with a derisive sneer. He turned back to the captives, who were hurriedly slipping their stolen weapons into the sleeves of their shirts. "I have heard that tale too many times before."

Aziz stole a look at Kokachin; something about him had changed. He was staring blankly ahead, the expression drained from his eyes. His plan did not seem to take the khan's arrival into account.

The khan looked to Amelio, the first of the prisoners kneeling before him. "So, tell me, what do you bring? If you are not a trespasser looking to do us harm, but instead a worshipper donating riches to our kingdom and glory—then lay them all down at my feet. Give us the gifts that you've promised. Though if you have nothing to offer, you've earned your own death, my friend."

Recognizing it was time for a new plan, Aziz looked up at the khan and spoke clearly. "Great khan, my name is Aziz Be'Nai," Aziz said. "We have met once before—you know me. Do you remember?"

"You dare speak when not spoken to?" the khan said, whipping around toward Aziz. "Do you *want* your head and your body to quickly part ways?" Then, taking Aziz in, the khan's demeanor began to change. "Wait one moment. I *do* know you," he said. "Look at me, look me in the face. Tell me where I would know you from." He approached, genuinely wanting to understand.

As the khan came closer, the royal guardsman and Mongol soldiers grew alert, watching to ensure the prisoners made no sudden moves.

With the khan standing just in front of him, and commanding his full attention, Aziz continued. "My name is Aziz Be'Nai," Aziz repeated, "and I have been your guest here in the past. I came with a band of Western traders, the Polos and their men. We spoke of trading routes between the East and West, and remained for quite some time. I have told your soldiers this, but they did not believe me. Do you remember?"

The khan's face clouded as he listened to Aziz, impossible to read, and when he didn't respond after several moments Marco grew fearful he was about to call Aziz's words a lie.

Then a gleam of recognition appeared in the khan's eyes and his mouth spread into a wide grin. "Of course! The traders from Venice with the extraordinary wares. You've returned with new companions!" The khan turned to the guard and his soldiers. "This has been a mistake. As he stated, Aziz Be'Nai means us no harm—and I'd wager his friends mean no harm alongside him. You may untie them, untie them at once!"

The Mongol soldiers who captured them in the desert, as if their time together had never occurred, now advanced quickly toward them to untie the knots that bound their wrists. As fast as he could, Sarap hid himself away inside Amelio's pocket. When the soldiers circled around they were shocked to find all of their hands already freed, but the khan continued speaking before they could say a word.

"Aziz Be'Nai's new companions, each of you, stand and tell me your names. And dear guardsman and soldiers," the khan said, nodding toward them, "you had no way of knowing my familiarity with Aziz. You have done well, and may now take your leave."

The soldiers all lowered themselves into a deep bow, their hands held in front of them in supplication to the khan. Then they hurried off into the alley to the left of the wooden platform.

With the soldiers gone, and the procession remaining silent just behind him, the khan turned the entirety of his attention to his new guests. "Please. Present yourselves."

Marco, astonished first to find himself freed, and then doubly so to be standing in the presence of the king of the Mongols, staggered forward. "My name is Marco Polo, your greatness," he said. "I've been told you met my father and uncle, Niccolo and Maffeo, when they were on a prior journey. It is truly an honor to be here in your presence."

"And it is truly a pleasure to have you as my guest," the khan said as Marco bowed deeply before him.

Amelio was the next to step forward. Once a lowly servant boy, he was now amazed to find himself personally received by the khan. "My name is Amelio Strauss, sir, and this is an enormous privilege."

The khan nodded respectfully and said, "Welcome to our court, my friend."

Though Kokachin should have been next, he did not acknowledge the khan or move from where he stood. Marco, Amelio, and Aziz looked quizzically at one another, and murmurs of disapproval rose up from the procession crowd.

"Your masked companion does not greet me with the same

enthusiasm as you and your friends," the khan said, looking to Aziz. "Come," he said, turning to Kokachin. "Remove your headdress and make yourself known."

Kokachin remained where he was, betraying nothing.

"The khan saved our lives," Marco said, not understanding. Then he turned to the khan, trying to explain. "This is our—"

"You care as little for the deaths of your subjects as you do for their lives. It is only your own reputation that you find of interest. You should not have been here to witness this today," Kokachin said.

In an instant, the entire courtyard grew deathly silent. The khan's whole demeanor changed.

"You dare?"

"You never interfere in the work of your guardsmen—you never come to the trials. You should not have been present in this courtyard today."

Several shirtless men holding blades pushed forward from the khan's procession, then spread out to circle Kokachin all around.

"Who are you? Remove your headscarf and make yourself known, and I will help you make sense of everything," the khan said.

"What are you doing, Kokachin? What's going on?" Marco whispered.

"This is impossible. I have come too far for this to end here," Kokachin said. "I have learned too much, and come too close— the guardsman would have fallen and we would have escaped, exactly as I planned—"

Seeing the shirtless men with swords beginning to close in, and the khan himself preparing to draw his enormous blade,

Kokachin realized there was little choice left. There were too many of them. There was no way out of this.

"Fine. Then the Fates have decided, and I must be resigned to my fate. Do you wish to see my face?" With trembling hands, the dark fabric was unwrapped and allowed to fall to the ground.

"It's you . . . ," the khan said quietly.

A series of gasps and half-whispered exclamations spread through the procession like an electric current—members of the court turned to one another, put their hands to their mouths, each of their faces consumed with surprise. In the midst of which, Marco, Amelio, and Aziz's own shock went entirely unnoticed as they discovered what lay under the shroud of their traveling companion for the first time—the jet-black hair, defiant gaze, pale skin, and delicate features of a young woman.

Chapter 67

The khan stared at Kokachin, who was steely-eyed and silent amidst the sea of rising voices all around them.

"Silence!" the khan roared. Every voice went quiet, and all eyes looked toward the khan—an entire courtyard of people waiting expectantly for his reaction and his next words. "Clear the court."

"*Clear the court, now!*" the shirtless men with blades repeated at the top of their lungs.

Instantly, every nobleman, servant, and soldier in the courtyard scrambled back into the marble hall. Marco, Amelio, and Aziz looked to one another, not knowing what to do, until a raised hand from the khan stopped them in their place.

"Please," he said in a neutral tone. "You and your friends may stay."

"What's going on?" Marco whispered to Amelio.

"I have no idea," was all Amelio could say.

Less than a minute later, the courtyard that had just been

bustling with dozens of voices was as deserted and whisper-quiet as an ancient ruin.

The khan stepped over to Kokachin, looking her directly in the face. She gazed back defiantly.

And there they stood for quite some time, their eyes burning into each other, each implicitly daring the other to look away first.

After several minutes the khan laughed quietly and, turning away, began pacing slowly back and forth.

"So much to say," he began without looking back at Kokachin. "Maybe you can start by answering a simple question," he said after a moment. "Why?"

Marco, Amelio, and Aziz listened without speaking, desperate to understand what was happening.

"You know perfectly well."

"I understand your loss. I do. But you must understand we were all betrayed, all of us disgraced!" the khan said with genuine emotion. "And I devoted armies, countless armies. I did what I could to make things right! But it was never enough."

Kokachin's expression remained hard and impassive, and there was another long pause as the khan continued pacing.

"When I found you gone—did you ever worry about how I'd feel?"

Silence.

"What about your obligations to the Mongol people?" the khan began again. "We both have obligations to this nation, do we not? And when you were not there to fulfill them, what was I supposed to say?" he said, starting to stir himself into a rage. "That the one and only daughter of the khan, the princess of Mongolia, had simply *run away*?"

"Daughter of the khan?" Marco whispered to himself.

"Princess of Mongolia?" Amelio echoed.

"If you had to announce something," Kokachin said solemnly, "it could have been that I was fulfilling my obligation to my loved ones and the nation by not giving up. That I insisted on doing everything I could to free them from living in the shadow of Arghun. Instead of lying about his death, I was intent on bringing it about."

The khan had heard enough. As soon as he snapped his fingers, two menacing guards made their way from the hall.

"Take her to her quarters. You know better than to struggle," the khan said, looking Kokachin in the eyes. Then, turning to the guards: "See to it that she doesn't disappear again."

And with that, Kokachin begrudgingly allowed the two guards to escort her up the steps of the marble hall until they disappeared down a long, column-lined hallway.

No one spoke for a long while. Then the khan looked to Aziz and broke the silence.

"My daughter was gone when you were first a guest at my palace, was she not?"

"She was," Aziz said.

"And you . . . you told my soldiers you came bearing a gift. I don't know how you found her. But for returning my daughter to me, I am now deeply in your debt."

The khan clapped his hands, and three more soldiers arrived from the marble hall. "There is much to discuss. My soldiers will escort you to private quarters, where you'll have an hour to clean yourselves and change into proper attire. At that point, I would be honored if you would join me for dinner in the Royal Hall."

Chapter 68

After recording everything in his journal, and quickly changing into formal garments supplied by the khan's servants, Marco was led into the Royal Hall. Amelio and Aziz were already seated across from the khan.

Marco hurried along the banquet table, piled high with delicious-smelling food, and was directed to take a seat at the khan's side. Then he did his best not to look amazed in the face of the hall's extravagance. Though it was only the four of them, ornate metal chandeliers hung from the vaulted ceiling, twenty wax candles blazing in each. Garlands of red and white flowers hung generously from the rafters. Enormous and beautiful paintings decorated every wall. And, as Marco watched, servants continued serving food—wild boar on roasting spits, plates of carved duck, and golden platters stacked high with all manner of spicy grains.

The khan did not acknowledge his servants as they swarmed around them. Instead he looked squarely at his guests, neither smiling nor scowling, not saying a word. It was only once all of the food had been distributed, and the servants scattered to the far ends of the room, that the khan finally began to speak.

"I thank you for being here with me tonight. And, from the bottom of my heart, I thank you for returning my daughter," he said in his deep, commanding voice.

Marco, Amelio, and Aziz each shifted uncomfortably in their seats. No matter how hard they tried, they hadn't yet grown used to the idea that their fierce guide had been a girl not much older than Marco and Amelio themselves; not to mention the fact that she was also the one and only daughter of the great khan. These discoveries would take some time to sink in.

"I would like to explain the circumstances surrounding my daughter's disappearance," the khan continued, oblivious to their discomfort. "While I anticipate she may have told you a story of her own, it is important that I set the record straight. It would be . . . unfortunate . . . if her tale caused you to come here thinking poorly of me, or if it reflected badly upon your opinion of our empire."

Looking pained, the khan continued. "First, I must ask you to understand that the Mongol empire is large. While I am beloved by many of my subjects, there will always be those who, for reasons of their own, would seek to do me or my family harm.

"To guard against such treachery, all of my offspring are trained from an early age in the art of war. By my decree they remain in peak physical condition at all times, trained in every form of martial arts, able to wield any weapon with unparalleled skill. Learning under the close tutelage of ancient masters, my children's strength, discipline, and ferocity is second to none.

"As a result, should any member of my family be taken by an aggressor, the fiend would not find themselves with a groveling pawn. Instead, regardless of whether they've taken my youngest or my oldest, they would be in the presence of a child capable of immediate and deadly force. Though my offspring may look harmless, each is capable of slaying even the mightiest foe, then quickly and safely returning home.

"This is why I was amazed when whispers grew louder that my daughter had been kidnapped by Arghun. Both because Arghun had already fallen at the hands of my soldiers," the khan said, pausing to issue each of them a hard look, almost a dare, to say otherwise, "and because, even if Arghun were still amongst the living and had taken my daughter, she would have made fast work of the fire mage. Killing Arghun was never our problem. The challenge lay in finding the elusive sorcerer and his lair.

"But forgive me—in telling our story, I have already spoken out of turn. To fully understand my daughter's disappearance we must go back before it occurred, before Aziz and his companions first came to me. This tale begins in our court before it was disgraced."

Chapter 69

"It was not so far in the past that my daughter was happy," the khan said, allowing himself a small sigh as he looked over Marco, Amelio, and Aziz.

"As you have seen, though there are dangers in these lands, our kingdom is largely blessed. Especially between these palace walls, there are few wants that cannot be met, few desires that cannot be catered to. It is a wonderful existence.

"My daughter, the light of my life, was engaged to be married to a man named Affat. Affat was of a high-ranking family and had grown into a powerful and widely known earth mage, performing many feats of magic in our court. It was a splendid pairing, and the two of them were very much in love.

"Shortly after the engagement was announced, Affat—informed by his connections throughout our kingdom—came to me with stories about a fire mage named Arghun. It was said Arghun had an aptitude for magic, a hunger for knowledge, and a certain charm that lifted him above ordinary men. The spells he cast excited many. Intrigued, Affat recommended I summon Arghun to the palace so that we might all take measure of his abilities. On his word I did so.

"Just as in the stories that are now widely told, upon meeting Arghun we were immediately impressed. With wondrous tricks and a smooth, supple tongue, he awed our court into a quick, almost dreamlike submission. Though he lacked experience, Arghun's connection with the fire dragon was unusually strong, and in no time at all he was able to perform spells even our most senior mages were afraid to cast. We began to turn to Arghun for strategies and advice. And, when not otherwise engaged, Arghun spent every free moment charming myself, my advisors, and the populace at large.

"When, after several months, citizens began demanding Arghun be appointed chief magician, I listened. And, though I am dishonored to say it, I allowed their demands to influence my choice. It was my decision to bypass the established order. It was by my words that his title was named, and by the touch of my hands that the role of chief magician was bestowed upon him.

"Throughout his rapid rise, the only ones in our court Arghun failed to charm were his fellow mages. Perhaps he suspected they didn't trust him. Perhaps he knew they would only try to slow his ascent. Either way, in remaining apart from them, it became easier for the rest of us to believe their claims against him were only the sins of their own pride. No matter what they felt or said, it could all be chalked up to the irrational anger of the old guard against the new.

"Affat, in particular, grew to distrust the fire mage he first brought into our court. One afternoon, when Affat told my daughter and me he saw real danger in Arghun's ambitions, I listened. Sometime later, when he claimed Arghun was plotting something dreadful and the access we gave him posed a threat, I let his words drift by. But when, without evidence, Affat ascribed Arghun specific motives—saying he would soon try to break into the archives, driven to unearth the forbidden summoning spells—I had had enough, delivered a stinging rebuke, and ejected Affat from my chambers. At the time, Affat's words sounded like the claims of a bitter man who thought, in marrying my daughter, he married himself to the role of chief magician as well. I came to the conclusion that his grievances were imagined, and that his anger and jealousy had left him momentarily unhinged.

"In my foolishness, I mentioned this conversation to Arghun. And it was not long afterward that Affat disappeared.

"My daughter was devastated, suspecting foul play from the start. But from where I stood it seemed Affat's jealousies had driven him away.

"Then additional members of the court began to vanish. Three other mages disappeared without a trace, followed by five more, then more still. The royal guard could find no information as to their whereabouts, and the public grew increasingly concerned.

"Weeks passed and the situation only worsened, another mage disappearing each day. That's when Affat's warnings about Arghun and his intentions began to plague me. One dark night I found myself traveling along the narrow underground tunnels that housed the palace archives. And, unable to stop my feet, I took the hidden route to the Forbidden Tomes. When I saw fresh footprints in the dirt in front of me my heart began to beat faster. And when the ancient door that should have led to the summoning scrolls revealed an empty chamber . . . that's when I knew Affat had been right all along.

"The royal guard surrounded Arghun's quarters within the hour. But when they burst inside, swords drawn, the mage was already gone.

"It was my daughter who, several days later, was scouring every inch of Arghun's quarters and found the secret handle in the floor. She pulled it to discover stairs, and a hidden chamber carved out beneath the palace stone.

"What resided in that chamber is almost too terrible to describe, a hollow filled with remnants of dark magic and even darker deeds. The bodies of the first who had gone missing were there, victims of horrible tortures. Their legs were twisted, bodies covered in strange and hardened scales, lips and mouths torn apart after sprouting hundreds of shining teeth. These were experiments of the flesh. Arghun had attempted the summoning spells, and in doing so he'd drawn too deeply from the fire dragon. From what we found, it was clear the experience had driven him mad.

"Affat's ruined body was found at the bottom of the chamber that day, and my daughter, consumed with rage, demanded revenge. Our honor, our subjects, our entire kingdom insisted we make these injustices right. Thus we sent armies across the land, spies into every city, rugged bounty hunters into every remote region. It was widely known, for his treason, Arghun would be tracked down and killed in the most terrible ways imaginable.

"That said, while whispers of Arghun's deeds only multiplied once he fled from the palace, no one had any clues as to the whereabouts of the fire mage. Months passed in this fashion, and doubts began to emerge whether we would find him at all—whether this single mage was now more powerful than all the soldiers in our empire, whether one man could evade us and make fools of the Mongol race.

"My daughter could not bear the humiliation. She blamed me for our failure and swore, even if it meant her own death, Arghun would pay. And one day, when we looked to her chambers, my daughter was gone as well.

"No man can hide forever, and over the course of the following weeks my soldiers finally saw to it that Arghun was found. They strung him up and killed him like an animal. But my daughter did not come back to me. Now our armies, in secret, looked for her, combing the lands for many months to no avail. Because I knew her departure would make her a target—and I knew it would be seen as a sign of weakness by our enemies, one they would happily exploit—the entire time she was gone, I had no choice but to insist she remained within the palace walls.

"But now this terrible chapter has come to a close. Arghun is dead. You've brought my daughter back to me, offering her as a gift. You are what I've hoped and prayed for. So tonight you dine as the heroes you are, and in return I offer whatever you might desire. Only name it—for restoring my daughter to me, any wish you have will be gladly fulfilled."

Chapter 70

Aziz and Amelio looked at each other, speechless, astonished by the tale they'd just been told.

But Marco's mind was in another place entirely. It involved incredible risk, but an opportunity now lay before them. Marco summoned every last reserve of courage he had left, then, before anyone could stop him, he stood up, cleared his throat, and began to speak.

"Great khan, we are truly humbled that you chose to share your story with us."

Aziz and Amelio looked up at Marco in surprise.

"We are humbled, and for the return of your daughter— whether intended or not—we accept your gracious thanks. While she was gone we understand the pain you must have felt. I'm missing a loved one as well, and I know the pain can be great."

Aziz and Amelio were trying to figure out what Marco was up to, but he ignored their glances and barreled on.

"Great khan, seconds ago, as a reward, you promised us anything we desired. And, though I know exactly what we desire, I must confess that I'm afraid to ask it."

The khan said nothing, studying Marco's face. Then he cast his arm out toward the grand table in front of them, still crowded with plates of delicious food. "Our empire is wealthier than all others in the world. Look at the splendor all around you—do you think I cannot provide you with anything you wish?"

"It's not whether you can provide it," Marco said, his voice shaking slightly. "It's whether you will."

"I have just said that I will." The khan noticed Marco's strange expression. "Why do you hesitate?"

Marco forced his own tongue. "Because in asking this of you, I would have no choice but to contradict what you have told us."

At all corners of the room servants snapped to attention.

The khan's eyes slowly narrowed. "You would dare to contradict me?"

"I would. And I must," Marco said. "Great khan, in telling your story you spoke falsely no fewer than three times, and in making our request we must be honest about that now. Despite what you say, we know your soldiers never found the fire mage. I say this because we know his whereabouts now. We know where Arghun resides, and we know that the traitorous wizard is still very much alive."

The entire hall was gripped with a sudden and deathly silence.

When Kublai Khan spoke next, his voice was little more than a whisper. "You dare? He is *dead*. I have decreed it."

Aziz rose from his chair and stood in solidarity with Marco. "Great khan, the last time I had the honor to visit this hall I heard you make another decree. You swore that your daughter still remained safe in her room in the palace. In bringing her back to you—to our own surprise—we seem to have proved that your decrees could still be untrue."

Now Amelio stood in support. "We know you had no choice but to declare Arghun dead. After months of searching, you couldn't risk the strength of your army being further undermined. But none of that changes your need for revenge. Or our own."

"For returning your daughter, you promised anything that's in your power to provide. Arghun kidnapped my father, but his

Abarimon revealed the location of their lair in the process. We are now on a quest to Mount Dragoian to rescue my father and slay the fire mage. Help us. Supplement our numbers with your armies, and put an end to the great evil in your lands once and for all."

The khan was silent for some time, impossible to read.

After a long pause, he clapped his hands twice. Without delay a flurry of servants rushed in from the corners of the room and fell upon the table, removing every last dish and tray, then wiping the entire surface clean. Just as suddenly all of them rushed out, leaving Marco, Amelio, Aziz, and the khan alone in the massive chamber.

"Because I am a man of honor, and I have promised you anything you wished, you shall have the army you seek," the khan said, his deep voice booming. "I keep my promises. And I, too, desire revenge." The khan's words echoed off the walls.

"But there will be conditions that you will meet. In the first, none shall be told of this army's purpose, including the soldiers themselves. If Arghun is not where you say, or if he were to escape, I would not have your actions embarrass me or my soldiers. Is this understood?"

"It is," Aziz said, amazed by this turn of events.

"In the second, the Mongol army does not go into battle with children by their side. This has nothing to do with your courage. It is simply a fact. Aziz, you may lead the troops I provide. Marco and Amelio, you will remain with me here in the palace."

"What?" Marco said, shocked. "But it's my *father*—I've come this far to—"

The khan looked at Marco sharply. "Show your wisdom,

boy. Even without you, in these last few moments your father's chances of survival have dramatically improved. If I provide the army you wish, you will accept my conditions. Is that understood?"

Marco's face grew flush, his breathing quickened, and he felt a strange tightening in his chest. But he knew he had no choice; there could be no doubt this was for the best. "I . . . it's understood," he said in a choked whisper.

"Good. My servants will provide simple quarters in the meantime."

The khan forcefully stood, then looked over each one of them. "All of you," he said. "If this is a trick, I tell you now that I will have you strung up and killed in the public square. None shall know your names, and they will not be remembered. But if everything is as you say, and you slay the mage Arghun—you shall be immortalized as heroes and have anything in my lands you desire."

Then he turned to Aziz. "You leave tonight. It will be a full day's ride to reach the barracks with our troops, and two of our guards will escort you under cover of darkness. From there it's another three days' ride to Mount Dragoian. Come. If this is your path, we have many things to discuss."

With that, and without another look at Marco or Amelio, the khan started toward the hall's exit, beckoning for Aziz to follow just behind him.

Marco nearly said something in protest but Amelio squeezed his arm, silencing him. Marco sighed and his eyes dropped down to the marble floor beneath him. He could see the reflection of his heavy eyes and furrowed brow in the polished surface.

Before he reached the exit Aziz turned back to whisper to the boys. "Both of you—it's going to be all right. This is for the best. You got us here, and your courage will have been the first and greatest step in your father's rescue. You needn't ever—"

"Aziz!" the khan's voice boomed from just over the threshold of the exit.

Without another word Aziz turned and followed the khan.

In a moment they were both gone, leaving Marco and Amelio in the giant hall, by themselves, at the end of the enormous table.

This was Marco's idea and it worked. The khan hadn't killed them—instead, he gave them an army to rescue Marco's father. Both boys should have rejoiced.

Instead they both felt very small, and very much alone.

Chapter 72

"Marco! Marco, you have to wake up!"

Marco hugged his pillow to his chest, lost in the haze of another dream about his father.

"Marco, come on! Open your eyes! It's important!"

Under Amelio's verbal onslaught, the dream began to crack apart and drift away.

"Marco, now!"

Marco's eyes flickered open. His dreamscape was quickly replaced by plain bamboo walls, a simple mattress, and the figure of an agitated Amelio standing just over him, Sarap perched precariously on his shoulder.

"What's happening? What's going on?" Marco said, sitting up in bed and rubbing his eyes in the basic quarters the khan supplied them until Aziz returned.

"They don't know what to do," Amelio said, breathing heavily, his eyes manic. "Ever since I found out . . . I spoke to four guards already, four, but no one seems to know more than any-one else. They're all panicking—"

"Calm down!" Marco said, realizing something was very wrong and snapping to full attention. "Start from the beginning—ever since you found out. Ever since you found out what?"

"Aziz," Amelio said, slumping down on the bed next to Marco as Sarap jumped into his lap. "Last night."

"Last night he went off with two of the khan's soldiers. To ride to the barracks, to raise an army."

"No, that's what *should* have happened," Amelio said.

"What are you talking about?" Marco said, his tone growing grave.

"I woke up two hours ago and I couldn't fall back asleep. I didn't want to wake you so I went for a walk on the palace grounds. That's when I saw the guard, he was terrified. A ferocious Mongol soldier . . . scared."

"What was it?" Marco asked, his heart now pounding in his chest.

"Late last night, a pack of disguised Abarimon entered Peking. They killed four guards on their way to the palace gates and six more just outside them. Then they waited. When a group of three men finally left the gates the Abarimon pounced. Two guards were left dead, and the third . . . they took the third man with them."

Marco's face went pale. "Aziz . . ."

"Arghun was the palace's chief magician for too long. Despite everything he's done, they say some here are still loyal to him. Someone must have told him what Aziz had planned; he knew.

"By the time more guards arrived at the gates, it was too late. The Abarimon were transformed and had taken off with Aziz. The guard I spoke with was one of the reinforcements, he saw the bodies of his comrades and watched the Abarimon disappear into the distance.

"Marco—Aziz told the khan about the pearl. There were going to be two sets of soldiers waiting for him at the barracks. One set was to guard the pearl; the other was to travel with him to Mount Dragoian. But Aziz, he still had the pearl when he was taken. The Abarimon took Aziz *and* the pearl."

Marco felt an icy chill seize hold of his body, and everything around him seemed to slow down. This was impossible. It couldn't be happening. . . .

"Does the khan know?" Marco whispered.

"Everyone knows. The Abarimon left a trail of bodies all throughout Peking. The khan sent word to mobilize the armies in the barracks just the same, but it will take time to reach them. And another two days for them to arrive at Mount Dragoian. The Abarimon will get Aziz and the pearl to Arghun in half that."

Marco pulled himself together and steeled his resolve. There was no time to panic, they had to act. "Amelio and Sarap, grab your things. We have to go find Kokachin."

Chapter 73

Marco and Amelio got the location of Kokachin's quarters from a terrified servant running across the palace grounds. Word was spreading about the previous night's attack, the farthest the Abarimon had ever ventured into Peking, and the tenuous lie the khan had told about Arghun's death was now completely unraveling.

To reach Kokachin, Marco and Amelio took a shortcut through the Imperial Gardens. They hurried past several lines of small wooden benches, pine trees with twisting, knotted trunks, and patches of carefully tended rock gardens ringed with sticks of smoking incense. An enormous gray hawk circled overhead, eyeing them from above.

Kokachin's quarters were surrounded by the khan's guards—there to make sure she didn't run off again—but Marco and Amelio were allowed through, since they were the ones who had returned her to the palace in the first place. The guards wordlessly stepped aside and let them pass.

Marco rapped his knuckles against her heavy wooden door. When both boys heard Kokachin's voice telling them to enter, Marco pushed open the door to her large, sparsely decorated quarters and found her sitting at her dressing table.

As Marco and Amelio gazed in surprise, Kokachin's dark hair reflected the light of a single candle. No longer wearing clothes prepared for combat, she wore a purple robe fastened by a row of delicate buttons and twined with silken thread. She looked entirely different from the fierce, unyielding warrior they had come to know—if they passed this girl anywhere else, they wouldn't have recognized her at all.

Noting their stunned expressions, Kokachin spoke for them. "You're seeing who I was—the girl I used to be. Thanks to Arghun, she doesn't exist any longer."

"Kokachin," Marco began, leading with an apology. "You know, all along—we had no idea you were Kublai Khan's—"

Kokachin shook her head, dismissing him. "How could you have known? I gave you no reason to suspect it." Then she paused, her tone softening. "But I am glad you came here to see me after finding out."

"Kokachin, we need to talk about—"

"Before you start," Kokachin said, cutting Marco off with a wave of her hand, "you must understand, though I am not of many words, my convictions are strong. I know you have spoken with my father, and I am sure he has told you certain things. You should know, his story is not wrong. His armies did look long and hard for Arghun. But at a certain point, when they did not find him, my father felt it was more important that his people believed in the strength of their soldiers than it was to capture the fire mage. To maintain this belief, he told them Arghun was found and killed.

"This is how my father perceives his duty. He does not see himself as a man—he is the living embodiment of his kingdom, and its needs subsume his own. His personal desire for revenge is cast aside to maintain confidence in our military might. His love for his children is immaterial; he trains us harshly so he might guard against our being used as pawns of war. He no longer attends the trials of his citizens in case he might know them and allow his emotions to obscure his logic.

"But, in removing himself so completely, his judgment is clouded; being nothing but the kingdom turns him rigid and selfish, as the kingdom must have its way. It deprives his rule of its compassion and heart.

"I could not live, or rule, in the same way. When Arghun went unfound, my father felt he served his empire by denying himself and calling off his soldiers. I felt I served my empire by following the heat in my blood and the pain in my heart. So against my father's wishes I left the palace to soldier on.

"I traveled from city to city, learning much before eventually finding my way to Bukhara. In the border town, tales of Abarimon were increasing and rumor of Arghun was ripe. I took what Bukhara had to offer; then, when Aziz told me your story and asked me to be your guide, I agreed out of selfishness, thinking additional clues about Arghun's whereabouts could be gleaned. When it became apparent we were on a common mission, and drawing closer to our goal, I agreed to stick around.

"I knew, when Aziz was hurt, there was risk in letting the soldiers bring us back to the palace. But his injuries were great enough that we had no choice. And I was sure, with my knowledge of the palace, we could quickly escape and continue on our way without my identity being found. I was wrong.

"Yesterday afternoon I spoke at length with my guards. They told me what my father decided. Where he would not send more armies against Arghun for me, it appears he has agreed to do so for Aziz. I never imagined my father would submit to this; Aziz must have been quite compelling. Though I wished to kill the fire mage myself, I am heartened to hear that, under Aziz, steps are again being taken toward his death."

Chapter 74

Marco's eyes were steely as he took in his unmasked friend.

"Kokachin—all that is what we came here to speak with you about. Your father gave Aziz the army he requested. But, on his way from Peking to the army barracks, Aziz was ambushed by a pack of Abarimon. Arghun has him now. He has the pearl."

Kokachin stared at Marco blankly, unable to believe what she had just heard. "What?" she whispered.

"Your father knows. He's sending troops to Mount Dragoian," Amelio said.

"It will be days before they arrive. They'll never reach Arghun in time," Kokachin said.

"Amelio spoke with a guard. It's the best they can do."

"And what of us?" Kokachin said, the warrior they'd known fast returning. "What's the best *we* can do?"

Kokachin reached beneath her dressing table and removed a bundle of cloth with several large items inside it.

She removed the objects one by one: a collection of swords and knives. "I have armor as well, hidden from months before. Against all odds, a warrior always makes sure she has the supplies she needs."

Marco's eyes glowed brighter as he took in the weapons.

"But there are six soldiers outside your door," Amelio said, bringing them back to reality. "They'll never let you leave. The same goes for Marco and me if we try to get past the palace gates."

"What about Sarap?" Kokachin said, eyeing the small green creature poking its head out from the collar of Amelio's shirt. "He still owes us two boons, doesn't he? Perhaps he could—"

"Only one," Sarap interjected in his strange, squeaky voice. "Only one boon left to serve."

"One? But all you've done so far is untie us back in the courtyard," Marco said.

"Not exactly," Amelio chimed in, looking slightly guilty.

"What?"

"Back in the Shrine of the Eternal Order, when I first got Sarap. The rest of you disappeared with Kar-wai and left me on my own. And I wanted to try Sarap out."

"So you wasted one of your wishes?" Kokachin said, her voice incredulous.

"I don't know if I *wasted* it. . . ." Amelio reached into his pocket and took out four vials of brightly colored liquid. "I had Sarap fly over and take these from the shelf. I thought they could prove useful down the line, and if anyone noticed they were missing, we could just blame it on Sarap. Small price to pay for letting him out of his bottle."

Marco stared at the vials, his mind starting to race, and Amelio handed them all to his friend. "I had Sarap take four of them, one for each of us, but now we have an extra. Since Aziz . . ." Amelio let his sentence drift off into silence.

Marco took a deep breath. "We have to escape from the palace and quickly cover the distance to Mount Dragoian." He looked at Sarap. "We have one boon left. How fast can you fly?"

"Fast, fast, fast when I fly on my own," Sarap said.

"I'm not sure that helps us any," Kokachin said.

"It doesn't right now, when we're so big Sarap could never carry us," Marco said. His eyes narrowed in on a metal thimble on Kokachin's dresser. "But if we were much, much smaller, it might not be a problem."

"Even if that helped us escape the palace and make our way to Mount Dragoian," Amelio said, "what would we do once we got there? We won't have much time, and we'll have to avoid the Abarimon, get inside Mount Dragoian itself, then get close to Arghun before he can use the pearls."

"Kokachin," Marco said, "how well did you know Arghun when he was chief magician?"

"Well enough. Enough to see through to his hatred and envy of my father, his ambition to have everything he has."

Marco handed Amelio a vial, then gave another to Kokachin. He kept one in his own hand, then slipped the last one into his shirt. "This isn't going to be easy. And Sarap, you'll be free to go off on your own once your boon is done. But I think I have a plan to get us into Mount Dragoian and close to Arghun before he can resurrect the dragon."

Chapter 75

In no time at all, a small green creature with tiny wings on its back soared out Kokachin's window and over the palace walls. The creature carried a metal thimble, and three miniscule people were crouched inside.

As Sarap flew them higher and higher into the air—zipping bravely in the direction of Mt. Dragoian—all of them could see their reflections in the polished metal of the thimble's insides. They each looked warped, their features stretched and bulging, the entire world distorted as they made their way toward Arghun and the dragon's pearls.

"In the center of the marble platform, Arghun unleashed an explosive circle of heat. Enormous white flames billowed up and roared in a solid ring all around him, stretching twenty feet into the air, hot enough to incinerate everything they touched.

It was beginning. . . ."

—FROM THE JOURNALS OF MARCO POLO

Part Six

DRAGONS

Chapter 76

Just outside a small village on the path to Mt. Dragoian, Kokachin breathed in deeply, opened her eyes, and found herself returned to normal size.

Buzzing overhead, Sarap wished Kokachin luck. Then, all three boons fulfilled, he flew off to newfound freedom.

Kokachin watched him go.

She held on to the thimble in her hand that contained her two still-small friends. Then she prepared herself.

"Here goes nothing. And everything."

Kokachin turned toward the village and narrowed her eyes. She didn't have much time, and she needed to buy their fastest horse.

Chapter 77

Alone on a powerful mare, her dark hair tied behind her and her sword by her side, Kokachin continued on her journey toward Mt. Dragoian.

There was a dense pine forest before she could reach her destination and Kokachin navigated quickly through it, riding along narrow dirt paths surrounded by enormous trees.

When the forest thinned, and Kokachin began to hear voices all around her, she brought her horse to a halt alongside a gigantic cedar.

"What is that . . . ?" she whispered.

The voices continued, too low to make out any specific words. Kokachin waited silently.

Finally, the voices began to grow in volume . . . a murmur, then a buzz . . . little bursts of riot . . . the occasional scream, a throaty groan, coming from the forest just behind her . . .

Kokachin turned. Then she saw them—Abarimon. There were only a few toward the front, but there were dozens behind them, and hundreds after that, all moving in an enormous pack toward Mt. Dragoian. Some were fully transformed, traveling more quickly, sniffing the air with flared nostrils. Others were still in the midst of a transformation, walking as thin, bony men before stopping, snapping themselves into an erect stance, and letting loose a horrifying scream. Torsos inflated with muscle and sinew, talons burst out of fingers, and knees collapsed above twisting feet.

Kokachin's eyes grew wide as she saw them all. She thought she might encounter a few at Mt. Dragoian, but it was terrifying to see them this soon, and in these numbers, all at once. For now they were oblivious to her presence, but she knew that couldn't last long. . . .

Kokachin's pulse quickened just as her horse realized their predicament, grew spooked, and started whinnying.

"Quiet, be quiet!" Kokachin whispered, stroking its mane as she tried to figure out a plan. But her horse paid her no mind, continuing to whinny and bucking in place.

And just like that, with her horse's last outburst, the air around her changed. Everything grew still. Even the Abarimon's snorts, grunts, and screams petered out. Kokachin knew what this meant. "They're fast, so you're just going to have to be faster," she whispered to her horse. "On my count. One . . . two . . ."

Before she could reach three, in horrifying unison, the whole of the Abarimon horde screamed loudly enough to be heard all the way back at the palace. There was no more hiding now.

"Yah!" Kokachin screamed, kicking her horse into a gallop.

As soon as her horse burst into motion the Abarimon erupted in pursuit. Her horse whipped frantically ahead, Kokachin strong and focused on its back, as the Abarimon drooled and howled, trampling through the forest, their claws bared, with Kokachin reflected in each of their horrifying eyes.

Kokachin kept straight and steady, refusing to turn around, her horse's mighty legs crushing foliage underfoot. "Keep going, keep going," Kokachin whispered, the wind stealing the words from her mouth.

Before she could say anything else, an Abarimon crouched down, leaped through the air, and smashed down on top of her horse. The horse's legs buckled; it nearly toppled under the weight. But it was somehow able to recover and keep on charging with the Abarimon standing on its back.

Kokachin, her legs wrapped tightly around the horse's midsection, grabbed a dagger tucked inside her boot and turned. The Abarimon was standing at its full height, the talons on its feet keeping it steady, nails sunken in and drawing blood from the horse's back. Its mouth foamed, and it lunged toward Kokachin just as she thrust her dagger forward, plunging it deep into the creature's chest. The impact was enough to loosen the grip of the Abarimon's taloned feet, and it fell off her horse and landed hard on the ground with Kokachin's dagger still buried deep.

Kokachin turned and continued racing, refusing to stop, ignoring all the groups of Abarimon gaining on her from behind. She didn't stop even when the shrieks of the Abarimon were replaced by great bangs, accompanied by the cracks of timber. At first she thought the beasts might be breaking off branches from the trees. Then, when the entire tree next to her toppled over and fell to the ground with an enormous crash, she understood.

She had too much of a head start and the Abarimon were unable to catch her, so they were throwing themselves into trees. They threw themselves again and again, their powerful bodies splintering and knocking over the centuries-old pines, each tree cascading into another and knocking it over as well. If they couldn't catch her, they would knock down the forest and try to crush her under its weight.

Her horse continued to gallop, faster than ever, as trees started falling all around them. "Yah! Yah!" Kokachin shouted, her horse leaping over an obstruction. The air was full of the crack of timber, another tree falling, then another, dominos set into motion. Soon the chain reaction took on a life of its own—to her horror, Kokachin saw Abarimon charging from every corner with the forest collapsing all around them, each tree that crashed to the ground bringing the tide of destruction closer to her and her exhausted mare.

Kokachin could do nothing but shut her eyes and pray the speed of her horse would save them.

And when she opened her eyes again, the tree branches had begun to thin over her head. What had been a dense ceiling now let in sky. She was almost free of the forest!

Kokachin sped into a clearing, just past the reach of any of the trees, the last one falling with an enormous crash behind her. Breathing heavily, her heart pounding in her chest, Kokachin turned back toward the decimated forest. Moving through the wreckage she saw hundreds of Abarimon, all transformed into ravenous beasts, all pushing steadily toward her.

And in front of her the odds were no better. Immediately there was the steep rock wall of an enormous volcano—Mt. Dragoian. And no fewer than a hundred transformed Abarimon stood, waiting, at the cavelike entrance to the volcano's inner depths.

Kokachin halted her horse and placed her hand on her sword, but the Abarimon in front of her didn't make a move. Behind her, as more Abarimon made their way out of the forest, they stayed in place as well, drooling and panting anxiously.

Finally, as Kokachin watched, a solitary figure stepped out from the entrance to Mt. Dragoian, Abarimon shuffling aside to let him through. With a tight flick of the figure's wrist, Kokachin's horse dropped to its knees, forcing Kokachin to disembark and stand on her own.

The figure wore a simple black robe. He was slim but muscled, stood nearly as tall as Aziz, and had pale skin, delicate features, and black hair. He advanced fearlessly, with strength and purpose, stopping several yards away from Kokachin. Every Abarimon watched his approach, and none dared to move or utter a sound.

Kokachin rested her hand on her weapon.

"Hello, Princess Kokachin. I haven't seen you in some time."

While Kokachin had spent countless hours imagining what it would be like to face what Arghun had become, nothing prepared her for this. Where, in his early days at her father's court, Arghun was simply a powerful young fire mage, his time with the summoning spells warped him more entirely, in mind and in body, than she had imagined.

In the face of a man, Arghun's eyes were entirely black—a black so deep even the slightest glance made you feel as though you were falling forever and would never stop, swallowed entirely by the dark. His voice was the sound of metal scraped hard across stone, each word almost painful to hear. When he said Kokachin's name her face grew hot and her skin began to tingle, as though thousands of tiny insects were running up and down her body at once, each drawing blood. And, just below his skin, all of his veins pulsed black, his body etched with the foul knowledge he'd collected. No human was meant to draw this strongly from their dragon; it had corrupted him utterly.

In the face of this creature, Kokachin had to force herself to speak. "Arghun—I've found you. I'm here to kill you for all that you've done."

"I'm sure you are," Arghun said calmly, and Kokachin was unable to help breathing in sharply each time she heard his voice.

Arghun took another few steps toward Kokachin until they were face-to-face, his dark hair waving gently in the wind. Then, as if this was the only and perfect act of greeting, Arghun met Kokachin's eyes and ran a cold hand over her cheek.

Before Kokachin could respond, a mouth nested inside the palm of Arghun's hand began to shriek, a tiny dragon's maw. Kokachin did all that she could to fight as the pain exploded in her head, dropping her to her knees, turning her body useless and immobile while Arghun walked back inside the cavern, and several Abarimon stepped forward to drag Kokachin painfully into Mt. Dragoian in Arghun's wake.

Chapter 78

Kokachin regained consciousness slowly, her impressions scattered in the dark. They were inside Mt. Dragoian. Stone walls all around them, a damp and filthy floor. Her vision bounced with each step—she was being carried over the shoulder of an untransformed Abarimon. Many more Abarimon were following just behind, each one encased in a thin layer of mud, clothes tattered and moldy. Frail and hollow-cheeked, all of their arms and legs were covered in red sores.

Then Kokachin heard the sound of a heavy bolt sliding to one side, followed by an iron door swinging open on rusty hinges.

Before long they were in an enormous chamber, stretching out both before them and hundreds of feet into the air. As Kokachin's eyes adjusted to the dim light she saw a network of scaffolding and tunnels that honeycombed the chamber's upper walls. At the very top of the chamber a hole let in the starry sky. Mt. Dragoian was a volcano, and this was its heart.

Beneath them, a narrow stone path led to a smooth marble floor that took up the majority of the enormous chamber. Hot and bubbling lava rose up along the very edges of the marble.

The Abarimon procession marched to a long and wide metal post erected in the far corner of the marble floor. As Arghun, already waiting, calmly looked on, the Abarimon carrying Kokachin grabbed her off its back and slung her body roughly against the metal post. Two Abarimon just behind it carried rope, and they quickly tied Kokachin into place. Then all of the Abarimon retreated to the outer perimeter of the marble floor and waited, evenly spaced, an unbroken chain of death from which Kokachin could not escape.

Arghun looked at Kokachin, her eyes now open and filled with hate.

"I'm glad you came," Arghun said, his black robe hanging lightly off his shoulders. "For some time I've heard it rumored that you were my prisoner. Now the rumor finally appears to be true."

"What have you done with Aziz?" Kokachin said, her voice icily calm. "What have you done with Niccolo Polo?"

"I destroyed them."

"What?" Quickly, Kokachin's calm was broken.

"They each had something I required. I took what I needed and did away with the rest. Much as I did with—what was his name?"

"Affat," Kokachin whispered.

"Yes. Affat." Arghun's black eyes scanned Kokachin's face. "I learned from Affat. So difficult to master the summoning spells, to turn a man from one thing to the next. It can all go so painfully wrong," Arghun said. "Affat screamed for days. In fact, he was one of the reasons I left Kublai Khan's palace; there was too much to be learned, and I grew tired of having to cover up his shouting. If his pain was necessary to perfect the spell, so be it. I had to kill him in the end—I believe you found his body. But here at Mount Dragoian I do entirely as I wish."

"You're a monster," Kokachin spat, hating him with every inch of her being.

"I'm far beyond a monster," Arghun said with that same terrible calm. "I've pulled so much from my connection with the fire dragon that I've started to become . . . a part of it. Only a small part of it—the human body can only handle so much. But a part just the same."

At that, Arghun held up his hands for Kokachin to see. And, nestled in the center of each palm, she saw angry mouths with four rows of sharp and gleaming teeth. Each one like the miniature maw of a dragon.

Arghun dropped his hands, and throughout the rest of his body, Kokachin could see the black, pulsing blood running through his veins, different enough from a human's to show beneath his skin. And his skin itself, up close, had changed in composition, now beginning to take on the characteristics of . . . scales.

"I am a work in progress," Arghun continued, seeing Koachin's horror. "A weak mortal frame continually being perfected. My Abarimon, as well—I have helped them, but they are limited by their own mortality. Did you know, thousands of years ago, Abarimon were naturally occurring? A little-known offshoot of man's evolution from beast. Abarimon were among the first sentient creatures to worship the fire dragon, but they became extinct during the height of man's rise. I've taken it upon myself to bring them back, forcing fire dragon essence into men. I find the result to be quite efficient."

Arghun looked down at his hands, at the scaly mouths with their teeth hungrily gnashing. "At one point, I hoped to draw as much as my frame would allow from the fire dragon. Then I realized the potential of having a dragon of my own. There were the two living dragons, but to control them I would have to slay them and take their pearls, and even I could not kill a dragon on my own. Then there were the slain Western dragons, of water and of wind, but no one had seen their pearls in generations.

"Until the Westerner, Niccolo Polo, traveled into our Unknown Lands and visited the khan with a world in his pocket. I thought he had both of the wind dragon's pearls, but he was only one piece of the puzzle."

At that, the mouth in the center of Arghun's left palm opened wide, and from within its depths the swirling red pearl rose to the surface and was clenched between its teeth.

"But it's a funny thing with the dragon pearls. The universe has always managed to keep them together, even when mortals try to carry them apart. If Niccolo Polo had one of the pearls, I was fairly certain another Polo would have its twin. And if I couldn't wrest it from them by force, there was as much a likelihood they would unwittingly bring the pearl straight to me."

With that, the mouth in the center of Arghun's right palm opened and gnashed against the blue pearl that lay between its teeth.

"A very recent acquisition," Arghun said. "Now, with both pearls, I shall summon Shen Lung as my own. I shall possess the wind dragon and all will tremble. It is only fitting that you be here as it starts, as your father's kingdom will soon be subsumed by the empire of a god."

Kokachin, her hands fighting against their constraints the entire time Arghun spoke, was finally able to grab the small metal thimble that she had tucked away in her sleeve. "I've gotten us inside, and you're as close to him as you'll ever be," she whispered. "I've played my part—it's up to you now. Good luck."

Then Kokachin opened the hand holding the thimble and let it tumble imperceptibly to the ground.

Chapter 79

As soon as the thimble hit the marble floor, Marco and Amelio closed their eyes, cast off the effects of the shrinking liquid, and sprang up to their normal height.

Fully dressed in Mongol armor, with their swords at the ready, both boys held their ground between Kokachin and Arghun.

Arghun looked at the two intruders with his cold black eyes, his expression unchanging. But the Abarimon around the perimeter of the marble floor began breathing in deeply, snorting, their mouths foaming. In an instant any untransformed Abarimon standing nearby began their hideous metamorphosis, bones cracking, claws extending, legs breaking and growing stronger.

From his pocket, Marco grabbed the water stone Kar-wai had given him back at the Shrine of the Eternal Order. He held it in his hand, squeezed it gently, then threw it toward the center of the marble floor.

With a great surge, an incredibly strong jet of water blasted out from the bottom of the stone. The jet pushed the stone higher and higher into the air, the stone spinning rapidly all the while. Then, with a boom akin to the crashing of two ships, the stone began pouring hundreds of streams of water in a constant arc from every side, creating a powerful wall of water all around. Each of the snarling Abarimon standing on the outer perimeter found himself trapped between the burning lava on one end and the wall of water on the other. One Abarimon tried to cross the wall and immediately fell to the ground, sizzling and burning, helpless against the element. The rest of the Abarimon screamed and spat, punching their chests and pacing furiously, but they could not cross the water wall to attack.

As Arghun took in the impact of Marco's actions, Amelio quickly cut through Kokachin's bindings and she dropped to the floor in a battle crouch. Amelio slipped her a pair of daggers and she held them like natural extensions of her hands. Flanking her on either side, beads of raindrops glistened on Marco's and Amelio's metal armor.

"What you've done is unfortunate," Arghun said coldly, cupping his hands together and bringing them to his lips. As he blew into his hands his breath turned to flames, and within seconds he was holding an enormous ball of fire.

"You are mistaken to think I need Abarimon for my protection," Arghun said, steam rising around him as drops of water fell and were vaporized on the flame. "The truth is, Abarimon are far more merciful than I. They quickly tear into you with their claws; you're dead by the time they're finished. But me, I prolong the process. I am a patient student of suffering. I use it for my own ends until you beg for the grave."

Marco, Amelio, and Kokachin dove for the ground just in time. The fireball flew over their heads, its heat so intense they could feel their eyelashes crisping and burning away.

A second later Marco rolled one way, Kokachin and Amelio the other, as an even bigger fireball crashed into the ground just between them.

There was a moment of relative quiet as the three of them got to their feet—the only sounds they heard were the hiss of Arghun's flames, the wall of water hitting the ground and the deep roar of lava just below.

Arghun tore off his robe, and beneath it, every inch of his body was covered in the pulsing black veins and hard, red scales of the Fire Dragon. Some red scales were large and jutted out from his chest, others were small and lined the creases of his arms and legs. But across them all, it was abundantly clear that Arghun was no longer human.

As if to further prove the point, Arghun took two steps toward them and held up his arms in front of his body. The mouths on each hand opened wide. Then, like silver tongues, enormous steel blades slid out from each of his palms, glimmering menacingly in the dark lava light.

"These are my dragon claws," Arghun said. "They're about to feast on your flesh."

Chapter 80

With a roaring battle cry, Marco, Amelio, and Kokachin ran toward Arghun.

Marco took the first swing, his sword deftly blocked by Arghun's blade.

Kokachin and Amelio attacked from the other side, only to find each of their strikes parried as well.

Though Arghun was fighting against three adversaries, he matched his opponents blow for blow. The swordfight raged along, neither side getting the upper hand or showing signs of weakening.

Eventually, growing more aggressive, Amelio lunged. Arghun leaped back and used the boy's momentum to kick him into Marco, knocking them together.

As Arghun watched Amelio and Marco collide Kokachin thought she saw an opening and leaped forward, stabbing one of her daggers into the protruding red scales on Arghun's chest. It had no effect. When Kokachin did her best to rip her dagger free, Arghun smashed his forehead into her face, knocking her backward in a daze. Pressing his advantage, Arghun took another step toward Kokachin, then slammed the outside of his fist into the side of her head. Kokachin stumbled, her vision blurring. Finally, before she could recover, Arghun sliced his blade across her stomach.

Kokachin gasped. Her hands flew to the wound, blood leaking between her fingers.

Before Arghun could finish her off, Amelio charged up behind him and ran his own sword as hard as he could across Arghun's back. Several large scales splintered and cracked, but Arghun showed no sign of injury. Instead he reared back his arm and elbowed Amelio's stomach, hard.

Arghun's blow knocked the wind out of Amelio and he collapsed forward, momentarily unable to breathe. Before Amelio could force another breath Arghun whipped around and cracked him across the face with his knuckles. Amelio stumbled backward, then forced his sword up in defense. Sensing Amelio was weakening, Arghun became aggressive with his blades, bombarding Amelio with strike after strike, not giving him a chance to recover.

All Amelio saw was a shower of sparks.

Finally, with the mightiest swing he could manage, Arghun smashed his blade into Amelio's, and the impact knocked the boy to the ground. Amelio tried to get back up, but Arghun put one foot on his chest and the other on his knees, keeping him down. Arghun pressed the tip of his blade against Amelio's throat.

"No!" Marco shouted, his hands covered in Kokachin's blood, halfway to Arghun and Amelio.

"I grow tired of this," Arghun said, both blades sliding back into his hands. He slammed one foot down hard, breaking Amelio's legs. With a flick of his wrist a fireball crashed into Marco's chest, sending him flying back through the air.

"A pleasant diversion has become a distraction," Arghun said. "It is time for me to resurrect a god." He turned his black eyes to the center of the marble platform. On his palms, teeth drew back to reveal the blue and red pearls.

"Don't bleed to death too quickly, children," Arghun said with one last look at Marco, Amelio, and Kokachin. "They say dragons are very hungry when they're reborn."

Chapter 81

Marco tried to fight back the worst pain of his life. His body felt as if he'd been burned alive.

A short distance away, Kokachin was lying in a pool of blood.

Amelio, a bit farther off, was unconscious. Marco saw his legs bent at odd angles where Arghun had slammed his foot.

In the center of the marble platform, Arghun's hand began to glow. Then he snapped his fingers and immediately unleashed an explosive circle of heat. Enormous white flames billowed up and roared in a solid ring all around him, stretching twenty feet into the air, hot enough to incinerate everything they touched. It would be nearly impossible to get to him now. It was beginning.

"No!" Marco screamed as his eyes welled up with tears.

Through the incredibly hot white flames, Marco saw Arghun bend down, take his finger, and trace the image of a large triangle on the marble floor. He followed by tracing a second triangle within the first, half its size and upside down. Then, placing both pearls into its center, he stood and began muttering feverishly to himself, speaking so quickly the words tumbled over and quickly became one.

Amelio and Kokachin were in no position help him. If Arghun was to be stopped, Marco was going to have to do it himself.

For Aziz. For his uncle. For his father.

Arghun continued chanting, louder and louder, growing more incensed with each word. As he did, both pearls and the lines of the triangles he'd traced began to glow with a radiant blue light.

Marco forced himself up to his knees, pain exploding in his head.

Both pearls floated upward of their own accord, rising steadily until they were even with Arghun's hands. They hung next to each other in midair. Arghun looked at them breathlessly.

Then, without further warning, blue beams shot up from the three points of the large triangle to the hovering pearls themselves, creating a three-dimensional pyramid shape. The shape seemed to be charging the pearls with energy, and the pearls glowed with an increasingly bright and white light.

Amelio breathed in sharply and opened his eyes.

Just as suddenly, the pearls began projecting light upward into the air of the cavern, forming an enormous inverted light pyramid directly atop the original. In the space above everyone's heads, the light projected the vague and sketchlike outlines of a giant blue dragon.

"Yes, yes!" Arghun screamed from inside his circle of fire. "Awaken, Shen Lung!"

Amelio's eyes grew wider, realizing what was happening. He tried to get up but couldn't move his legs.

As the light grew brighter the wind dragon's soul began to be released. The blue lights progressively added layers of texture to the dragon: its lizardlike head and jaws, its powerful body and enormous wings, its long and curving tail. Shafts of white light traced in finer details: the long whiskers and bristling hairs, the layers of scales along its chest and back. The dragon's spirit, projected in the lights, started to take on substance and become flesh. A horrible roar filled the chamber.

Amelio saw Marco and shouted to him. "Marco!"

"Amelio, don't try to move! You're going to be all right."

"What do we do? Everything we were afraid of is happening! We have to stop him!"

Inside the circle of flames, the two pearls were both sucked back into the mouths in Arghun's palms, each one glowing madly. So long as he had those pearls, the wind dragon would be under Arghun's control.

Marco struggled to his feet, knowing he had to do something. He put up his hands to shield himself from the incredible heat of Arghun's fire-wall, blistering even from a distance—it would take the strength of a thousand water stones to put it out. Marco bent down to pick up his sword, and as he did, the last vial from the Shrine of the Eternal Order fell out of his shirt and onto the ground.

He stared at the vial, the liquid a strange yellow unlike the others they'd drank before.

Marco remembered, back at the Shrine, Kar-wai had said the liquid in each vial had a mind of its own. When Arghun drank a vial it nearly killed him. When Amelio took one it gave them Sarap.

The two vials Marco drank so far had made him smaller, just when he needed to be small.

Now, when he needed to be stronger—strong enough to put an end to Arghun—would the vial do the same?

Overhead the dragon continued taking shape, its wings now starting to twitch and shake.

Marco stood up, sword in one hand and the vial in the other. He was the only one left, and he couldn't let Arghun finish summoning Shen Lung. To stop him, Marco would have to get through the wall of fire and fight Arghun all over again, this time on his own. If he didn't drink the vial, his chances of surviving that were slim. And if he did—

Marco closed his eyes and put the vial to his lips.

Amelio, seeing this, cried out in alarm. "Marco, stop, what are you doing!?"

Marco prayed he wouldn't shrink. Then everything turned to black.

Chapter 82

When Marco next opened his eyes, his head was still pounding and he was still in pain. The vial hadn't healed him. And it didn't seem like it had given him strength.

He looked around. The water stone was still keeping the snarling Abarimon at bay. Kokachin was still motionless, Amelio's legs were twisted on the ground, Arghun was encased in his circle of flames. And the terrifying dragon was growing more real by the second above his head. All of this was happening, but everything was the same size as always. Marco didn't seem to have shrunk an inch.

To his dismay, the vial didn't seem to have done anything at all.

But his sword was still in his hand and there was some time left. He had to do what he could, even if it meant certain death—it was better to die trying than to die by a summoned dragon. Marco looked to Amelio. "No matter what happens, you're my best friend in the entire world. I'm so sorry I got you mixed up in all of this."

Then, before Amelio could reply, Marco closed his eyes and ran headfirst toward Arghun and the wall of fire.

Chapter 83

When he didn't feel his flesh burning and skin melting away, Marco opened his eyes, thinking he'd run in the wrong direction.

And he found himself in the middle of the wall, enormous flames covering him from every angle, beautiful and terrible all at once.

But he didn't feel a thing. There was no heat, no pain.

Marco pinched himself as hard as he could, then jerked his hand away when he realized he'd just cut his skin and bled. He was still alive. He was just . . .

Something had happened.

He was *fireproof*.

The liquid in the vial. It hadn't shrunk him, and it hadn't made him stronger. But it made him what he had to be. The flames whipping around him couldn't hurt him at all.

Up above, the dragon's head had turned entirely to flesh

and it let out an incredible roar, snapping Marco out of his thoughts. That dragon was unlike any creature Marco had ever seen. And, if he could help it, he wouldn't see any more of it. He had a job to do.

Marco continued walking through the flames, entirely unscathed. He tightened his hand on his sword.

As the flames began to thin, Marco saw Arghun's back, his arms stretched out alongside him, his palms holding the glowing pearls tilted up toward the sky. The scales growing on Arghun's back were hard and strong, with barely a dent from Amelio's blade.

But the scales on his wrists were small and thin.

Completely absorbed in the spectacle of the dragon coming to life, Arghun didn't seem to notice Marco at all.

Marco knew he would only get one shot. He charged out of the fire as hard as he could and swung his sword down once on the left. Then, before Arghun had time to react, he swung his sword down one more time on the right.

As Shen Lung's body became fully realized overhead, both of Arghun's hands fell twitching to the floor, each one sliced off at the wrist by Marco's blade.

But Marco was too late. Shen Lung was reborn.

Arghun spun around, staring at Marco in disbelief, the flame wall crackling all alongside them. "You?"

In an instant, Arghun's black eyes turned red with fire, and a pair of monstrous flaming hands shot out from each of his wrists. "You dare to strike at me? I am a god, and you are less than a worm! In the name of the fire dragon, I will *incinerate* you!" he screamed.

Marco glanced down, bracing himself for a blow, and saw Arghun's severed hands give one last twitch on the ground. The mouths in his palms—absent the rest of his body—abruptly went slack and released their grip on the pearls.

The second the pearls were free again, their power over Shen Lung was broken; a pair of mighty dragon jaws slammed down from the sky and closed entirely over Arghun. Marco heard Arghun scream as the wind dragon chewed once, twice, three times, then it raised its snakelike neck into the air and swallowed the rest of Arghun whole.

Marco collapsed to the ground in terror. Seeing both pearls only inches away he scooped them up into his hands, not knowing what else to do.

And, moments later, Marco found himself face-to-face with Shen Lung the dragon.

Chapter 84

What would you have me do?

Shen Lung didn't speak the words, but Marco heard them clearly in his head just the same. The enormous creature, twice as large as the demon worm they'd faced back in the desert, was flying in place in the center of the cave and staring directly at Marco, waiting for his reply.

"Ex . . . excuse me?" Marco said, in shock.

You now possess the twin pearls of the wind dragon. I am under your command. What would you have me do?

Finally taking in the dragon, Marco was amazed at Shen Lung's surprisingly soft visage—the long whiskers, bristling hairs, and layers of blue scales that ran across its face.

"What would I have you do? You're a great dragon."

Yes. And for so long as you bear my pearls, I will ask it again. What would you have me do?

All around them the flames still raged. Just out of sight, his friends were badly injured and a water stone just barely held an army of Abarimon at bay.

"What would I have you do? Put an end to all this," Marco said. "Help my friends. If you can, help me bring my loved ones back. Stop all this destruction. And make sure the Abarimon never hurt anyone again." Marco looked down at the two softly glowing pearls in his lap, red and blue, finally reunited. He thought of everyone who had wanted them, everyone who tried to take them along the way. Then he met the wind dragon's eyes. "And take your pearls. They're yours, freely given. Keep them safe, and make sure they don't fall into any man's hands again."

As soon as Marco said the words, the pearls began to glow brighter and brighter, the glow exploding out from their center until the entire cave was filled with a blinding light.

Chapter 85

The mighty Shen Lung, both pearls glowing brightly from its forehead, flapped its massive wings just over the marble platform.

I am Shen Lung, the wind dragon of the West, and I am reborn.

Marco looked up at the dragon in awe, amazed that anyone would seek to control such an incredible being.

As young Marco Polo has asked—the human Arghun took much from my brother, the fire dragon. I now return to the fire dragon's essence everything that was his.

With that, a powerful wind tore through the insides of Mt. Dragoian, coming from everywhere and nowhere all at once. The water stone was knocked from the sky. Arghun's flames flickered and died away. Kokachin woke, her hands flying to her stomach to find her wounds healed, no longer bleeding. And Amelio was able to stand as if nothing had ever been wrong with his legs at all.

In Amelio's head, he heard the dragon speak.

Amelio Strauss, know that you are of my tribe. Had I been whole before, we would have had . . . a connection. Now that I have returned, a part of me shall always be there when you call.

Then Shen Lung beat its mighty wings, turned its head to the skies above that were rapidly turning bright, and flew free from the open maw of Mt. Dragoian.

Chapter 86

Kokachin and Amelio ran over to Marco in stunned disbelief, each tripping over the other's words.

"How did you—"

"A great dragon—"

"Arghun, did you—"

"Is he—"

"What about—"

"It's over," Marco said. "It's over."

Marco finally let his sword slip to the ground with a mighty clank. It fell just next to the water stone and Arghun's already stiffening hands.

The water stone . . .

All three of them noticed the water stone on the ground, no longer spinning, and whipped around.

Just in time to see no fewer than fifty transformed Abarimon, suddenly free, snorting, their mouths foaming, their sharp claws extended and ready to fight.

Chapter 87

Marco, Kokachin, and Amelio backed away as the Abarimon started to advance.

"No . . . ," Amelio whispered. "We've come so far. . . ."

"There's too many of them," Kokachin said.

Marco ducked down and grabbed his sword.

That's when he saw Arghun's hands. In the center of their palms the gnashing mouths were finally still. But in that instant the mouths began to glow. It was a deep red glow, almost imperceptible at first, then it began to get brighter. "Amelio, Kokachin, look . . . what's going on?" Marco said.

"It's happening to the Abarimon, too!" Amelio said, pointing to the snarling creatures in front of them.

As Marco looked on, the glow in the center of Arghun's palms grew almost blindingly bright. Then, in a burst of red light, the glow broke free of the palms and began slowly rising up through the air. It rose and rose, heading toward the top of Mt. Dragoian, and when Marco looked back to Arghun's hands the teeth and mouths were entirely gone.

"The Abarimon!"

Now the Abarimon, too, were each covered in the deep red light, their prey momentarily forgotten as they looked at one another in puzzlement. The light grew brighter, then the first Abarimon jerked back. Its hair began filling in, the color in its eyes and face returned, and its sharpened claws receded into hands. Its knees pushed forward with a dull crack, its feet twisted back into place, and, as a burst of red light broke free from its body and rose up to the top of Mt. Dragoian, a very confused man was left in tattered clothing on the ground.

One by one, each Abarimon found itself bathed in the red light, its body shifting and changing against its will. Soon the air was full of red sparks, passing by one another and colliding as they rose toward the ceiling, and the floor was filled with half-clothed and disoriented men.

"It's just like the wind dragon said. The essence of the fire dragon is all being returned," Marco said, the red glow shining on his face as hundreds of sparks filled the air and the skies.

But Kokachin didn't hear him, because she was too busy charging forward into the arms of Aziz. "You're alive!"

"And more than a little confused," Aziz said, hugging Kokachin back nonetheless. "Why am I wearing these tattered rags? And where are we in the first place? The last thing I remember, I was on my way to meet your father's men—"

"Mr. Polo! Mr. Polo, over here!" Amelio shouted, picking Niccolo Polo out from the crowd.

At first Niccolo didn't recognize the blond boy running toward him with his arms newly muscled and his expression both confident and strong. Then Niccolo's eyes softened. "Amelio Strauss," he said in a dry whisper. "What are you doing here, halfway around the world? If your father could see you now he'd have my head."

Amelio wanted to laugh and cry all at once. And Marco seemed to be doing just that as he barreled into his father's arms. "Father!" he shouted.

"Marco, my boy, my dear boy," Niccolo said as he hugged his son as tightly as he could. "How long have I been here? How long have I been out?"

"I don't know," Marco said, refusing to let his father go, barely able to believe after all this time they'd found each other. "It feels like a lifetime. But we did it. . . . Amelio and I, we found you."

With tears in his eyes, Niccolo looked at them both. Still the boys that he knew, but also far, far more.

"And now that you're here, we can finally make our way home," Marco added.

Epilogue

"Amelio, Kokachin, Aziz, my father, and I led the way back to the palace of Kublai Khan, followed by hundreds of men Arghun had turned into Abarimon.

A day into our travels we ran into the army of the khan's soldiers that Aziz would have commanded, ready for battle against Arghun. But upon hearing our story, and seeing some of their missing companions among our ranks, they turned and joined us on our return.

Back at the palace the khan listen quietly to the full tale of our quest as it unfolded. Then, amazed, he declared five days of celebration in our honor.

On the first day, in an official address to his subjects, the khan announced his daughter had returned. Naming all of us and Kokachin as heroes, the khan said we had done what entire armies could not and finally put an end to the fire mage Arghun's reign of terror.

Over the following weeks, as we rested and recovered, I finally caught up with my father. And for the first time in our lives, I was the one telling him about my adventures.

Amelio, after days of strange dreams, began taking long walks throughout the palace. I overheard a young palace maid whisper that a strong breeze seemed to accompany him everywhere he went, and to her delight, every surface was completely free of dust by the time he walked out of a room. Perhaps because of this—and perhaps not—Amelio soon became quite popular with several young ladies in the palace.

The khan, after hearing details of Kokachin's travels, realized his resourceful daughter had now been to parts of his kingdom that even he had not. Asking her for advice dealing with certain territories and subjects, and finding it exceedingly wise, Kublai Khan began to treat his daughter as his most trusted council. Kokachin, in turn, found herself in far less of a rush to return to her days living outside the palace.

And Aziz, training in the courtyard one morning, found himself watched by the head of the Mongol royal guard. Intrigued by Aziz's fighting style, and amazed by the stories he had heard, the Mongol warrior asked Aziz to work with him to train a new platoon of Mongol soldiers. Aziz accepted, and soon found himself training a small army of his very own. He worked hard each day, and each night—to their mutual surprise—Aziz spent increasing amounts of time with Kokachin.

After just over a month of life in this fashion, the khan called us into his quarters. He had grown fond of us, and offered us all permanent positions within his empire as highly paid liaisons for trade. After consulting with my father, and making sure he could still work with his Mongol army, Aziz accepted. However, needing to return to our loved ones in Venice to assure them we were all safe, for the moment the rest of us were forced to decline.

In response, the khan gave us parting gifts of exotic spices and permission for an exclusive route of trade. He also asked, now that the wind dragon had returned, if we might have our leaders send one hundred of their wisest men to the Unknown Lands in the hope of sharing knowledge. If they were interested, the Mongols would send the same.

I thought that might be a great adventure for the future, one I could take side by side with my father and my best friend. But, for the time being, my memories would hold me over. And, just ahead, I had a feeling our long journey home would prove to be travel enough."

—FROM THE JOURNALS OF MARCO POLO